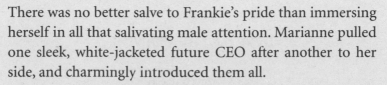

There was no better salve to Frankie's pride than immersing herself in all that salivating male attention. Marianne pulled one sleek, white-jacketed future CEO after another to her side, and charmingly introduced them all.

It meant nothing to them; it was a life lesson for her: kisses didn't lead to anything but sex, and sex led to someone's gratification—probably not hers. It was good to know how to deal with them, entice them, use them in the same ways they wanted to entice and use her.

"You have to make sure you get yours," Marianne told her. "Enjoy the kisses, the attention, the hot feelings—and go as far as you feel comfortable. We all practice on each other, you know; we play with each other, and sleep with each other. Sometimes a newcomer sweetens the game."

Praise for Thea Devine

"Wickedly delicious erotica with an OMIGOD twist!"
—Bertrice Small, author of *A Dangerous Love* on
His Little Black Book

"A multilayered story that sizzles with sexual energy from start to finish."
—*Publishers Weekly* on *Seductive*

"Devine's deft plotting and searing sensuality wrap around you like a silken web . . . holding us captive with her prose and passion for her story and characters."
—*Romantic Times* on *Sensation*

Also by THEA DEVINE

His Little Black Book

Bad as She Wants to Be

THEA DEVINE

POCKET BOOKS
New York   London   Toronto   Sydney

POCKET BOOKS
A Division of Simon & Schuster, Inc.
1230 Avenue of the Americas
New York, NY 10020

First Pocket Books trade paperback edition June 2007

POCKET and colophon are registered trademarks of Simon & Schuster, Inc.

For information about special discounts for bulk purchases,
please contact Simon & Schuster Special Sales at 1-800-456-6798
or business@simonandschuster.com

Manufactured in the United States of America

10   9   8   7   6   5   4   3   2   1

Library of Congress Cataloging-in-Publication Data

Devine, Thea.
     Bad as she wants to be / Thea Devine.—1st Pocket Books trade pbk. ed.
        p. cm.
     1. Young women—Fiction. 2. Life change events—Fiction. I. Title.
PS3554.E928175B33 2007
813'.54—dc22   2007000267

ISBN-13: 978-1-4165-2416-8
ISBN-10:   1-4165-2416-9

To John, who makes all things possible

Bad
as She
Wants
to Be

Chapter One

Bar Harbor, Maine
Summer 2003

The day Frannie Luttrell saved Marianne from drowning, she also fell in love with Dax Cordrey.

The whole thing played out in slow motion. A splash, a bloodcurdling scream, and everything stopped. No one moved. On the deck of the yacht anchored closest to the pier, people stood frozen.

Frannie stripped off her shorts and tee and dove off the pier. She didn't know that behind her, Dax had leapt into his speedboat to follow her; she was only aware of people pointing to where the girl had disappeared.

She didn't think—she grabbed a deep breath and went down, immediately seeing the slack body of a slender girl descending toward bottom. Grasping the girl's arm, she pulled her hard and explosively up to the surface. As she broke, she heard a commanding voice—"Here!"—and a strong hand reached out to her and hauled the victim up into the motorboat.

She nearly fell on board next to the girl's limp body and felt for signs of life. There was no breath, no pulse, and she immediately began mouth-to-mouth resuscitation as if she were on auto-pilot.

The commanding voice was speaking into his cell phone. "Almost there," she heard him say through her panic. "They're on their way."

No breath, no breath—but just as the boat veered toward the dock, the girl suddenly choked and spewed seawater. Frannie thought her heart would stop.

Only then did she look up at *her* savior, her hair bedraggled, her eyes tearing up, her mouth vulnerable. She wore no makeup, her face was burned and freckled, her bikini plastered to her slender, boyish body, and she looked right into his intense blue gaze—and her heart stopped.

The rest was like snapshots in her memory: the EMTs carefully lifting the girl into the ambulance, the applause from onlookers, the heat of the sun on her wet skin, the fact she was barely dressed, *him* standing so close to her.

But most of all she remembered that he scared the hell out of her. She wasn't supposed to meet someone like him when she was seventeen and looked like hell. And he surely wasn't supposed to look like *him* either: tall, angular, elegant, not remotely handsome. Not anything she wanted or expected or needed now. Just *him*, strong and long and elusively magnetic, with a perfect mouth and that cool, assessing blue gaze that made her heart stop.

And then she became aware people were watching them.

She remembered slanting an uncertain look at him. "I have to go."

His gaze flickered slightly. "Her name is Marianne Nyland." His voice was deep, rich, faintly accented. "She'll want to meet you."

"I'll—meet you there then," she said, trying to sound nonchalant.

He vaulted onto the dock and held out his hand. She had to take it, though she didn't want to touch him. His grip was enfolding and warm; she felt as if she were melting into it, and that she never wanted to let go.

She stepped up and quickly relinquished his hand. Someone handed her a shirt and she bundled up, feeling suddenly exposed.

"What's your name?"

She froze. She just couldn't give him her plain-Jane name, she just couldn't. She needed a pseudonym fast—something exotic, sexy, memorable, romantic—everything she wasn't.

"F-Frankie," she stammered after a moment.

He absorbed that, sweeping her with another one of those looks. "I'm Dax. I'll drive you."

"I don't know you."

"You know the important things," he said cryptically. "Come on."

She did. She thought she did. But she didn't know that he drove a new $45,000 Mercedes, that he was the son of one of the elusive, exclusive summer scions, that he would kiss her and she wouldn't deny him, and that everything was going to change.

* * *

A girl's life was defined by lines: fine lines, hairlines, bikini lines, class lines, the tightrope line between being a good girl and a slut. But there was always a moment when the lines blurred and a good girl had to decide whether to toe the line, cross the line, or stay safe behind the line that guarded her virtue.

Frannie knew she'd pole vaulted over that line the moment she'd agreed to let Dax drive her to the hospital, and she didn't care.

When he stopped the car in the parking lot, and just sat looking at her as if he were wrestling with his better instincts . . . her bones melted.

"How old are you anyway?"

Shit. The chasm. "Eighteen," she lied.

He made a sound. "I think I need to kiss you."

The lines dissolved. *Need* was grown-up stuff.

If he had any reservations, they didn't matter. The tension had already escalated to the screaming point, and every cell in her body wanted him to touch her. Taste her. Want her.

She wasn't conscious of leaning toward him, but she felt him cup her cheek; she closed her eyes as his mouth touched hers gently at first, and then he became a marauding pirate; he probed her mouth deeply and her whole body turned to tallow: thick, rich, hot, moist, malleable, ready to mold him to her burgeoning desire.

This was beyond . . . anything—any other guy, any other make out; this wasn't casual, he wasn't even touching her and she was nearly naked. His tongue . . . oh God . . . she was going to die from the pleasure of tasting him and those tangy little orgasmic darts piercing her everywhere—

He pulled away slowly, leaving the taste of him still in her mouth, and she opened her eyes and stared into his for what seemed like forever.

"Marianne . . ." he murmured, easing her away.

Oh. . . . Damn. She'd almost forgotten about Marianne in her consuming need for his mouth. The hell with Marianne. She didn't care if she ever met Marianne, for God's sake. Who the hell was Marianne, anyway? She leaned toward him again hungrily.

But he was already out his door and coming around to the passenger side to open hers.

She never forgot her first sight of Marianne. Marianne was absolutely beautiful, with thick blonde hair and doll-like features—those deep set cornflower blue eyes, that perfect translucent skin, those perfectly arched eyebrows, her perfect pink mouth, and a wand-thin body any model would kill for.

She was sitting up in bed, primping in a handheld mirror, when Dax knocked.

"Dax!" she greeted him joyfully.

"This is Frankie," Dax said, diverting the joy. "She pulled you out of the water."

Marianne looked at Frankie, then at Dax, and then at Frankie again, hard. "Oh—oh! You're . . ."

"Frankie," she jumped in.

"Omigod—I owe you my life!"

Frankie held up her hand. "Anyone would have done what I did."

"Anyone didn't," Dax said pointedly.

"I have to do something to thank her. Don't I, Dax?"

"If you must," Dax said, with a shrug.

"I'll think of something wonderful," Marianne said, slanting a scathing glance at Dax and then turning to Frankie. "Saving a life is not something that should be rewarded lightly. I'm perfectly aware of that, Dax."

"I never thought you weren't," Dax murmured, and Frankie wondered how the touch of irony in his voice utterly escaped Marianne.

But Marianne was still staring at Frankie. "You're not one of the gang."

"Hell no," Dax said. "They didn't have the balls. They just stared at their Ballys."

Marianne shot him another look, and then stared long and consideringly at Frankie. "I know what we're going to do. I'm going to take you over altogether, Frankie. Introduce you to everyone. Take you everywhere. All you have to do is give me your life for the next month, in exchange for your saving mine. How does that sound? Don't think. Just say yes."

How could she say no? Another line crossed, the wide unbridgeable line between the townies and the wealthy summer residents who ruled the harbor for three months of the year.

This, secretly, was the life Frankie yearned for—where you called a cleaning service to open the house and paraded your limousine up Main Street to the family's fifteen-room summer cottage overlooking the harbor. Who wouldn't want to be one of them? They had the most fun, the best times. They did everything and anything they wanted, with little supervision and no constraints.

They were all decadently rich, like Marianne, who was the only child of parents who were the sole surviving progeny of either family. Her father had retired, she told Frankie, and was now a consultant on the board of the investment company his great-grandfather had founded. Which meant his name was still on the letterhead to assure the investors that a Nyland was still in charge while he watched the money roll in.

Frankie couldn't conceive of that kind of life, that much money, that much excess, that much anything. Which amazed Marianne, all of whose friends *were* that rich. "Well, you're going to live how the other half lives for the rest of this summer. That's the least I can do, for what *you* did."

Frankie didn't protest. She'd grown up in a rural town, not far from the harbor; she'd worked every summer since she was twelve, whether blueberry picking up north, mucking stables, or the counseling gig she'd had for the past two summers.

She didn't have clothes or connections. She barely had conversation. She could do a few athletic things well: swim, ice skate, ski. She had a passable game of tennis and she could ride, skills she wasn't willing to test with Marianne's set. She played a mean game of Ping-Pong, chess, and checkers, and she'd learned rudimentary chording so she could accompany songs on a guitar around a campfire.

Not real useful things in Marianne's world.

The next evening as she walked up the steps to the country club where Marianne had invited her to the dance, she felt like she was Cinderella and Marianne her fairy godmother.

"There will be a ticket for you at the door," Marianne had told her.

"*Me*? I don't even have a dress for a dance at a country club."

"Sure you do. I have enough dresses to outfit the whole town. I'll send my driver with a couple, then he can bring you up to the club when you're ready."

This was so beyond Frankie's everyday life—a world where you had scads of clothes, maids picked up after you, and drivers took you places and waited for you. She was out of her depth in just hours, utterly swallowed up in the ocean of Marianne's odd desire to befriend her.

The chauffeur came as promised, waited for her to change, and then delivered her to the alien world of the country club. She emerged into a fairy tale of bright lights and music, underscored by the low buzz of conversation and the gauzy whirl of couples on the dance floor, the girls all dressed in light-as-a-soufflé dresses, looking like ethereal flowers you could puff away with a breath.

She eased in among them, looking for Marianne. When she saw Dax, she stopped dead short. Dax in evening clothes was devastating—tall and elegant, seemingly years older and miles apart from everyone, contained and austere, reserved and remote, but his intense blue eyes missed nothing. Not even her.

Her body went weak, her mind went blank, everything inside her reached out to him as he came to her and swept her onto the dance floor.

Another social grace she lacked, but Dax made it easy. He held her just right, just close enough, just perfectly. She wanted to tell him—she was falling in love with him.

He saw it in her eyes and shook his head. "Not yet. It's too soon."

What? "Dax—"

"Shhh . . . it's too soon. For *anything*."

She didn't understand, she didn't want to understand. As he guided her around the floor, she caught sight of people watching them. Marianne watching them with disappointment that she didn't bother to conceal.

Too soon, too late . . .

Nothing was going to happen between her and Dax; she saw it in his eyes, she knew it with a painful finality that cut like a knife as she caught sight of Marianne.

She pulled tight on her emotions and pulled away from him, but she hated that he just let her go. She wheeled away from him and nearly ran into Marianne, who gave Dax a furious look, and then she smiled at Frankie as Dax turned and walked away.

"He's such a snob," Marianne said, her voice soft but laced with malice. "Dear Daniel Alexander. Dax—sounds a little like a dog—you know—here, Dax, come, Dax. Sit, Dax. Dax usually doesn't dance with anyone. Lucky you. Do you wonder everyone was staring?"

"I didn't know," Frankie murmured. What could she say?

Two humiliations in one night was almost too much. And maybe what she'd expected among the sharks Marianne called friends.

"Well," Marianne said, her voice tempered now, "Dax notwithstanding, *you* are here to dance. That's why I invited you: to get to know people. Connections count, Frankie. So forget about Dax and just be real friendly to everyone. If the guys like you—well, you'll see . . ."

Frankie saw. There was no better salve to her pride than immersing herself in all that salivating male attention. The inquiries into pedigree would come later.

Marianne pulled one sleek white-jacketed future CEO after another to her side, and charmingly introduced them all. Some of them were her age, some already in college, others graduated and working. They politely asked her to dance and twirled her around the dance floor, and sometimes out onto the piazza, to steal a kiss.

She had never been the focus of that kind of sexual barrage before, and these were grown-up, dominating rich-man kisses that presupposed a lot of things she wasn't initially prepared for.

It meant nothing to them; it was a life lesson for her: kisses didn't lead to anything but sex, and sex led to someone's gratification—probably not hers. It was good to know how to deal with them, entice them, use them in the same ways that they wanted to entice and use her.

"You have to make sure you get yours," Marianne told her the next day. "Enjoy the kisses, the attention, the hot feelings—and go as far as you feel comfortable. We all practice on each other, you know; we play with each other, and sleep with each other. Sometimes a newcomer sweetens the game."

"But *you're* not playing," Frankie pointed out.

"They bore me," Marianne said, "but they don't bore *you*. And that entertains me. So have a good time with them—as long as you remember that they always marry their own in the end."

Frankie spent all her free evenings with Marianne. It seemed to her that Marianne refused to talk about the accident. Didn't care to remember, didn't want to speculate or discuss whether she'd fallen, was pushed, or deliberately jumped. She sloughed it off as the "thing that happened" and as if it had never happened.

So it became the thing that was never talked about even as they spent time together every day. A tightrope that Frankie walked between gratitude and concern, curiosity and hands-off altogether.

She played tennis, she rode, she sailed, she cheered on the sidelines at softball games and polo matches, and she pitched headlong into a new world of wanton sensuality.

She didn't know that there were ground rules, but Marianne laid them out for her.

"Of course they pay attention," Marianne said. "You're striking, athletic, you wear clothes well. Trust me, you'll never have another chance to experiment with the best. These guys are born and bred knowing how to screw. So go to it, *but* you have to tell me everything."

Frankie found it easy to tell Marianne everything: how

she loved French kissing, and what she was learning about herself and her body, her dormant sensual nature—and those hot-handed randy boys. She was smart enough not to allow penetration, but she adored them fondling her between her legs and she learned how to give good head. And between those two "gets," she reveled in being the go-to girl that summer.

"Just don't get pregnant," Marianne told her. "They'd kill us."

"I know; I'll get pills. It just feels so good—it's like you're floating on this pillow of . . . I can't even describe it, it's so— lush . . ."

"So how many have you let diddle you now?"

"Four. They're all different too, the way they do things and handle you . . . honestly, Marianne, you really should—"

"No! No, I'm saving myself."

That sounded lofty, but it never occurred to Frankie to ask for what, and why Marianne had no compunction about Frankie's experimenting with the outer edges of sex.

"Has Dax approached you?"

Frankie squirmed. It was crystal clear that Marianne wanted Dax and Dax didn't want anyone. He was always there, watching from afar, his expression impassive. And Frankie knew everyone in that set gossiped and Dax had to be aware of just what she was doing in the dark, but she didn't care. If it was too soon for him, it wasn't fast enough for her. It was his choice, and she was perfectly willing to play it his way and take advantage of all those hot, randy playboys.

"I heard he went back to New York."

Marianne's face closed up. "So tell me again how it feels when they play with your nipples."

There was no end to them playing with her nipples, and goading her to go all the way. When Dax wasn't around, she let herself drown in the fondle fests. When Dax was there, prowling around the edges, she felt edgy and restless.

"I wish he would lighten up," Marianne said one afternoon when they were at the club, lazing on the patio that overlooked the harbor.

"Does he ever have a conversation with anyone?" Frankie asked idly, following his movements from under her eyelashes.

"Not even his parents," Marianne snorted. "A goddamned saint, our Dax."

Or maybe he had standards, Frankie thought. But it didn't matter. She had a date with Rob Gildred that night—delicious, handsome Rob Gildred who kissed like a dream, handled her like a beloved sports car, and promised untold pleasure whenever she was ready.

She didn't expect much from her first time, but she was determined to lose her virginity this summer and that Rob would be the one, because Rob attracted her the most.

Only—*I wish it were Dax.*

But Dax didn't play those games. By every account, he wasn't a make-out and break-up kind of guy. And he seemed to avoid Marianne.

It made her wonder about Marianne's feelings for Dax. But since she owed Marianne so much for this magical summer, she wouldn't think such disloyal thoughts. Marianne came first, and her own unrequited crush on Dax was unimportant next to that.

She dressed for Rob that night in a flirty summer dress of lime green knit that clung to her breasts, draped over her hips, and flared out around her tanned legs. She left her sun-streaked auburn hair loose around her shoulders, wore makeup that emphasized her eyes, and minimal jewelry—earrings, a bracelet—so nothing would catch if they happened to . . .

They met at the club, where they danced and nibbled hors d'oeuvres for about an hour while Rob nibbled on her ear. But it was obvious he wanted to get to the main course. And it wasn't the prime rib.

"Prime Frankie," he whispered against her cheek as they swayed to the music hip to hip and he rubbed his erection tight against her belly.

"Prime *you.*" She'd learned the right things to say, the erotic arousing things, the coy exchanges that pumped up the volume.

"Let me prime *you.*" He ran his hands over her back coaxingly, and, when they were turned away from the rest of the crowd, he cupped her buttocks and pulled her tight against his hips. "Oh my God, Frankie. Do we *have* to have appetizers?"

She loved the way he caressed her. She felt stoked, golden, the familiar curl of desire ruffling between her legs. But she wasn't quite there yet, wasn't feeling that molten melt, the telltale darts, the cream of her desire . . . not feeling the way Dax had made her feel, and she wanted to want that, badly.

She closed her eyes and swayed against his strong body. This was the night, the time, the man, the moment.

But suddenly his arms were not around her, someone else had caught her up and held her convulsively close.

She opened her eyes in surprise.

"Dax?"

"I've been watching you. Don't do it. Don't sleep with him."

Her legs nearly went out from under her, and he held her hard until she steadied. She couldn't breathe, couldn't find a word to say, felt resentful and delirious both, especially after she caught sight of Rob's expression.

"Not your call," she murmured.

"Just don't." He pulled her closer.

"Dax . . ." She started to say, she *wanted* to say, she loved him.

"Don't say anything else. You'll do what you want to do, obviously."

And you know what I'm going to do, and you're going to let it happen. She couldn't believe it. She stared up into his shuttered eyes, willing him to tell her *he* would make love to her instead, that he wanted to be the one, because he couldn't stay away.

But then Rob was there, cutting back in, and Dax relinquished her without a word. Rob's embrace suddenly seemed paltry next to the confident way Dax held her.

"God, he's such a . . ." Words failed him. Even he didn't know how to describe Dax. "What did he say to you?"

"Nothing worth mentioning," Frankie said. "Idle chitchat.

15

Rob gave her a skeptical look that plainly said *Dax?* "Let's get out of here."

"My thought, too." Because otherwise she would dwell on Dax, and Dax was the last person she wanted to think about tonight.

An hour later, they lay side by side on the deserted beach, making out and goading each other with deep lush kisses and erotic whispers.

"God . . . your tits . . ."

". . . so hard . . ."

". . . let me suck—"

"Anything . . ." She cupped his erection, he lifted her skirt, and rooted between her legs. "Perfect . . . love it . . ."

"Hot . . . wet . . ."

"You do that to me . . ." She knew the exact words . . . no matter what, it was going to get done—*tonight* . . .

"Insane for you . . ."

"All the boys say that."

"No . . ." he breathed around her well-sucked and distended nipple.

"Ask them." Her body pumped against his questing fingers. "Ummm . . ." She swallowed hard. "More, deeper . . ." She canted her hips. "Love that." She knew what to say.

"Frankie . . ."

"Yes, yes, yes . . ."

It was so dark, she couldn't see him yank down his pants, but she felt his shaft, suddenly, poking at her cleft. Now what now what now what? Oh God, it's here, he's there . . . oh Lord, now what? Does he even know? Why didn't I find out?

16

It didn't matter; she pushed every thought from her mind, wrapping herself around Rob in blatant invitation. She wanted it done, here, now, with *him*. But the thought surfaced anyway, just as Rob jammed his heft and heat hard between her legs and made her a woman forever: *I wish it had been Dax.*

And so it went the rest of the summer. Frankie was the lucky townie who had the coveted invitation to the party, to the yacht races, the country club dances, the tennis and croquet matches, the afternoons of sailing and sex, horseback and humping, bridge and boffing—all the genteel pursuits of the wearily wealthy who were taking a month to wind down from their hectic city lives.

Rob was endlessly hers that summer. In the gardens, in his bed, in hers, in the woods, on the sailboat, in the stable . . . September was coming way too soon. They were already talking about packing up, about going back to school, about the winter social season, about things Frankie would never be part of once the summer ended.

But until then, with Marianne abetting her every step of the way, Frankie blossomed in Marianne's high-stakes, high-end world, took it for granted and took it all with both hands, while Marianne watched from the sidelines. And Frankie never thought to wonder why.

Chapter Two

And then they were gone, all of them, and Frankie felt like she'd been dropped from the fifty-foot cliff outside Marianne's family's summer cottage.

Back to reality. Cinderella, nursing her foot from the shards of her broken glass slipper. No longer the exotic and sexy Frankie. Back to being Frannie again, in her country double-wide, keeping company with her hardworking, long-divorced mom.

Maybe it was for the best. There was no one to testify to all the things she'd done this summer she'd rather not think about. No witnesses to the fact Rob said he'd call, email, text, never forget, always remember . . . but, she learned, they always said that after sex.

"I promise to stay in touch," Marianne had said, but Frankie knew once back in the whirl of her social life, Marianne would forget all about the summer—and her.

Dax, of course, had been nowhere around at the end. It was time to leave the fantasy behind and gear herself up for her first weeks at the state university.

Freshman year was a bitch—so hard to come down from the high of the summer with just intermittent emails from Rob, and even those petered out before the end of the first semester.

It's over, it's over, it's over.

The next summer was rough—Frankie worked in a law office in Portland so she wouldn't mourn the summer crowd, who that year, Marianne emailed her, were off to Europe and various islands around the world to play.

Frankie dated a lot that summer. Had lots of awful sex. Kept in intermittent touch with Marianne, who rarely bothered to answer.

Then, the summer before Frankie's senior year, Marianne's parents were killed in a plane crash as Mr. Nyland, an experienced pilot, was flying them to their summer compound in Nantucket for the weekend.

Frankie got word from Rob, and she sent condolences, which were formally acknowledged.

And she got a senior-year internship at a New York publishing house.

She debated whether to send an email to Marianne—or Rob.

Probably Marianne was the better choice; it was the polite thing to do, right? She impulsively shot one off very late at night: *Coming to Manhattan for a six-month internship at Barton House. Love to see you . . .*

See you, see Rob, see . . . Dax.

A week later, she was shocked to receive a reply from Marianne: *Omigod, when are you coming? Where are staying?*

Forget it. Stay with me. I'm rattling around in this big old apartment and I need company. Call me! Followed by a phone number.

Faster than Frankie could outline the details of her work-study program, she was boarding a commuter jet to New York at the tail end of the New Year, barely in time to settle into Marianne's apartment and get to her new office the following day.

Marianne lived on Central Park West in a huge, old-fashioned two-bedroom apartment in a prewar building with marble floors and walls. Leather club chairs were grouped around the lobby fireplace, oriental rugs were strewn everywhere, cut-glass chandeliers reflected in gilt-framed mirrors on the walls, and the elevator was paneled in mahogany and decorated with brass fittings.

Frankie was dumbstruck by the elegance, the space, the city, the noise . . .

And the apartment! With its huge sunken living room, commodious galley kitchen, massively large bedrooms, *and* every window, except the kitchen and dining room, facing the park. Frankie had a bare inkling who could afford an apartment like this and it wasn't Frannie Luttrell.

"*Mi casa es su casa,*" Marianne said carelessly, dropping onto the sofa. "It'll be so nice to have company. Everyone's so busy these days."

"What are you busy with?"

"Not much," Marianne admitted. "I couldn't go on with school after my—parents . . ."

"Of course not," Frankie said sympathetically.

"We'll throw a party," Marianne said, brightening. "This weekend."

"That would be great."

"Good. It's been too many days since the last party, and you need to decompress."

Frankie hadn't been aware she *was* compressed, but perhaps the strain of starting a new job was more obvious than she knew. "I'd love that."

Marianne arranged it for Friday night, three days after Frankie started in the publicity department of the venerable publisher, having no clue what interns did. She found out: everything from coffee to compiling lists and cold-calling obscure media outlets to fielding phone calls from nervous new authors to running publicity profiles.

It was tiring, some of the work was menial, but it was also exhilarating. And it was an eye-opening shock to realize that her paltry weekly salary would barely cover an hour of maid service to clean Marianne's apartment.

"Oh, don't even think about that. I have more money than I know what to do with," Marianne told her.

Now she met Marianne's inner circle—the cynical, comedic Becca, slightly older than the rest, chicly blonde and rail thin; and the high-powered and superconfident Nina, a writer, another glossy blonde; both totally immersed in themselves and immediate gratification entertainment.

"Ladies, this is Frankie, who saved my life four summers ago. Frankie, Becca manages an antique store, and Nina is a freelance travel writer."

"Oh, and here's Rob. And Andy and Chip—Timon—

JG—come, come . . . the bar's by the fireplace . . . Geoff's hosting . . ."

They poured into the apartment—surely at one point there were fifty people wandering around with drinks and hors d'oeuvres from the endlessly full platters on the dining room table.

Rob was at her side within thirty seconds of sighting her, and he still wanted her. Maybe Rob wanted everyone, but after four years of an arid go-nowhere sex life, and the memories of him stirring sensually within her the minute she saw him, Frankie was hot to get naked.

"God—pick a corner," he muttered, as he peeked in the bedrooms. "Shit. Full to blasting. I know—the coat closet right by the kitchen. Come on."

She came, with her skirt hiked high, pinned against a wall of cashmere coats. He held her hard and tight in the dark, whispering erotic nothings in her ear until she moaned and begged for more. "God, you're hot," he breathed against her lips.

"And you're so hard—fuck me again . . . I *need* a good hard fuck—*now*." She bit down on his lip and he rammed himself between her legs like a piston.

"That hard enough? That? That?"

Hard and heaven. She arched her body, spread her legs, and took him as deep and hard as he could go. "Don't move," he whispered as he rocked her body, locked tight between her legs, goading her moans and sighs with erotic words, with heat, with a suppressed violence that somewhere he perceived aroused her still more.

She knew it too suddenly—she felt it more, the harder he pumped, the more of his penis she wanted, and the harder he drove into her, priming her, pushing her, feeling her whole body gather and reach for the breaking point . . . coming, coming . . . and over, her orgasm breaking convulsively through her body . . . coming all on him, his bone-hard shaft drowning her in this insensate pleasure as he spent himself on the hard edge of her orgasm.

"Whoa."

That was a fitting finish to a ten-minute fly-by. "Was it good for you?" Frankie murmured, with a touch of irony.

"I'm still majorly hard for you, babe. You're better than ever. Let's do it again."

"It *was* a feel-good fuck," Frankie agreed. "Why not? Let's do it again."

She emerged from the closet the next morning to find bodies entwined and entangled all over the apartment, and Marianne in the kitchen sipping coffee.

"Oh, there you are," Marianne said. "Where's Rob?"

"Sound asleep on your cashmere coat."

"Guess it needs to be cleaned now."

Frankie took a cup of coffee. "Guess so."

"Was it good for you?"

"Still want the details?"

"Always," Marianne murmured.

"He got off, I got off. What about you?"

"*I,*" Marianne said portentously, "am the ringmaster." She

tipped her cup at Frankie. "I create the fun and games, and everyone dances to my tune."

Frankie blinked. "No sex?"

"What fun is sex, next to pulling all the strings?"

Was Marianne putting her on? Hard to tell this late in the morning when her senses were still blurry from all that sex and her body still dripping with Rob's semen.

Coffee was a good antidote to riddles and mind games. Fifteen minutes later, Rob came looking for her. "Come on. I'm not fucked out yet."

She looked at Marianne. "Neither am I."

"Good." He led her back to the closet. It was a hot little womb now, wholly suffused with the scent of their sex. He closed the door and backed her up against it, and, lifting her skirt, he embedded his penis fast, tight, and hard.

"Hot," he grunted, supporting her against the door by the thrust of his hips as he ripped open her blouse. "Tits . . ." He cupped one naked breast and felt for her nipple and fondled it. "Hard." He spurted. "You're so juicy, so hot. I"—he bucked against her—"can't . . ." trying to control his out-of-control penis . . . "—stop . . ." and he let it rip—a long, slow soaking spume of cum, while jamming her hard against the door.

"Oh God—Frankie . . . so sorry, didn't intend . . ."

"It's okay . . ." Women had said this forever as they rode a premature ejaculation, she was certain of it. It was wired into her organs. *It's okay. Not.*

"Make it up to you . . ."

"Really, it's okay . . ." He was moving away from the door,

24

holding her tight on his distended penis as he eased down to his knees, and laid her on the bed of coats they'd pulled on the floor sometime during the night.

"Don't want to go . . ."

"It's okay . . ." she murmured like a mantra, stroking his hair, his back, his flanks, and easing her legs to the floor. His cum flooded out from between her legs, all over his ripening penis, soaking everything beneath them.

"It's getting okay." He nuzzled her nipples one after the other, licking and sucking, squeezing the hard tips between his lips.

"Don't get cocky," Frankie whispered as he hardened appreciably.

"I'm cocked up as hell already."

"Just keep feeling my nipples."

"Just keep feeling my penis."

"It's so big, how can I help feeling it?" she whispered, giving it a Kegel squeeze.

"It is. It's one big fucker. It loves your tits."

"You could do my tits," Frankie whispered daringly.

"Nah—I'd rather do your cunt." He thrust at her suddenly. "I like *sucking* your tits."

She moved restlessly beneath him. "Let me on top and you can do both."

He reached for both nipples as she braced herself above him. "Oh, that's it, babe . . ." He fastened his mouth to one nipple, and his fingers to the other with a convulsive compression.

Her body jolted, she threw her head back, arched her

body closer, and let him take all of her nipple while she writhed a sinuous belly dance around the pole of his penis.

She adored how he played with her nipples, she adored the thrust and heft of his penis inside her and the rhythm of her hips grinding back down on him . . . she might even say she . . .

There was a thunderous knock on the door.

Shit—"SHIT . . ." Rob shouted disgustedly. "WHAT???"

"Just checking." Marianne. "Breakfast is served."

"Go away!"

"Frankie?"

"Go away."

"Ooh-kay . . ."

Silence. The darkness enfolding them. The two of them trying to recapture the thick, lush moment before Marianne knocked.

"Oh shit," Rob muttered, thrusting once and releasing his cum. "Sorry, babe," as he climbed out from under the very irritated Frankie. "I'm hungry."

She learned quickly to be that casual about sex. And that life with Marianne was just one long continuous sex-larded party.

"I don't cook, by the way," Marianne had told her the first day. "I'm great at takeout." It saved a lot of time and energy, Frankie found, because after a day at work, with the probability of sex always looming in Marianne's nighttime world, she was too enervated to cook anything beyond making coffee in the morning and toasting some bread or pouring cereal, and she felt barely energetic enough to go out to the next hip restaurant, club, or social event.

She learned about good haircuts, designer clothes, luxury spas that pampered you, fine dining, gorgeous music, weekend trips to the Vineyard or Aspen.

One day, Marianne decided she wanted to spend two days in France.

"You don't have a passport, do you?" Marianne said suddenly, when Frankie kept refusing the invitation. "You *don't!*" As if she couldn't imagine anyone not having gotten her passport along with her birth certificate. "Well, we have to remedy that. Tell your mom to send your birth certificate."

"I can't just take off midweek and go to Paris," Frankie protested. "Even if I had a passport."

"Why not?"

"They're paying me to *work*," Frankie whispered as if she were revealing a secret.

"Well, then, don't take their money and don't work."

Some days, it was almost as if she weren't working; they'd be out late clubbing and drinking—big-time drinking, drunk dancing-on-tables drinking—and Frankie would oversleep, and either call in sick or be late, hating herself when that happened.

More, she hated the growing feeling that Marianne was siphoning off her energy. When they were together, Marianne seemed more alive, more engaged. When she was among her friends, she seemed subsumed by the same insolent, indolent boredom that sent them out every night careening from restaurant to club to after-hours lounges, and finally home in the wee hours to collapse, exhausted, from excessive dancing, dining, drinking, and covert doping.

Frankie's bank account looked like hell after a month of that, and her credit wasn't much better. But she just couldn't allow Marianne to pay for everything. Except, of course, in the end she did.

"I'm bored," Marianne said early one morning when they were in the after-hours lounge of Cellar am:pm in the meatpacking district. Frankie shook her head groggily. How could Marianne be bored after hours of drinking and flashing their naked bottoms table dancing at a nearby club? They'd left with two great-looking guys who'd left them an hour ago when they realized that hand jobs were all they'd get.

"Those two were losers. I got nothing. What about you?"

Frankie was wrenched out. It didn't take five minutes for her guy to insinuate his fingers under her skirt, find her naked cleft, and initiate a seductive finger fuck under the table. She couldn't do anything else but reciprocate. Safe sex, mundane and unmemorable. "It was okay."

"Okay is *not* okay," Marianne said. "Random fucks are the pits. I hate this. I'm bored."

Frankie was tired; she had to go to work in five hours. She curled up on the banquette and closed her eyes.

"We have to do something about this," Marianne said.

Which meant Marianne would do something about it.

Two nights later, Marianne called Becca and Nina to join them for a girls' night out.

"We're going to a tasting party," she announced as they

piled into a cab, all of them sleekly dressed in satiny slip dresses and not much else. Less was more; skin was in; bling was verboten; the body was the story.

"Don't ask," Becca whispered to Frankie. "You'll see."

There was an element of excitement in her voice—Becca was stoked and Marianne was wired, an odd combination when Becca seemed the sanest of all of them. "It's a private event," Becca added as the cab drew up to an industrial building within the shadow of the Manhattan Bridge. "Come on, this will be fun."

Nina paid for the cab; Marianne had some sort of members' key to the fifteen-foot iron outer doors, and a moment later, they were in an elevator, rising to a floor where the iron filigree gates opened to a panoramic view of the East River that dwarfed the high-ceilinged candlelit space, including the people milling and talking, drinking and eating finger food, and shifting subtly and purposefully from one guest to the next.

"Now this is what I'm talking about," Marianne said, leading the way into the crowd. Immediately, they were swarmed by a dozen good-looking men who introduced themselves and offered drinks. Nina immediately paired off while Marianne watched and Becca turned to Frankie.

"Choose your partner, Miss Innocent. This is a *tasting* party—not wine—tongues. And here comes a tasty tongue for me to sample . . ." as a tall, sinuous man who might well have been a model approached her. "Hello, lover," she murmured as he swept her into his arms and kissed her deeply and thoroughly.

"Ummm . . . oh, I'd like to give you a hot tongue bath," she whispered, and he put his arm around her and guided her away to a more private place.

"Your turn, Frankie," Marianne said.

"Do I have to kiss and tell?" She wasn't even certain she wanted to participate. She eyed the good-looking man approaching her. Maybe she did.

"Always," Marianne murmured, moving away.

"Can I offer you a tequila? A tongue?" the man said.

Frankie shot Marianne a cynical look. "How about both?" she said, her voice slightly husky. Maybe this could be fun.

"Which one first?"

"Which do you think?" Oh, now that was a true bad-girl line. She loved that he immediately took her arm possessively and moved her into the crowd. Now that she was accustomed to the lighting, she could see she was in a big building-width room with that fabulous floor-to-ceiling window and view. On one side of the room there was a bar; on the other side, piled with floor pillows, couples were deep and hot into making out, or deep into making conversation and connections.

He eased her down onto a pillow and climbed on top of her and just gave her his tongue, thrusting it forcibly, deep and wet, into her mouth.

She was shocked that her body cringed with pleasure, as if somehow she had wanted this hot invasion of sex and dominance. Maybe she did. Maybe this odyssey with Marianne was all about the freedom to be a bad girl—because she was loving this stranger's kisses. She sank deep into the pillows and pulled him tighter and harder against her body and into her mouth.

She was barely aware when another mouth took his place. But it was a different movement of the tongue, a different wetness and taste. Not so much this time, but she couldn't squirm out from under him. She had to endure until yet another tongue slipped into her mouth and took her.

Her dress was hiked up at this point, her naked lower torso exposed. She didn't care. She lusted after the tongues, one after the other, as they penetrated her mouth.

So bad. So yummy good.

She lost track of time, of everything but the soft creaminess of her body and her bare naked need to have a tongue in her mouth constantly. The insensate pleasures of a dozen hot, randy tongues . . . how could she have known?

Hands all over her, probing, parting, petting. Her body molten, pliant, succulent from the onslaught of torrid kisses.

Just a tasting party . . . whose tongue was the yummiest of them all when you didn't know whose tongue was in your mouth one moment to the next. It was a thought to contemplate as a subtle little gong sounded and all activity suddenly ceased and the men who had avidly been tonguing their partners on the pillows withdrew from the room like ghosts.

"It's almost time for the tasting room." The announcement swept through the crowd like a wave. Everyone began righting their clothes and lining up near the bar, taking the moment to get another drink, to talk in low tones about the night's tasting.

Frankie found Becca. "What do you think?" Becca whispered.

"I love it," Frankie whispered back. Because there was such a hush in the room, speaking felt almost irreverent.

"Good, because there's more."

A few minutes later, another gong sounded and an unobtrusive door opened into yet another large, spacious room, empty except for the atmospheric candlelight and a curtain strung across its width, from which protruded a line of penises in various states of arousal.

"This is the tasting room," Becca murmured. "And guess what's on the menu?"

"Cream soup," Frankie retorted.

Everyone crowded around as the most eager to give head chose a penis, got on their knees, and began the succulent job of blowing it off.

"Go go go . . ." The chant began softly and ratcheted up as the action got heavier and more purposeful. The hand jobs came first, spewing and spurting thick luscious cream that was offered to the assemblage.

"Best hand cream ever," Becca told Frankie as she swiped her hands over one of the distended penises and made room for Frankie.

The intermittent sound of the blow jobs reaching culmination was a chorus under the soft murmuring of those fondling the already-spent penises, after which everyone got to play.

After about ten minutes of this, the gong sounded again. The action stopped, everyone moved to the door back into the main salon. The door opened, and the elevator arrived and dispersed what Becca called "fresh tongue," two dozen more beautiful men for them to taste.

"Go on, take one," Becca urged her. "Look at the guy Nina got hold of . . ." They were already deep into each other's mouths winding and grinding, silhouetted against the backlights of the city outside the huge window.

Frankie's whole body went buttery with lust. "You . . ." She grasped the arm of one of the passing man-guests. "Tongue . . ." He gave it to her. He was tall, muscular, dark, and he tasted real good, and he manipulated her tongue like the expert he was.

They found a pillow. "Were you one of the penises?"

"I'm in the tasting room next week. You've got a great mouth. I'd love your blow job."

"I'd love your tongue fuck . . ."

"No sex permitted. Only touching, mouths, and kissing."

"I didn't know," Frankie murmured. She was so ripe she thought she'd burst, and all she was allowed was touching and tongue? "So kiss me . . ."

"You're my first tonight. I'm really hot for you."

"Good . . . give it to me . . ."

He had a long, strong tongue, and she arched her body upward into the kiss, into his thrumming erection and against his sinuously moving hips. But just when she was deeply engaged and superaroused by the erotic stroking of his tongue, he left her. "Sorry . . ." The barest whisper. "Time's up . . ." And another body, another mouth, another tongue took his place.

It didn't matter. It was hot, delicious tongue deep in her mouth and her body responded as it had to her previous tongue lover.

In the swooning dark, with two dozen feminine shadows dominated by a male tongue hotly making out with them, it was the most seductive, alluring world, totally focused the hedonistically arousing movement of the body and the tongue.

Another partner, another tongue, wet, hot, probing, making her feel like a flower unfurling, pliant, open for anything.

Another tongue . . . and another, her body writhing and reaching with no satisfaction but the voluptuous possession of her mouth by yet another tongue.

Frankie had no idea how long she'd been spread out for her last tongue lover. No idea how long they'd been there, or where the others were, no sense of anything but her swollen yearning for a penis between her legs, the one thing she could not have.

At some point, she fell asleep—except she thought she felt, or maybe she dreamt, one of those expert tongues licking and sucking at her cleft. Except—she wakened groggily sometime really early in the morning still in heat.

In the guttering candlelight, there were bodies all around, fast asleep, all the tongue lovers, all her friends, all the other guests.

She eased herself up, tiptoed to the bar at the far end of the room to find some water to rinse her mouth, her well-used, voraciously kissed mouth, her lips swollen with those hard, hot kisses . . .

There was someone else awake. She felt it. She turned and there was one of the beautiful men. Maybe a man who had been her tongue lover. Maybe she hadn't tasted him yet. She felt a roaring need to taste his tongue—*now*.

He saw it in her eyes. "I need more tongue, too," he whispered roughly. "I need *your* tongue. Come on." She came into his arms, he slipped his tongue into her mouth, and they made out until it was time to go home.

Frankie felt like an overripe plum, tender, juicy, oozing heat and sex, ready to burst at the first bite. Of course, she couldn't go to work after the tasting party. She would have exploded just thinking about penetration all day long.

"I loved that tasting party," she said languorously as she reclined on the couch. They were all back in the apartment having breakfast and comparing notes and probing Frankie for her reactions and her intentions. "I want to go to another one. Now."

"Marianne arranges them," Becca said. "Chooses the men and everything. Great tongue this time, Marianne."

"Delicious penis, too," Nina added, delicately sipping her tea.

"Much more satisfying than random head. More control over the product. I have a fabulous catalogue of delicious tongues and erect penises to choose from every week."

Frankie bolted upright. "What a minute—you mean—literally, a catalogue?"

"I mean photographs. Beautiful life-sized photographs. You could get off without a vibrator, they're so luscious."

"I don't want photographs or a vibrator," Frankie said with a petulant growl in her voice. "I want a real thick juicy penis between my legs."

"And you shall have a penis, my dear," Marianne said. "Tonight."

"We can't wait that long," Frankie said. "*I* can't wait that long."

Marianne eyed them. "Everyone wants penis for lunch? Show of hands . . ." She waited a moment, watching their edgy sensual reactions. They were all squirming with voluptuous anticipation. They all raised their hands.

"Like *now*," Nina growled.

"Wow," Marianne breathed. "That was *some* tasting party if you all got so hot and bothered you can't wait. Let me make some arrangements." She grabbed her cell and went off into her bedroom.

She was back in five minutes. "Okay. Let's make this apartment into a sex hole. Dim the lights. Get the pillows. Let's figure out who's going to fuck where. Your penises will be here in ten minutes."

They dimmed the lights and spread comforters and pillows in the living room and bedrooms. They waited breathlessly right by the door, with Marianne as lookout, Becca first, then Nina and Frankie.

"They're here." Her words barely above a breath, Marianne opened the door, and five of the beautiful men from the tasting party entered. One by one they paired off, as Marianne watched, watched all of them eagerly get naked, watched them spread their legs wide, watched the tasting lovers penetrate hotly, watched the hard ride to each explosive climax.

And only then, as the lovers withdrew their naked rampaging penises, changed partners, and fucked each of them again in turn, did she leave the room.

The dim room was like a cave, primitive and reeking of sex and lust. And it wasn't over yet. The tasting lovers made it an orgy of feeling, fondling, tasting, and fucking. Whoever was horniest, hottest, most voluptuously aroused, and needed a penis . . . she was the one serviced by whichever lover was hard and ripe for penetration. No one wanted oral stimulation, no one wanted tongue. All they wanted was a penis, jammed hard and deep between their legs.

"I know you," Frankie panted at one point as one of the tasting lovers rode her for the third time.

"You know me better now," he growled, pounding against her belly-dancing hips.

"Did I taste you?"

"See if you remember." He dipped his tongue into her mouth.

"I think I did . . ." She sighed, her tongue on the tip of his.

"Maybe you didn't . . . maybe this is your first taste." He rooted into her mouth again.

"Your penis tastes good, too," she breathed when she could speak again.

"Everything about me tastes good." He swooped into her mouth again, lusciously dueling with her tongue, making certain the taste of him and the feel of him were imprinted everywhere, from her mouth to her cunt.

In the dark, in this cavern of sex and sin, her body was an engine of lust and longing. She couldn't get enough, she couldn't figure out why or how she was so creamy and malleable and explosively orgasmic. She never wanted it to end.

A long time later, spent and exhausted, the tasting lovers reluctantly were chased out, amply paid off by Marianne who patiently waited until they had recovered enough to leave under their own steam, and then she woke up the others.

"Where are the penises?" Nina demanded groggily. "I need a penis."

"They're gone, darling," Marianne said gently. "And they're mere shadows of their former selves. You rode them down to the nub, all of you bad girls. It was something to behold. Now, rise and shine—it's nine o'clock, nearly time to fly out into the night, and you need something to wake you up. My-jitos, anyone?"

She had made a tray of her own special twist on the mojito and she handed them around as they lounged on the floor of the living room, struggling to galvanize themselves to get up and get made up.

"You babies. Just because you've come off eight hours of humping and bumping doesn't mean you have to give up the night."

"I need sleep," Frankie moaned. "I'm so tired."

Marianne ignored her. "You're so bad. I have a great idea for tonight."

"How do you top a tasting party and a humping orgy?" Becca asked.

"Depends on if you're sexed out," Marianne said cagily.

"I'm never sexed out," Nina said. "What's going on in that deviant mind of yours?"

Marianne ignored her. "You'll need to shower—or not, if you love the musk—and change. You have permission to raid my closet. Something simple, sexy, and sinuous, ladies. Easy in, easy out. Just like your lovers today . . ."

Obviously Marianne had another sex-fest in mind somewhere.

"Do we have to?" Frankie muttered so only Becca could hear.

"Absolutely," Becca said. "Come on. We'll get you up for work tomorrow, if you have to go."

"Absolutely. I can't let it slide anymore."

"Okay. We'll figure something out."

They were in an orgy of trying on Marianne's clothes again when her cell rang, loudly and insistently.

"Ignore it," she said airily.

It stopped. Rang again, that loud irritating squawk that Marianne had for some reason chosen as her signature tone.

"For God's sake, at least see who it is," Becca said, through a slide of silvery satin around her neck.

It rang again, and Marianne picked it up, looked at it as if she were about to throw it against the wall, and then she looked at the caller ID.

"Oh shit. Dax is back in town." She looked at them in irritation. "He always spoils everything."

Chapter Three

Or calmed things down, Frankie thought, when, after a week, Marianne hadn't led any expeditions to her salacious hangouts.

"So what did Dax say when you spoke to him?"

"I haven't spoken to him. He effing left a message," Marianne spat. "He's an associate at the family law firm. He was up to Nantucket. I finally got rid of the compound—"

She took a deep breath as she realized how peevish she sounded. She gave Frankie a long, measured look. "You know what? I made a decision. I'm going to hire Dax to take care of my day-to-day estate business. Reward him for getting such a good settlement on the sale. I didn't have to outlay a cent on the deal."

"Ooo-kay. TMI, by the way," Frankie said. This was none of her business.

"Nonsense, you're like a sister. I owe you my life."

"You keep saying that, and it's embarrassing. I did nothing anyone wouldn't have done. And *you* have never dealt with what happened."

"I don't need to."

"You don't want to."

"Whatever. And *anyone* didn't do a thing, as you well know, and you did."

Score another stonewall for Marianne. Marianne's indebtedness was like an empty well that could never be filled. And she continually refused to talk about that day. To anyone.

"Forget that awful day. Let's go get a massage."

Thank God, it was Saturday. A quick call to the inner circle, and the girls all converged at the Red Door for an afternoon languid massage, super pampering, and intimate gossip.

"I feel like so voluptuous after a day like this." Nina sighed as they were leaving. "And it's all going to go to waste."

"It doesn't have to," Marianne said coyly. "What do you think? Want to put our buffed-up bodies to good use?"

"I knew she'd come up with something," Becca said to Frankie. "You up for something?"

"What I want to know is, can she top last week's over-the-top party?" Nina said.

"Forget that," Marianne said severely. "That was nothing. What I have in mind is going to test your mettle. I want to see how far the bad girl in Frankie will go."

"As far as you can dream up," Frankie said, "if that's the challenge."

"Maybe it is," Marianne retorted. "An orgy in my living room isn't quite the same as getting naked outside your comfort zone. You all ready for that?"

"Bring it on," Nina goaded her. "I haven't seen naked action since the tasting party."

"Everyone in?" Marianne asked, looking around at them all in the bright streetlights of Fifth Avenue.

They said in a chorus, "I'm in," "me, too," "I'm coming."

"Okay. Downtown we go."

The club was called Plumb. It was on a side street way west in the Village, down a long flight of stairs in a very old Federal building that had once housed a shipping office.

It was cramped and narrow, and there was low jazzy music playing as they emerged into the dimly lit entrance.

The gatekeeper, a young woman, asked, "How many?"

"Four," Marianne said, handing her a credit card.

"The lockers are that way." She pointed behind her. "They'll give you a numbered wristband."

"Okay, ladies. It's time to get naked." Marianne removed her coat and started stripping off her clothes. "I brought protection for everyone. Diaphragm, condom, spermicide. Then choose a penis and get it on."

"Or one will choose you," the clothes-check girl said. "Doesn't take but a minute around here." She handed out the numbered bands which corresponded to the locker numbers she put their clothes in. "The rules: Whoever chooses can't be refused. You can take on one guy or as many as you want. We're open twenty-four hours. Nonstop fucking all the time. The naked lounge is straight ahead. Get a drink, get a penis, get a good fuck."

"I'm cold," Frankie whispered to Becca as they filed into the lounge after a pit stop in the ladies' room.

"You're scared," Becca said. "This'll be good."

"But this is random penises. I thought Marianne was against random penises."

"But she loves the thrill of the unknown. That way, she never gets bored."

"Works for me." But did it really? How bad a bad girl was she, deep inside? This was way outside her comfort zone: narrow curtain-shrouded cubicles and no soundproofing. The customer was here for a good hard ride on a good stiff penis and then on to the next hardass bucking cowboy.

"Come on." Marianne wrangled them into the dim lounge. Naked guys, sprawled on the sofa, stroking themselves, waiting, watching. Jumping up as they entered, choosing among them with nothing more than a terse, "Let's go . . ."

And they went. Into the cubicles, onto velvet-spread beds, spreading their legs and feeling the vibrating thrill of a stranger penetrating velvet. It was, sometimes, orgasmic. An unfamiliar, hard-muscled stranger, the anonymity, the ride, the spasms of pleasure, and on to the ravishing stimulation of the new.

A circular orgy of strangers, in the dark, no other connection but a rock-hard shaft tightly crammed into a cunt. Elemental. Primitive. Male/female hot, hard pumping, plunging into the hot honey of a woman's body for his pleasure, and if she were smart and cunning, her own.

So insane to be so intensely aroused all the time. Desire was like honey inside her—thick, viscous, lush, molten. The sex was rough, raw, insanely intensely exciting. Frankie couldn't get enough, and the freedom of it all, the volup-tuousness of it all, was as heady as wine.

"What do you think?" Becca asked Frankie when they were in a lull and having a drink in the lounge.

She thought she was learning things about herself. "Two months ago—omigod—I never knew—who knew I was like that?"

"Marianne brings out the best *for* all of us," Becca said with a touch of irony. "The best food, the best drink, the best fucking. A girl has to know a good fuck from bad, Frankie. You never know about guys, or relationships. But knowing a good fuck is priceless."

"What time is it?" Nina asked lazily. "Who has a watch?"

"Hey, everyone's naked," Marianne said. "Time doesn't exist here."

"I'm soooo worn out." Frankie curled up on one of the couches. "I can't take another penis. I'm tired. I want to sleep."

"I don't," Marianne said. "I'm not tired. I want as much sex as I can handle tonight. Anybody have pressing busi-ness tomorrow? A hot date you have to prepare for? Any-thing to do that's more important than getting laid right now? No? Good." She turned to Frankie. "We're staying the night."

They called the place Plumb, Frankie decided later, because by the time you left, you felt thoroughly completely probed, poked, and plugged, like you wanted to live your life naked and on your back with a hard muscle pumping between your legs forever.

But damn, you had to go back into the real world where getting sex was *not* the primary objective of the day. Too bad. It was almost three in the afternoon when they finally left Plumb, and Marianne was up for drinks before dinner. "And maybe," she added suggestively, "we can pick up some company for tonight. Or I could call the tasty boys again."

"You're insatiable," Nina said.

Marianne leapt on that. "Omigod, that's what we'll call ourselves—the Insatiables. We're sex whores anyway. Did we not screw the night away and we're still hot for more? I call that insatiable."

"*You* are," Becca said meaningfully.

Marianne sent her a freezing look. "I'm hungry. For cum."

Frankie murmured, "I'm tired. I really need to go home."

"I have work to do." Nina. "Deadlines, you know."

"Spoilsports." Marianne looked sulky.

"Enough," Becca said, the voice of reason. "We're done being insatiable today. It's exhausting. You're exhausting sometimes. You guys have fun. I'll call you."

They parted at Sixth Avenue, grabbing cabs as they came. "The hell with them," Marianne snapped, waving at the oncoming traffic. "We'll have our own party. We'll order takeout and make out, how does that sound?"

"Exhausting," Frankie said, mimicking Becca.

"That's what we want," Marianne said. "To sex ourselves to exhaustion because the pleasure is so fleeting, we have to continually seek it all the time."

"I *have* to get some sleep," Frankie protested.

"Fine. I'll go entertain myself," Marianne said peevishly, as if Frankie had let her down somehow. "I know just the place." A cab braked sharply in front of her.

Marianne knew too many *just the place*s. Frankie hesitated. Oh God, was she that jaded that she'd blow off everything to find a blow job?

"Look," she said finally, placatingly, "I'm as insatiable as the next guy, but I *have* to get some sleep. Work-study, remember? Tomorrow? Office, work, money to live."

"You could call screwing around work-study," Marianne pointed out.

"I could, but that would spoil the pleasure."

"Fine. Go. I'll go play, and we'll figure out something sexy for tonight."

"Perfect." She hoped not. She was pumped out. She didn't have the energy or the juice for anything else. "I'll take the subway home."

"If that's what you really want." Marianne climbed into the cab, waved, and was gone.

Frankie felt a momentary wash of relief. She needed a break from Marianne. Apart from work, which was getting more and more problematical, she was with Marianne all the time. And Marianne had men and sex on her mind *all* the time.

Frankie felt like a kid with a sack of Halloween candy, stuffing herself full of goodies in the dark before her parents caught her. Cum was such a luscious, delicious, irresistible goody.

God, she was thinking about orgasms already and she was barely at the subway. The ride uptown felt interminable; there were any number of interesting men with whom she could have hooked up in a second if she'd wanted to.

It was a powerful feeling, addictive, one to which she was almost tempted to succumb. Tempting, tormenting . . .

A new penis rooted between her legs for another night . . .

You are insatiable . . .

She greeted the doorman, who motioned behind him as she entered the marbled lobby. There was someone waiting, reclined in one of the leather club chairs in the reception area, deeply absorbed in reading some papers.

She whirled to look at the doorman. "Mr. Cordrey," he mouthed.

Her heart plummeted; she stopped short. *Not today, not now, not after last night . . .*

She had to move; the doorman would wonder why she was just standing there like a dumbstruck teenager.

Because I am—

Or because there was something so powerful between them that Dax just knew she was there and that she was waiting for him to acknowledge her.

He looked up and his bolt blue gaze took her in wholly and completely in that one instant, and she knew two things: that the connection between them was still there, and that she couldn't hide.

He levered himself up and she moved, stunned that her legs, wobbly in her strappy stilettos, could still support her.

"Dax." He made her breathless, he was so tall and so elegantly dressed.

"Where's Marianne?"

"Off somewhere, doing the things Marianne does." Her voice was steady, too. "Come up for a drink."

He gathered his coat, his papers, his attaché. "I'll take coffee, thanks."

"I can do that." She lived on coffee; it was the only thing they—she—used the kitchen for. Marianne believed in three-meal-a-day takeout, no work, no fuss, no mess.

The elevator was too crowded with him beside her. His presence sucked the air out, made her heart throb, her knees weak, her whole three months' sexual odyssey with Marianne flash before her eyes.

"I've never been here," Dax commented as she opened the door and preceded him into the apartment. She flipped on lights, hung her coat, hated that she was dressed for invitation and innuendo and she couldn't possibly hide or explain that.

"*Don't* slip into something more comfortable on my account," Dax said wryly as he set his things down on a dining room chair.

"I need a sweater or something." Like he wouldn't know what that was about. She was naked beneath the thinnest of thin royal blue silk slip dresses, her nipples were erect, pressed tightly against the bodice, and the material draped sensually over every curve and hollow of her body. Her studded stilettos barely had two straps to support her bare feet, and everything about her was up front and out there.

No hiding anything.

"You need a keeper. Bad idea, letting Marianne convince you to stay with her. Where's the coffee? I'll make it."

She waved toward the kitchen. "In there."

He disappeared, and she debated changing her clothes. But it wouldn't change his assumption that she'd been out on the prowl, so what was the point? Anyway, maybe it would be good for Dax to salivate over her for a change.

Except Dax wouldn't salivate over anything. He made coffee swiftly, competently, and just watching him move made her go soft with desire.

"There you are. Sit." Like it was his place. She sat. She felt as if the heat of her body would melt off the dress. She felt naked. She wanted him and she was burning to see some sign that he wanted her—wanted her naked, right there, right on the kitchen floor. This was not going to be easy.

"Dax . . . I—"

"No." No compassion in his icy gaze, either. Nor was he avoiding looking at her. She hated him. Strangers had been falling over themselves all night to get to her. Men on the subway had fantasized about her. What the hell was wrong with him, that when he had her alone, and virtually willing to strip and lay herself bare for him, he *rejected* her?

Her lips compressed into a moue of testiness. "Why not?"

"You do *not* want me to tell you why not." His expression was unyielding, which made her want to provoke him all the more.

"But I do," she retorted.

He gave her a long, level look. "I'm fully aware of Mari-

49

anne's lifestyle and how she draws the innocent and unwary into her web. Is that enough?"

He knew too much, damn him.

"Just tell me when she'll be back."

This was not how her fantasies about him ended. "I don't know," she said tightly. "I don't know where she went or when she'll return; I just came back to get some sleep." Belatedly she heard how that sounded—and how he'd interpret it.

"Coffee's ready," he said, turning on his heel. "Cups are where?"

"Cabinet above," Frankie said, clenching her fists and her legs.

He found mugs, poured the coffee, got out some sugar and the creamer, and set them down emphatically, while she simmered.

He gazed at her grimly over the rim of his mug. She tossed her hair and stared back.

He made a sound. "Not gonna happen, Frankie."

"Why not?" There was a peevish tone in her voice. Damn. But she hadn't had to beg anyone for any sexual favors, for God's sake.

"Because I choose *not* to let it happen." He sipped his coffee and she watched his mouth avidly, her imagination running rampant. "That's what a man does, Frankie. He doesn't take the easy way. You're still a baby, with all of a baby's worst traits. You're greedy, needy, selfish, and parasitic. *And* you're vain, promiscuous, and an exhibitionist to boot. Not so sexy, actually."

"You shit." Frankie blasted out of her chair like a volcano, so incensed, so enraged by his rejection, she dumped her coffee all over him. "You son of a bitch, you *asshole*! You're probably *gay*."

"*Dax*? Don't be insane."

And there was Marianne, hanging on the swinging door, her bright gaze taking in Frankie's fury and Dax's drenched suit and shirt with unusually malicious glee.

While Dax cleaned himself up, Marianne signed papers, and Frankie changed into jeans, sneakers, a tee-shirt and sweater, and scrubbed the porn queen makeup from her face.

Shit shit shit shit. She'd wasted four years fantasizing about a guy who'd barely thought about her for four minutes, and then reamed her out as thoroughly as a lemon zester when she offered him her naked body.

The hell with him. Let his root rot. Let him fantasize about *her*, let him jerk off the rest of his life imagining what he could have had. Let him die wishing he *had*. Shit—damn, hell . . .

But this was good, that he finally showed her just what he was. She'd had him on a pedestal, and now she was free to sample the hundreds of other men who would want her.

And she wouldn't apologize.

The hell with him.

She stamped into the living room. "Where's Dax?"

"Oh, he's gone," Marianne said. "But—he came to me. That's not like Dax. That's weird. He said *he* made the coffee?"

"I wouldn't drink it; it's probably full of cooties." Oh God, that was juvenile.

"So he was waiting downstairs?"

Frankie threw herself on the sofa. "Uh-huh. It's pretty good coffee actually."

"I didn't know we had coffee in the house."

Sure she did; Frankie made it every day. "I have to have coffee, Marianne. How else can I operate under these conditions?"

"Such onerous conditions," Marianne mocked her. "Did you ever get to sleep?"

"No, I never got my nap. And Dax was a shit. And now I'm so wired, I don't know what to do."

"You need some downtime," Marianne said. "Or rather— some *up* time. I suggested takeout and make out. How about just make out?"

She didn't even have to give it a thought: she wanted hot anonymous sex, she wanted what Dax refused her, just to *show* him . . .

"Why don't you just get naked? It'll be five minutes tops . . ."

"They're already on their way?"

The buzzer sounded. Marianne winked. "I guess they are . . . on their way *up*." She pressed the button that released the inner door.

Two of the beautiful model men from the tasting party came in bearing wine and erections. Wine first. After which Frankie invited them to do their best to seduce her into bed. Marianne watched as they simultaneously kissed and stroked her, stripped off her jeans, her shirt, caressed her naked body, worked her nipples, slipped their fingers between her legs, her bottom, everywhere she felt rejected, injured, wounded. Two sets of hands arousing her, soothing her ego, her vanity, everywhere.

"Take them both," Marianne whispered, dimming the lights until there was just a shimmer limning Frankie's sinuous body movements.

One took her mouth, one took her between her legs, each of them rooting with their long strong expert tongues the places she most needed surcease. She bucked and writhed and shimmied, her hips bearing down, her body arching up into a hand that was cupping and playing with one pebble-hard nipple.

She grabbed a penis as she bore down on a tongue and her body spasmed gold, pure molten gold slipping and sliding all the way down between her legs to explode on the tip of the expert tongue that worked her clit and her cunt.

"Omigod . . ." barely a whisper.

"He's mine now," Marianne growled, grabbing the tasty boy from between Frankie's legs. The tongue lover, who was still kissing Frankie and squeezing her nipple, mounted her and stuffed his thick to bursting penis into her honey hole, and she arched and stretched beneath him as her body spasmed again at the feel of his heft and thickness inside her.

There was nothing like the keen thrust of naked male need filling her with tasty goodness.

She knew that kiss. She pulled back against his lips.

"Remember me?" he whispered.

"Tasty Man, from the party. No touch, all tongue."

"Not now."

"No, now you're all penis all tongue all the time man. I love it."

"I can tell."

"So stop talking and give me more penis and tongue."

They rocked that way for a long time, his penis rooted to his hips which were jammed against hers so she could feel every inch of it, and his tongue deep in her mouth so she could feel every inch of it.

It was perfect. She wanted to hire his penis and tongue to come live inside her, just like this, all the time. She didn't want to know his name. Tasty Man was the perfect name for him. He was very tasty, every delicious inch of his penis and tongue.

His lips moved against hers, while he was still in her mouth. "Coming now . . ."

"No no no . . ."

"Hold on . . ." He thrust, his hips twisting against hers, once, twice . . . and gone in short, hard-bucking spurts.

She felt like crying. Everything had stopped feeling good. What was the point? He wasn't Dax.

"I have to go to work."

"The six words I most hate hearing in the morning," Marianne said grumpily.

Frankie ignored her. Every day recently, she found herself struggling to wake up, fighting to get ready, and wresting herself away from Marianne, who only wanted a permanent party pal.

So when did ethical behavior start sounding like an excuse and a mantra?

"Remember? Self-sufficiency? Self-support? Pay bills?"

"Forget about work. I have money. You don't have to work."

"Ooohh no, I absolutely do." The horror of being supported for the next three and a half months by Marianne was enough to send anyone racing out the door.

But today especially she didn't want to blow off work; she was having lunch with Becca. And she wasn't sure Marianne knew about it.

She was super-busy that morning, too—setting up book signings, making travel arrangements for a best-selling author's tour, drafting press releases, proofreading copy. She barely got out at noon to meet Becca at a French brasserie a couple of blocks from the office.

Becca had been shopping. "Well, Bloomie's was *that* close. I couldn't help it," she said defensively. "Just a little nothing dress and some bling to make the afternoon more interesting. What shall we have?" They settled on a lobster *tartine*, which sounded exotic and excellent.

"I think it's time to play Momma," Becca said after they'd ordered and had their Perrier and lemon in hand. "Because Marianne is like a tsunami and you're drowning in her undertow."

That was a sucker punch, wholly unexpected. "I'm okay," Frankie said. "I get it about her."

"But at what price?" Becca asked. "I bet you didn't slut around like this before you met Marianne."

That stung. Like, if you were rich, there was no stigma attached to slutting around? *Okay, I'll be grown-up; I won't ask that obvious question.*

"No, I was a latchkey kid living in a double-wide in a trailer park, working menial jobs and desperate to get out. I got lucky. Who doesn't go a little wild the first time they're away from home? Especially in Manhattan."

"But what happens when you have to go home?"

I'm never going home. "I haven't thought that far ahead."

"Listen, I'm not sure you're thinking with anything but your genitals right now. Instant gratification is delicious, addictive. And men offering themselves to you can turn your whole perception of reality upside down. But you don't have the funds to handle this lifestyle, Frankie, and it's going to kill you when you have to go."

"Gee, Becca, why don't you say what you *really* mean?"

"I mean, Marianne can afford the men, the clubs, the sex. It keeps her busy. Gives her a purpose. She's never going to work. She doesn't manage her assets. She's always wanted Dax, so she'll wait him out and wear him down eventually, but she's not getting married anytime soon. So she has to do something, but she can afford to do nothing. And we—the Insatiables—can afford Marianne. You can't."

The food arrived, but Frankie had lost her appetite. She picked at her salad and then she looked up at Becca. "You know what? I don't care. I'm loving this. When, in my mediocre life, would I ever have had an opportunity like

this? I want everything: all the men, all the sex, all the attention, and I'll do whatever it takes while I'm here. I don't care
if I'm in debt forever."

Becca was silent a long moment. "O-kay."

They ate for a while and then Becca said, "Tell me about
the day you saved her life. She never talks about it."

Frankie hesitated. "I know," she said finally. "She just
sloughs it off. Even back then. Never said a word. Just decided
it never happened, and then, she kind of took over my life."

"And she turned your life inside out, as far as I can tell. So
what really happened?"

Frankie described it—the weird sense that no one was
moving, the slow-motion feeling, the yacht, the well-heeled
crowd that perhaps didn't want to risk their Tod's diving
into the bay. Dax right there as she broke water with Marianne's limp body in tow.

"Dax took me to the hospital and . . ." And then he kissed
her. But that, too, felt like it had never happened.

Becca perked up. "Dax?"

Frankie quickly distracted her. "And there was Marianne
in bed, looking into a mirror, and acting as if nothing had
happened."

She couldn't fool Becca. "*Dax* took you?"

"Dax kindly offered to give me a lift," Frankie corrected
firmly. Had her tone of voice given her suppressed feelings
away? Another game she didn't know how to play.

"Ummm." Becca was marinating that little tidbit, Frankie
could tell. Damn and blast. Worse, since she liked Becca the
best, and she wanted to be her friend.

"Of course, it would be Dax," Becca said finally. "Dax always does the right thing."

Time for a smokescreen. "What do you think he'll do when Marianne asks him to handle her affairs?"

That got an immediate and horrified reaction. "Oh dear God, are you serious?"

"She said so. He dropped over with some papers yesterday."

"Did he? After you two had spent the night catting around?" Becca got the picture clearly, completely, immediately.

"Me? Catting around? No. I was home. I dumped my coffee on him."

Becca burst out laughing. "I like you. I wish you could've talked Marianne out of this idiot idea of hiring Dax, but I suppose that's like trying to talk to the moon." She reached across and patted Frankie's hand. "I just want you to be real careful, totally protected, and very, very smart from now on."

That was a coded message, if ever there was one. "I can do that," Frankie said. "I won't take advantage of Marianne."

Becca laughed again. "Obviously you haven't—you're *working*. You have no idea what a novelty that is for her."

"I'm starting to find out. Lots of things."

"Sex is the least of it, Frankie. You're very, very young. Just don't be so cavalier—about anything."

"I'm not."

"You're not? All those men? All that sex? All in three or so months?"

No defense there. Time for another distraction. "Does Marianne know we're having lunch today?"

Becca's face closed up. "Maybe."

"Not, then."

"No."

Frankie looked past her, over her shoulder. "Well, I guess she does now."

Chapter Four

The thing was, Marianne didn't say a word. She was with Nina, and they settled in at the table as if they'd planned to have lunch together all along.

"Let's have some nice creamy dessert," Marianne said. "I know just the guys." She looked at Frankie. "Don't go back to work."

"I have to," Frankie said.

"Your priorities are screwed up," Marianne said. "Screwing is the first priority, everything else comes after. Becca?"

"I think I'd just like to have some coffee. I have to be back at the office at one."

"What office is that?"

"The one in the antique gallery I run."

"They won't miss you."

"But I can miss some afternoon delight. Waiter—four coffees, please. Frankie, dessert?"

Frankie wanted the dessert Marianne was offering, but she shook her head. Her stomach was in knots, her libido aching to tell Marianne she'd changed her mind, and her ethical voice berating her worst instincts.

"Well," Becca said, "coffee then."

During which they looked at Becca's new dress and accessories and talked about nothing.

"You're going to wish you'd come with us," Marianne said, when Becca finally paid the bill and they were escorting Frankie back to her office.

"I *do* wish," Frankie said, giving her that at least.

"Changes must be made, then, because this is unacceptable."

Instantly, Frankie imagined Marianne and Nina at Plumb, naked and writhing behind the privacy curtains. Or maybe Marianne had ordered up some tasty boys for them and even now, late in the afternoon, while she was making phone calls at the office, Marianne and Nina were making out on the living room floor.

She had to stop this. Becca was right. She was getting jaded about the whole bad-girl thing, thinking that all she had to do was crook her finger and quick, hot gratification would follow just because she *wanted* it.

Dax didn't, couldn't matter anymore. And maybe he never had, and all those feelings had been a figment of her imagination.

Which, if that were so, would remove any impediment to him sleeping with her. Nothing personal then. Just two bodies, hot for each other, one mounting the other, fitting tight, hard, deep . . .

Oh God. She put her burning forehead down on her desk. Someone should have warned her that unfettered sexual freedom led to enslavement of the body and the mind.

Get back to work . . . interning for the high-powered publicity director of a venerable publishing house, dealing with authors, and meeting all kinds of interesting people should have been a great job. Glamorous, even, worthy of the envy of her peers. But she was bored.

No, Marianne would be bored. *She* was restless, edgy, and testy because she was honor-bound to be at her desk when she wanted to be trolling for horny men with Marianne.

Listen to yourself . . .

I choose not to . . .

Three more months of this . . .

There was no one at the apartment when she came home, but Marianne had left her a note. *Rob's coming over tonight to console you.*

Pretty obvious what that meant.

She barely had time to change into something *easy on–easy off* before the buzzer sounded. She opened the door to Rob, walked right into his arms, and let him hold her.

"I hate working."

"Who doesn't?" Rob commiserated, guiding her into the living room. "Come on. Sit down. Put your head on my shoulder. Tell me how awful it is."

"It's awful. It's just that when Marianne invited me to stay with her, I never imagined it would be like this."

"Like what?" Rob started stroking her hair, her shoulders, her back.

"Like *this.*" Frankie sighed. "All this, all the time."

"Doesn't everybody live like this?"

"Everybody should," Frankie murmured, turning for his

kiss. Her whole body buckled into the pleasure of the known and the familiar where every movement was sweet and choreographed in a dance they had performed countless times. She just let it be—soft, pliant, willing, giving.

He gave. Her orgasm flowed like silver, sliding through her body in glowing ribbons until it burst between her legs. And then in the aftermath, him holding her tightly against his hot, pulsing, naked body.

And then the second time, and the third. Her on top. Him sucking her and guiding her. Next, him nuzzling her between her legs. And the fourth time, with him taking her from behind, this time almost as if he couldn't help himself, with a hard primitive violence. Collapsing on her, with her belly down, beneath him.

"I know a secret," Rob singsonged against her ear. "You like it ro-ough."

"Do not."

"Do too. I'll prove it."

"Not yet," she groaned.

"Yes, yet," Rob contradicted her, wrenching his penis out of her and masterfully grasping her hips and flipping her onto her back. "Now." He splayed her legs against his hips so that her lower torso was canted just at the angle for penetration, and then he drove his bulging penis ferociously between her legs.

In this position, she had no control. She was wholly at the mercy of his savage pounding of her body. All she could do was hang on, and feel.

Omigod *feel* . . . everything fell away against this primitive

63

possession of her body. He was everyone and anyone, lusting after her sex, his piston of a penis driving her fiercely over the edge.

Exhausted. Drained. Nothing more to give or take afterward.

Not even words.

"So glad Marianne called," he murmured as he kissed her good-bye later.

No offer of dinner, but she didn't care. Get him out and away. Done, finished, over.

The perfect end to a rotten day. Thanks to Marianne.

"I've solved all our problems," Marianne said the next morning at breakfast, which as usual she had ordered in.

"You know, I *can* boil an egg," Frankie told her.

Marianne waved the comment away as she always did. "First, I've hired Dax to take over my day-to-day legal stuff. Second, I'm going to hire you as my personal assistant so you don't have to work at that godawful job anymore. And you don't have to go back to Maine. You can transfer to NYU or Columbia."

"Are you crazy? I can't afford those schools."

"Get a scholarship."

"Jesus. I'm not quitting my job—and what kind of scholarship do you think I could get?"

"Well, you see—this is why you have the financial guy. He figures if your grades are good, and if you quit the job and just have the sole support of your mom, you could see a pretty nice aid package."

Frankie saw it clearly. It paid to have financial advice that you could freely dispense to other people you wanted to manipulate.

"Think about it," Marianne said. "Minimum, I could pay you what you're getting now."

"Hello-o-o." Frankie waved her hands in front of Marianne's eyes. "Remember the whole concept of internship? Work, study, grades? Graduation?"

"That can wait. Think about it."

"You just want someone to play with," Frankie shot back.

"So?" Marianne shrugged. "Think about it, at least. No getting up at seven. The whole day to relax and prepare all the sexy nights ahead of us—all those clubs, all those men, all that sex. How can you stand *not* to be out at night?"

"When I'm otherwise occupied," Frankie murmured, "I can stand it."

Marianne raised her eyebrows. "Rob was that good, huh? I knew that was what you needed."

Frankie squirmed. He *had* been better than good last night, but if Rob talked . . . This incestuously insular group talked all the time, gossiping about each other and everyone they knew. He could be telling bedroom stories about her right now, spilling her secrets during pillow talk.

But she wouldn't think about that.

That night they went dancing and drinking at a club on the way Upper West Side, under the highway. A "not yet discovered except by those in the know" club, that was frequented by celebrities who liked the low-key vibe, the out-of-the-way location, the superhot, nearly naked bodies gyrating on three dance floors to three different rhythms, and the privacy of the luxe secret penthouse VIP lounge.

You couldn't talk, you couldn't smoke—about all you could do was blow off sexual energy by diving into the music and hope someone fantastic was attracted enough to partner with you.

Preferably someone with a key to the VIP lounge.

Marianne was on the prowl, dressed in diaphanous silk and diamonds, so she lucked out. She pulled her panting celebrity over to meet Frankie, but the introduction failed to get Frankie the coveted entrée as the privileged friend of that night's hot girl.

The celeb looked her over like a piece of meat. "Not her." The most disdainful of dismissals.

"Send the car back," Marianne shouted as she melted into the crowd with him.

Not her . . . Frankie was steaming. Like her rural roots were showing or something. She stalked out of the club and threw herself into the limo.

Not her. Like she was a piece of shit. Not beautiful enough or naked enough or . . . She didn't know what enough. And he wasn't even an A-lister.

But then, Marianne was wearing diamonds. Of course, he'd go after a rich bitch: his plan B was a potential meal ticket. A source of secret funding. Maybe he was hoping Marianne would take him home, settle him in her bed, give him an allowance, and make him her new tasty boy . . .

Marianne was the one who needed a keeper. A buffer.

Someone more pragmatic and streetwise. Someone to temper her more outrageous impulses.

Damn, if she came home with that son of a bitch . . .

"Not a chance," Marianne said the next morning. "I blew him off. He wasn't famous enough."

"Thank heaven for small mercies," Frankie muttered under her breath.

Marianne gave her a look through her eyelashes. "That personal assistant position is still open."

Frankie threw up her hands. "Okay, I *am* thinking about it."

"I'll take that as a yes. The timing is perfect. It's almost the middle of the month, so you can give two weeks' notice."

Frankie wasn't so sure.

"Do it. We're having too much fun for your work life to interfere with my sex life. This way, you have the perfect excuse to get laid."

That was what was so seductive and scary. Full-bore immersion in Marianne's life meant she'd always be on call, constantly on the go, and invariably on her back.

Sounded *real* good to her.

"Oh, go ahead and do it. Call the school. Tell them something personal came up. Take an incomplete . . ."

This was getting scarier. These were things that Marianne wouldn't normally know. "You're amazingly well-versed in everything I need to do to save my ass."

"I made it my business to find out. Advisors, you know? So you'll write the resignation letter as of the thirty-first of the month."

"Which advisors?" Frankie asked curiously.

Marianne waved the question away. "I don't know. There are five dozen in that law firm. The letter, Frankie. Two weeks—that gives everyone enough time to adjust expectations. And then"—she smiled at her, catlike—"you can stay with me forever."

The logistics of leaving the job and leaving school were easy. Her mother took it hard, but Frankie talked her around. "It's a great opportunity, Mom. And Marianne doesn't want some stranger involved in her personal affairs. She's very rich, someone could take advantage. And she's very charitable, you know. We go to events all the time."

That was a big thumping lie. They'd been to one dinner to support the New York Public Library and one opening night at the Metropolitan Museum of Art. Marianne wasn't much interested in anything cultural, she didn't go to museums, and she disliked symphonies, opera, and art.

Nor did she have hobbies. She didn't like to read anything but *Vogue, Elle, Marie Claire,* and *W,* and she did nothing more strenuous than shop.

When she wasn't sleeping, going to her favorite day spa, or out to lunch, she watched TV or surfed gossip blogs on the web to see if her name had been mentioned.

"I always used to go to those charity and fashion events before my parents died . . ." She shook off that heavy thought. "You have no idea how often my name was mentioned then. But—you know what, I should blog about my sex life. That would get my name out there again."

"Maybe not about your sex life—but why don't you?"

"The advisors would kill me. They'd think it would open me up to all kinds of lunatics and fortune hunters."

"And they'd be right," Frankie said, gratified that there were wiser heads with influence over her. But there was also Dax, whom Marianne called endlessly on her cell, assuming he was at her beck and call now that she had hired him.

"We have to celebrate your last day of work," Marianne decided two days before Frankie was finished at the publishing house. "I'll plan a party."

"Your parties are starting to scare me to death," Frankie muttered.

"You haven't had sex since the last time Rob poked his rod into you," Marianne pointed out. "You're obviously saving yourself for the Big Moment."

"I have a big moment coming?"

"Yep. The big moment you gain your freedom from the drag of nine to five. I'll call the Insatiables. You seem to trust Becca's judgment more than mine. I'll let her plan the party."

Mound was located in the penthouse of a midsized old-world Midtown hotel. There were a half dozen tastefully decorated rooms for dining, drinking, and conversation and then there was the huge Olympic-sized pool with its floating lounges, half of which were occupied in sundry sexy ways.

"Bras only when we come here," Becca instructed Frankie. "That means tops on, bottoms off. Pussies rule at Mound."

This was a new sensation for Frankie, to have her lower torso utterly exposed in such a private venue. Everyone was bare, very bare down there. So bare, she couldn't bear to look. Time for a Brazilian. Time to samba.

Becca dove into the pool, climbed onto one of the lounges, and waved Frankie to join her. "Spread out, Frankie. It's your night."

"What does that mean?" Frankie asked suspiciously, looking around for Marianne and Nina.

"Oh, you'll see."

There were waiters who swam out to them and took their drink orders. There were waitresses with finger food. And then there were the beautiful naked young men who swam up to each lounge and offered their services.

"Choose," Becca invited her. "I recommend the full-body lick. Or maybe you're in the mood for a full oral. They specialize in pussies, but they do tits, toes, and anals, too. No fucking, though. It's up to you."

They were "up," too, those beautiful young men. She covertly looked around at the women who were splayed out and writhing, deep into sexual servicing on their lounges. She could have that, too. She had only to choose the waiter who attracted her the most.

Becca summoned one of them, whispered in his ear, and he promptly got to work on her. "Go on," she mouthed as she arched her hips upward to meet his questing tongue. ". . . ahhhh . . ." instantly drowning in her own private ecstasy.

The Insatiables were nowhere in sight. Time to take care

of her own gratification—but she hesitated, curiously disinterested.

She rolled off the mattress into the water and went to another lounge where she could be alone with the chosen instrument of her pleasure. Any of the service waiters would do. They were all around her, observing, offering themselves, or with their faces buried between the legs of a dozen half-naked women who didn't care who was watching.

It was odd to be so dispassionate in the midst of all that steam and sex. She ought to be panting for release instead of wondering how to escape.

She felt imprisoned suddenly—by need, by greed, by obligation, by necessity . . . she didn't know which. She felt out of place; all she wanted to do was leave.

Just as well the Insatiables were all occupied. That made it easier to get away without questions or excuses to Becca. She had no excuse. The service waiters weren't sexy enough? She wasn't sexed enough?

Still it wasn't so easy to just pick up and leave with the attendants eyeing her like she was abnormal or something.

She grabbed a cab back to the apartment and threw herself on her bed.

What is the point of all this?

She had never questioned it, not in the three months she'd been whoring around with Marianne. Stuffing herself with Halloween candy—and now she felt sick with it, her stomach full, with no gratification whatsoever for having gorged herself like that.

I want Dax.

71

But Dax didn't want her.

What if I called him? That was her forbidden fantasy.

And desperation—sneaking his number off of Marianne's cell had been an act of pure foolhardiness. But still—

She punched in his number and then switched off her cell before it rang.

Worse than a teenager making stupid cold calls to the fleeting object of her affections. She should either call him or stop acting like she was fifteen.

She felt paralyzed. Anguished. This was so unexpected, to feel like this.

Maybe I got lost the day I agreed to become Marianne's "assistant"—her sidekick and sexcapade partner. Maybe it's time to go home.

How? How could she go back to any kind of *normal* life after all this?

She punched in Dax's number again and this time, she let it ring. Once, twice . . . and then his voice, faintly impatient: "Cordrey."

"It's Frankie."

"What's up? Is it Marianne?"

"It's me. I need to talk to you."

"Now?"

Yes, damn it. Diva time. She could do imperious. "Now—unless it's wildly inconvenient."

"Inconvenient, but not wildly. Give me a half hour."

She changed out of her dress, washed away the industrial-strength makeup, put on jeans, a crisp white shirt, sneakers, and wound her hair up in a topknot.

Now she did look like a teenager.

Still, her fantasies ran wild, imagining he had been in the midst of making love to some perfect, gorgeous woman when she'd called, and now he had to extricate himself gracefully because his wealthiest client's *assistant* needed assistance.

What a mess.

She tortured the coffee maker instead of her imagination. Coffee was good. It put something hot and fragrant between her and something hot and flagrant. Like calling Dax for no reason except to feed her need and her libido.

Shit, hell. Call him back, tell him not to come.

Too late. The buzzer sounded and she waited breathlessly by the open door. Looking for clues that she'd disrupted his love life?

Well, if the way he was dressed—jeans, jacket, dark shirt—was any indication, he hadn't been up to much. Which was faintly reassuring. His expression was not.

She couldn't think of a thing to say as she closed the door behind him and leaned against it for support.

"Oh God," he muttered. "All the fucking got to you."

He wasn't supposed to know that or even surmise that. Damn him.

"I made the coffee," she said through gritted teeth.

"Hell, you don't expect me to walk into that trap again, do you?"

"You offered last time."

"Oh? Do I get to drown you this time? Because I feel like it."

"No, you get to be my friend," with just that little woeful break in her voice.

"I don't have a moment's sympathy for you," he said brutally. "Are we done?" He looked into her eyes and stalked into the living room. "Shit. Look, Frankie, you're not my client."

"What am I, then?" she whispered.

"A pain in the ass right now. You don't get access twenty-four-seven. You don't get a sympathetic ear because of your heedless, ill-considered choices. And you don't—"

"Dax—"

"—have a right to ask for—"

"Dax!"

"Crap. *What?*"

"Why didn't you tell me she was all about all sex, all the time?"

He gave her that look, the deep, knowing look that *saw* her, saw beyond her vanity and her recklessness right down to her core. It shook her that he saw so much, that he perceived too much and he knew her so well.

"It wouldn't have made a difference."

Damn him, he saw the truth, too. She stamped her foot. "I hate you."

"I know. You'll just have to find absolution elsewhere, Frankie. And preferably not on your back. Are we done now?"

Not if I can help it. "Not yet." She moved closer to him.

He shook his head, shaking her off. "Don't."

He was like a rock—light-years away from the guy who

needed to kiss her. But the man *wanted* to kiss her right this minute. She sensed it, she felt it, she *knew* it.

But he *chose* not to.

"Are we done?"

She was saved from answering by a commotion in the hall—Marianne and the Insatiables returning from their night of saturating sex. They tumbled into the apartment followed by two men whom Frankie recognized as two of the service waiters from Mound.

"Frankie!" Becca, obviously tipsy, stretched out her hands. "*This* is where you got to!"

Marianne stopped short as she caught sight of Frankie and Dax, her eyes narrowing slightly. "Or maybe it was Dax our Frankie *really* got."

"Today is Frankie's first day as my personal assistant," Marianne announced the next morning. The Insatiables had spent the night sprawled out on the floor, chairs, and couches. Frankie had made coffee again and handed out mugs before they headed off to shower and to dress from Marianne's closet. Now they were all gathered around the dining room table with a second cup and some fruit salad Frankie had hastily concocted. "So how does it feel?"

"Well, my first order of business was making coffee—*that* hasn't changed," Frankie said wryly.

But something *had* changed. Marianne had been extremely displeased last night, but now it was as if nothing had happened.

So she ignored the feeling. "What's next?"

"I need to get back in the game," Marianne said.

"Which means," Becca amplified, "she wants her name in the papers, the blogs, on the lips of every gossip hag. And a front-row seat at all those benefits, galas, and dinners she's shunned for the past two years. The ones they feature in *Town & Country* and get your name in the Sunday *Times*."

"Exactly," Marianne said. "I know people, you know people. We'll get our people together."

"Simple." Not so simple. Marianne meant the balls at iconic institutions, Southampton fund-raisers, horse shows, charity luncheons, runway seats at Fashion Week, yacht races at Newport—the kind of thing that Frankie had no idea how to accomplish or where to begin. "I'll start now."

"How do you start?" Marianne asked curiously.

Caught. "Online." Damn, she was fumbling the assignment already. "After you give me your wish list." Genius thought. "And of course you're a member of the Junior League?" Inspired. Surely they had some kind of charitable fund-raiser during the spring or summer.

Marianne looked at Becca. "Am I?"

"I think somewhere in your foggy past you were."

"Well, good. There you are. I don't have a wish list. Except—no fund-raisers for hospitals or illnesses. That's no fun. We're going shopping."

And there it was, from play pal to puppet in five minutes. Where money was involved, gratitude was a slippery slope. Marianne wanted value for her dollar even as she spent thousands on clothes she didn't need.

The online *In the Know City Social Calendar* gave her

what she needed. She had a list ready when Marianne and the others returned with their overstuffed shopping bags.

Marianne listened intently and ticked off those she was interested in.

"So, we have the Juilliard School dinner-dance." Yes. "City Harvest ball." Yes. "American Theatre Wing gala." Yes. "Junior League spring auction." Yes. "New York Philharmonic." Yes. "ASPCA benefit." Yes.

"Perfect. Make the arrangements—all of you going with me? Frankie? You should be charitable, too."

"Absolutely." To the tune of several thousand dollars for a half dozen events? She didn't know how she was going to manage that.

Something had changed. It niggled at her.

But when Marianne made up her mind, she dove right in—especially where there would be extensive media coverage.

Another thing about those events was that one couldn't possibly appear in the same dress twice. And there was only so much she could borrow from Marianne's closet. Which subtracted another chunk of change from Frankie's already decimated credit line.

Then there were the minor events: the American Musicals project, for which they attended only the benefit performance, the New York Ballet Tea Party, and an auction benefit at Brandeis High School, where most of Marianne's crowd—and Becca, Nina, Rob, and Dax—turned up.

And then Rob partnered with her for a half hour of tumultuous sex afterward when he escorted her home.

A girl had to keep in practice.

On the other hand, Becca was too right: she couldn't afford Marianne, even if Marianne could afford her. It was a vexing problem. Fifteen hundred dollars to attend a dinner-dance gala was off the charts for her, even on what Marianne paid her, and with no expenses.

"Working for me is not supposed to get in the way of our fun," Marianne complained.

"Fifteen hundred dollars got in the way," Frankie countered. "I just can't do it this month."

"Or maybe you're just looking for a good excuse to chow down on Rob."

"I don't need an excuse, and he rarely waits for an invitation."

As if Marianne didn't know. Marianne knew everything; she probably orchestrated what time Rob arrived and left.

"I'll tell him, he'll probably find a half hour for you. But it's your loss. You're going to miss a great party."

All of these gala functions were tame by Marianne's standards. However, she'd achieved two of her goals: a mention in the online *Gawker* and a photo in the *Evening Hours* page of the *Times* Sunday "Style" section. Now she was aiming for exposure in *Town & Country*.

It was exhausting dealing with all these change-ups, especially since none of it made any sense. Marianne was a wee-hours party animal, and staid society events were too constraining. And sex wasn't even on the radar. This non-stop display of social conscience was totally out of character.

But it was not for her to analyze: Marianne could afford

her whims. Frankie had her own character and conscience to wrestle with. And her checkbook. None of it looked promising.

Don't look in the mirror. She looked anyway; there was no one to see her, and she wondered when she had started veering out of control.

When Dax kissed you all those years ago . . .

That memorable kiss, forever frozen in time, suspended like fog over every other encounter, every other kiss. Over everything.

It blotted out reality. Any introspection was as futile as trying to pay off her massive credit card debt on a hundred dollars a month.

Thank God, Rob was consistent at least. Marianne waved a wand and he showed—like tonight, Cinderella's consolation prize for missing the ball: there was the buzzer, right on time.

She needed him as a respite from the maelstrom of Marianne's mercurial demands and to salve over the fact she couldn't afford to attend the gala.

But when she opened the door, it was Dax leaning against the frame. Dax, gorgeously dressed in a tux, giving her that steely I-know-what-you've-been-doing look that made her twinge inside. "Oh crap, you're here."

"Nice to see you, too," she murmured, stunned into momentary silence. "Come for coffee? Tea? Me?"

"You weren't with the Insupportables. I thought something might be up."

She clamped down on the urge to say, *Is it?* "Why do you care?"

"Hey, who wouldn't? You have brains, beauty, an intriguing innocence—*and* the heart and soul of a whore. Can't beat that combination."

She almost slammed the door in his face, but he caught it.

"*Don't* come in."

"I think I will, now."

"Screw you." She stalked into the living room and threw herself on the couch.

"Not on the docket tonight, Frankie." He followed her in and settled himself on an ottoman opposite her.

"Then why the hell are you here?"

"Damned if I know."

You know. "You're such a bastard."

"And I enjoy every moment of it."

She eyed him rebelliously. "You would." The equivalent of vocally stamping her foot?

"You look about fifteen right now."

"A veritable baby. Not so sexy in your book, as I recall."

"And you see a challenge."

It *was* a challenge. The air was thick with it. Hot with it. If he wasn't certain he wanted it, she was. She levered herself off the couch and onto the floor in front of him.

"I challenge you to kiss me."

"I'm a grown-up, Frankie. I can say no."

"But you want to, don't you?"

Again that long, level look. "Oh—absolutely."

She rose up on her knees. "Then . . ." She was that close to him now, she could see clearly, deeply into those bolt-blue eyes. Her mouth was inches away from his and she could feel the aura, the magnetism, the sex of him pulsating.

"Don't say no," she whispered, tilting her head slightly.

Her lips touched his, and she felt a swelling triumph that she had bent him to her desire. It wasn't even a deep kiss. All it took was a touch and her body softened like butter; a lick, and arousal swooped down like an eagle, feathering deep between her legs. A lush hot probing of his tongue, and she was home and she never wanted to leave.

He felt it, too. He visibly tensed, his body tightened. She opened her eyes as she whispered his name deep in his mouth and he cupped her face and took her again.

Don't stop, don't stop—she tore open her shirt and shrugged it off and then pulled at his tie and furiously worked the buttons of his shirt.

Big mistake.

He stopped her, his hands hard on hers, abruptly breaking the kiss. Slowly he pulled away from her soft, clinging lips, the look in his eyes mirroring what she felt and what he would not say.

"Make love with me, Dax." Her voice was barely a breath, she was so full of feeling for him.

"Make love with you—or fuck you?" He had retreated, his expression tight, all emotion wiped away as if it hadn't existed. "I don't think you know the difference."

His voice was so harsh, her eyes filled with tears. "Dax . . ." Her voice broke.

"Jesus God, Frankie . . ." He cupped her face again. A touch. It was enough, it had to be enough, it didn't need to be anything more. "This isn't going one inch further. Period."

His tone was plain, his voice rough. He was determined, no matter what he felt, and nothing she could do, even stripping naked and climbing all over him, would change his mind now.

She swallowed her tears and sat back on her heels, feeling exposed and vulnerable.

Only the sense that he was at war with his own emotions gave her any consolation when he walked out the door.

Chapter Five

"We're going to Paris this weekend," Marianne announced. "You, me, Becca, and Nina. We need a change of scenery. We need a change of men."

Now that Frankie had a passport, traveling anywhere was possible. But she barely had any money, and Marianne always flew first class. Thousands of dollars' worth of first class to France, with champagne flowing all the way.

"No problem," Marianne said, intuiting her hesitation. "I'll just advance you the money from your salary."

"We're talking *thousands*," Frankie protested, feeling a clutch at her vitals. "I'll be indebted to you forever."

"So, would that be so bad?"

The airfare alone was bad enough. But then there was the shopping spree in the First Arrondissement, just becoming *the* trendy avenue: the Galerie Véro-Dodat for shoes and dining, the trendy Surface to Air clothing boutique on the Rue de l'Arbre for Nina, who planned to write an article about on-the-edge designer shops.

No tourist sightseeing for them. No climbing the Eiffel Tower, no cruises on the Seine, no dancing on the Left Bank

·or dodging traffic around the Arc de Triomphe, no undiscovered bistros on out-of-the-way side streets, no tables for two on the Champs-Élysées, sipping wine. Paris wasn't about breathing the air of romance. It was wholly about shopping and sex.

And Frankie didn't even try to factor in the cost of the hotel. Or the raison d'être for the trip—le Boutique d'Accomodation, a sex spa for women who wished a long leisurely day of hedonistic self-indulgence. Women who were willing to pay for a day of unparalleled time and sexual attention they did not get from their hardworking and perhaps otherwise busy husbands, fiancés, or lovers.

Multiples, bondage, role playing, fantasies . . . everything was on the menu, everything was judiciously presented, everything was discriminating and discreet, and not a whisper about the well-heeled clientele's activities or proclivities ever went beyond the beautifully incised brass double doors.

Inside, it was the most elegant of salons. Everything was white, tipped in gold, refined, tasteful, luxurious. One waited in a beautifully appointed reception room. Albums were brought to be examined, and the menu discussed at length and in detail with the stamina and staying power of each select male guaranteed. Money changed hands somewhere behind the scenes, Marianne's treat.

They had a brief wait before a key was given to a particular room where their paramours awaited.

Marianne had opted for accommodations for the four of them together with their lovers: each of them had made a choice, according to her taste and preference, and appropriate precautions were handed around.

"Hell-*o* and start your engines," Marianne murmured as she opened the door to the penthouse suite. "Ladies, get naked."

Their paramours were spread out on two king-sized beds in the silk-draped bedroom, and they swung into sitting positions, their penises taut and bulging against their bare tanned bodies, as Marianne led the way in stripping off her clothes and climbing onto the bed with her amorist.

"Non, non, non . . ." The barest whisper as she slid her hand along his engorged shaft. Soft, fluid words in French to coax and goad—but he was in charge, he made it plain to her and to the others as they were mounted by their lovers as they climbed into their respective beds.

First, the hard-driving pleasure of a penis pumping and the first orgasm of the day with barely any arousal but the sight of the men and their equipment. They came almost in tandem, one after the other, soft soughing releases, and loud moaning goading—more more more more . . . Frankie's lover's penis was so relentless that even after she expelled her pleasure, he kept rocketing inside her.

And then it became a blur of bodies, penises, mouths, cunts, sucking . . . one of them at each nipple, one between her legs while Becca got serviced from behind. One lover roughly turning her on her knees to penetrate—*where*? God, it felt good . . . more more . . . On top now, and someone's fingers stroking and probing her crease as she pumped a hard-rock penis, inserting a finger—*where*? Two tongues sucking at her nipples—Marianne and Becca watching her hump her penis while their lovers got down on them and avidly began sucking.

Anyone, anywhere. One behind, one under, one sucking, one pumping, one spewing into a hand job, big, fat, thick penises spewing cream to spare . . .

A respite—kissing now, soft, tongue-lapping kisses all over their naked cream-soaked bodies, right down to the cleft, to the toes, until they were creamy with arousal. Now, side to side, in a three-way do-si-do—Nina first, penetrated from the rear and between her legs, sandwiched between lovers pumping her cunt and anally; Becca next with the remaining two lovers, front and back while Marianne avidly watched and Frankie looked faintly appalled.

And when they were done, the lovers, still throbbingly hard and coated with cream, took on Marianne and the reluctant Frankie.

They delighted in Frankie, the dual-penetration virgin, so awkward and so aroused, she didn't know how she could contain both penises in this dual invasion that seemed so physically impossible. And yet she managed, with her expert lovers coaxing and prodding her, filling her deeply and pumping her masterfully until her orgasm exploded like a geyser deep in her core.

More more more . . . a respite while the lovers played with each of them simultaneously and in turn as they lay languidly spread out, wholly open to the probing and stroking, the feeling and fondling of every part of their bodies.

At some point four pairs of hands grasped Frankie's arms

and legs individually, forcibly spread her out and held her immobile. No choice—maybe she never wanted one; maybe it was easier when others sexually imposed themselves on you, handled you, and penetrated you. No choice about where they insinuated any body part—her mouth, her cunt, her nipples, her ass, each individually, simultaneously and then one by one, each of the lovers fucked her and then inserted his penis in her mouth so she could suck off the cream.

She floated in a hazy orgasmic bubble somewhere outside of time with no sense of anything, of who was doing what to her, only conscious of the different thicknesses and lengths of penile penetration, of different hands, mouths, fingers dipping and stroking, pushing and pulling, and all the while she was held tight to the bed, only able to cant her hips to take the next hard orgasmic thrust.

Frankie, Frankie, Frankie—she heard her name murmured over and over in the romantic accent as the fucking diminished, and finally the lovers collapsed beside her on the bed. Her legs and wrists were released, her chosen lover rolled her into his arms and began petting her all over her body, and she dimly saw that Marianne, Becca, and Nina were being equally caressed by their lovers.

Another half hour of rest, of silence, except for the odd moan when a lover breached a pleasure point in the course of caressing. Frankie's body felt pillowy. Saturated. Well-used. Sated. Made for this continuous penetrating pleasure. She wanted more more more.

And finally, each of the lovers took them individually again in turn before their chosen lover came back to them and just planted his penis hard and deep between their legs and rested.

None of them moved. No pumping, no humping. Just hard penetrating possession right to the root. Staying power guaranteed.

Breathtaking endurance. Heart-stopping virility. Worth every *sou*.

Where did one find stamina like that in real life?

But that was tomorrow. Today, they were still naked in bed, screwing some of the most virile penises in Paris, and if they were lucky, maybe tomorrow would never come . . .

"That should hold me for about a day," Marianne said on the flight home the next day. "And isn't our Frankie the voluptuary? Who would have thought? Didn't you love all those luscious men? How could anyone be monogamous after a weekend like this?"

But that was a statement about Marianne's restive nature. She could not sit still from the moment they got back to the apartment to the next morning. She was up and out early, well before Frankie was awake, leaving a note that Frankie should tackle the mail, pay the bills, and return phone calls.

Which Frankie was in the midst of doing when Marianne returned.

"Has Dax called?"

She shouldn't jump every time Marianne said his name. He was over, dead, done. What was a chaste kiss, after the excesses of the weekend?

"Not yet." Keeping her tone as neutral as possible.

"*I'll* call him, then."

So Frankie wouldn't have to speak to him or see him. But there was another event that night at Lincoln Center, and the crowd would be there. Not that Marianne particularly cared about the Philharmonic, but she cared that there would be society reporters on the scene.

Becca pulled Frankie aside shortly after she and Marianne arrived. "How are you doing?"

"I'm just lovely."

Becca gave her that *motherly* eye. "Really?"

"Really."

"Hmmph. That was a barn full of sex this weekend."

"I haven't forgotten."

"How are your finances?"

"None of your business." That was rude; Becca was just concerned. "Smoking, at this point. Cinders, wafting away with every breath I take."

"I'll bet. Take it slow, Frankie. Don't let Marianne bamboozle you with her intrigues."

"What intrigues? It's all about the penises."

"That's what I'm talking about," Becca said playfully, tapping her shoulder with her *Playbill*. "Be wary," and she strolled off just as Marianne and Rob approached.

"You two are so cozy," Marianne commented, her eyes following Becca.

"Nothing cozy. She just asked how I was doing after the weekend."

"Funny. Rob was just asking that, too."

Rob leaned into her and whispered in her ear: "I know

what you did this weekend, and I'm so hot for you I could spew right now."

She gave him a faint smile. "And should I care—why?"

"Because now I know all your secrets, and I'll use them in any way I can."

"You're blackmailing me?" she asked in mock horror.

"How about, I'm balling you to keep your secrets. It's win-win: I get what I want, you get what you need—"

"Much subtler. And you are such a subtle guy."

"Okay, I'll be blatant. I want to fuck you—tonight."

"Rob! I'm exhausted."

"Not according to Marianne. Twelve straight hours? Come on, Frankie—" He put his arm around here. "I can compete with those fuckers."

"Think so? Twelve hours?"

"A man can but try."

"Marianne put you up to this?"

"Marianne's awestruck by your endurance. It just makes me hot thinking about it."

"We'll see." She eased out from under his arm.

"Sometimes," he said, pulling her back so he could still whisper in her ear, "what happens on another continent could become grist for the rumor mills on this continent." He relinquished her then. "See you tonight."

Oh God. Was Rob *threatening* her? She was no one, just a body he wanted to fuck because he could, because she made no demands. And she let him because he got her off, because he was reasonably nice and fairly good-looking, and a known commodity.

But now was there something more sinister involved?

Okay. Not happening. Didn't hear it. She pushed it aside and mingled some more, came back to Marianne and decided not to mention it.

The house lights lowered; the concert was about to start. Rob came up unexpectedly behind her, took her elbow, and propelled her toward the doors just as Dax entered the lobby.

She didn't glance at him. She had no idea what he saw, what he inferred, or even what she was doing, allowing Rob to take her over like this.

Except for the threat. She quelled her uneasy feeling. This was Rob, familiar, comfortable, available Rob. It hadn't been a threat; Rob was joking. He was old shoes. Her odyssey in Paris aroused him. That was all it was about.

It was an odd night; it felt as if Rob were trying to turn her inside out to find one part of her that had not been touched or compromised by her twelve-hour sex marathon in Paris. And he wanted to know every detail, every thought, every feeling, every position, *everything.*

She told him nothing, which made him want her even more.

He was still in the bedroom when she got up at seven and found that Marianne had already gone—or probably had never returned the previous night.

Whatever.

Oh no. Don't think like that. Working for Marianne is a blessing.

Whatever.

She made coffee and didn't even get out of her pajamas before she got down to the details of the day. A slow day, because there were no notations on Marianne's calendar and only a handful of written instructions.

Thank heaven for small mercies. She was restless this morning, feeling like she was on the edge of a cliff.

It was about all that money Marianne had laid out so she could get laid. Divide the dollars by number of orgasms, and you could say she'd gotten a lot of bang for the buck.

But meantime, Frankie felt as if she were in a golden cage.

How the hell did you escape a prison when you were indebted to the jailer? Shit.

God, what a bad idea to work for Marianne.

No, a bad idea to sleep with Rob again. And to let him stay till morning.

Too late now. He was at the doorway, bare-chested and barefoot, rubbing his hair and looking for coffee.

"Hey!" he said too brightly, settling himself at the dining room table, "just like we're living together."

"God, no," she murmured. "You'd hate it, and—*whatever.*"

She searched futilely for something else to talk about. It had to mean something if you couldn't find *anything* to say to your lover. *And* blessed the fact the phone was ringing.

It was Dax. Hell and damn.

"I'm on my way up. Marianne asked me to drop by."

"She did?" But he'd punched off before she could tell him Marianne wasn't there, and he was at the door before Rob could hide in the closet.

Shit.

Whatever.

They squared off like two pugnacious bulldogs.

"I swear to God, I'll drown the first one who throws a punch."

The pajama-clad warrior queen armed with boiling coffee and boiling temper. This was God's worst scenario—Dax and Rob in the same room—with her nearly naked, drenched with Rob's juices, and with a serious case of bed head.

She had the odd thought that Marianne had instigated all of this somehow. Conspiracy theories about Marianne? Not possible. *Whatever...*

Rob threw up his hands. "Hey. I'm a peaceful kind of guy. Dax is here for business, and I'm late for a meeting—or something..."

"More like 'or something,'" Dax muttered. They all knew Rob didn't do much at his father's holding company except pull a hefty salary he didn't earn.

"Like you don't have a trust fund," Rob shot back as he headed toward the bedroom.

Dax didn't say a word. He didn't have to.

"Marianne isn't here," Frankie finally said. "I don't think she came home last night." No reaction. "I can't imagine why she asked you to stop by."

He slanted a cold blue look at her. "Can't you?"

He couldn't have meant what she had thought he meant. No... "She's not that..." as Rob noisily made his way past them to leave, "... she's not like that."

"She is," Dax said in tandem with Rob slamming the door, almost as if to emphasize his point.

Now what? The silence thickened. He ought to just leave too, instead of sitting there, stewing. He was too formidable, with that look on his face. It wasn't even judgmental. It was pity. She stamped back into the kitchen; she should have gone to the bedroom.

No. *What was she thinking?*

·What she was always thinking.

"Hey." Dax at the door, perfection in a perfectly tailored Hugo Boss suit, blue shirt, and perfectly coordinated tie. "She's a bitch and Rob is a waste of your time."

"Thanks for the insight." She busied herself pouring another cup of coffee from the torture machine. "I'm there already."

"So why are you still here?"

"I have a—" He didn't know about her money problems. "I can't just walk away."

"Yes, you can."

"It's complicated."

"God, isn't everything."

"And you're the problem solver?"

"Somebody has to tell you, Frankie. You're standing in deep shit right now and you need a hand, if not a bulldozer, to shovel you out."

"I'm fine. I can take care of myself."

"You're not *fine*; you're obtuse and naïve, and you're in over your head."

"Is that your professional opinion? Do you charge by the

word? Because that's about all I can afford." She slammed her cup down in the sink and turned to face him. "You're the goddamned voice of doom. And you know what? I can't afford you. So go away."

She pushed herself away from the counter to leave the room. He grasped her arm as she passed and pulled her around to face him. And there was the look. She hated that look. It said he didn't hate her, but he didn't much like her at this moment either.

"Don't expect me to root around in another man's flower patch, Frankie. I don't play those games."

No? Then what was he doing in Marianne's garden, waiting for her to come home and play? His motives weren't so pure: everybody sold out on some level, even the rich and righteous.

"Sure, Dax, it's all about dedication to the job."

"Maybe it's all about you," he retorted, his voice rough and edgy.

That statement almost made her keel over. Except she knew it was really all about Marianne. And Marianne was always about sex.

She pushed past him into the living room. "Go away, Dax. I have work to do."

"It seems to me you've already earned your paycheck today."

That was so low, she almost doubled over. "Don't you have some hours to bill or something?"

"I'm still on the clock, Frankie."

And Marianne was going to pay for this folly big-time.

Saved by the ring tone. She dove for her cell on the dining room table before Dax could get to it.

It was Becca. A voice of sanity—thank God. "Hey. I'm with Marianne."

"Where?"

"You don't want to know. Rob leave?"

"Yes."

"Dax come?"

"What do you mean by that?" Frankie shot back without thinking. God, her life was becoming all sex all the time, too.

"Tell Marianne," Dax said clearly into the handset over her shoulder, "I'm making mad love to Frankie on the dining room table."

Becca heard and repeated what he said. "Marianne says if she believed that, she'd carve you up like the turkey you are."

But it was suddenly, explosively too late: too late to recant, way too late to pull back. He had come too close to the flame, to the heat of her body through the whisper-thin pajamas, and to the scent, seduction, attraction, and vulnerability of *her*, and it was as if nothing that had gone before mattered.

She blindly disconnected the cell and turned to give him her mouth.

"I'm goddamned *not* making love to you on the dining room table," he growled between kisses.

Dear heaven, what did it matter *where*? She was naked in a minute, everything so fast, so blinding hot, pulsing, breathtaking, two primitive forces colliding, coupling, fusing. On her back on the dining room table, their naked bodies joined to the hilt; she didn't care how where when what, just get there, right there, like that, deep tight *in . . . him . . .*

The connection was so emotionally shattering, it obliterated everything she'd ever thought, believed, experienced about sex.

Don't move—never move ever again . . . just . . . stay there, live there forever . . .

"Shhh . . ."

She could see every nuance of expression on his face, everything she was feeling reflected back in his intense blue gaze. Everything.

Just the most minuscule of movements sent molten rivulets of pleasure skeining through her veins. Just the feel of him between her legs, hot, deep, perfect length, perfect thickness, perfect fit.

Magic. His making love to her was like being enfolded in a hurricane, in the calm center, while her body raged out of control.

Nothing was forbidden. He explored her nakedness with heat, with suppressed passion, with reverence and violence, and with an erotic thoroughness that was both a claim and a denial.

She felt it with every fiber of her being. She hadn't been wrong about him, about them. But her endless orgasms were the easy part; for him, it wasn't only about the pleasure. It was about so much more, *too* much more for this to have happened now.

It shouldn't have happened now. And she shouldn't have fallen in love with him. Again. And not so soon after Paris.

Oh dear God . . . the Boutique—those men—her worst nightmare.

Afterward, she sat crossed-legged on the sofa, wearing her wispy pajamas, a glass of juice in her hands, watching him over the rim as he dressed. Beautiful Dax—long, lean, tall, athletically muscular like someone who'd played soccer or basketball. And those hands. And that mouth, dear Lord . . . that mouth . . . everywhere on her body—

Don't tell me it was a mistake.

Don't go.

If he said *I'll call you*, she'd die.

He picked up his jacket and turned to look at her. "There are consequences for fulfilling your fantasies, Frankie. That's the way it works in the real world. Are you prepared for that?"

Oh God, he was talking about the weekend in Paris. And there was that look, the one that she dreaded because it said he knew everything. She pushed back her unruly hair in a gesture of uncertainty.

"Are you?"

"Perfectly," he murmured, cupping her face. "As grown-ups should be."

The buzzer sounded. "Whoever that is, the timing is impeccable. What are the odds? Becca or Marianne? I pick Marianne, ten to one."

He opened the door and Marianne swept in on cue.

"I should fire you," she said coldly, giving Dax a hard assessing look.

"I wish you would," Dax said, matching her tone.

"Go to hell." She looked at Frankie, still disheveled with lust and faintly disoriented. "Cancel everything on my calendar today. You"—she turned to Dax—"get the fuck out." She turned and stalked down the hallway to her bedroom.

"That's my exit line," Dax said. "She'll get over it."

"She might mean it."

"I hope to hell she does," he said from the door. "It would make my life so much easier. Call Becca, Frankie. She'll take the edge off."

The wonder was, Marianne *didn't* fire her. Frankie showered and dressed before she called Becca, who suggested they go have a quick bite. At that point, she checked and Marianne was still sulking in her room.

She met Becca at a little restaurant a block away from the apartment on Columbus Avenue; they ordered a quick salad and iced tea.

"All right, chickie," Becca scolded, "I told you to be careful. Prudent even."

"I don't remember the prudent part."

"What if Marianne had come home sooner? I told you she wants Dax."

"He sure as hell doesn't want her."

"Well, no one knew he wanted *you*," Becca murmured. "What a mess. Why couldn't he have taken you to his place? Then no one would know anything."

"Let me point out that Miss Marianne made the appointment. Which I knew nothing about."

"Well, yes. You could draw a conclusion from that."

"Like, can you spell setup?"

"But you'd just spent the night with Rob."

"Who?"

"Oooo . . . he's vaporized already?"

"I can't remember who that is."

"Not good," Becca said. "Please tell me Dax doesn't know about Paris."

"He might."

Becca made a sound. "Not good."

"But Rob knows. Even made the suggestion his knowledge might be for sale."

"Holy hot shit. Who told him? No—let me take a wild guess. And he blackmailed you into sleeping with him last night."

"I prefer not to think that."

"Do what you must to live with it."

"She fired Dax."

"This is a black hole, Frankie."

"It could get worse: Marianne could fire *me*."

"Won't happen. She's too dependent on your presence and common sense. You're like family to her, Frankie. She'll pretend nothing happened."

Frankie shrugged. "This was probably the one and only time ever."

"Okay, maybe you gave in to the moment. But maybe not. Just be careful."

"I betrayed her."

"Marianne doesn't really *know* that. All she knows is that Dax came in time for an appointment *she* made, before you'd gotten dressed after Rob spent the night."

"True."

"Okay then, just stay away from Dax."

Exactly. Forget about Dax. How many times could you stir the same stew? It didn't change the ingredients and it didn't make it more palatable.

She went back to the apartment finally to find that Marianne was gone. No explanations necessary for now, which made everything easier. She did everything she could not to think about Dax.

To not think about the marathon of kinky random sex. To not think about the past, the future, anything that would mar the perfect memory of her intimate coupling with *him*.

Distractions did not work.

She thought for sure Marianne had felt it, tasted it, smelled it in the air, on her. But no, the next morning, Marianne came waltzing over to the office area she'd set up in the living room, sleepy and nearly naked, and peered over her shoulder as she read her email.

"So Rob slept over yesterday, huh?" It was as if she were concocting the palatable scenario to assuage her feelings.

"Yeah, and then Dax walked in before Rob left. You made the appointment, if I heard correctly."

"You know, I only remembered it later, which is why I had Becca call. Not a problem, right? He wasn't mad or anything, was he?"

"No," Frankie breathed. "I wouldn't say he was mad."

"I didn't think he would be," Marianne said. "Breakfast is coming. I hope to God there's still some coffee in the kitchen."

"There is," Frankie said. Not a problem? He wasn't mad?

They ate in the kitchen while Marianne detailed her night out.

"You know that show *Outrageous and Untamed*? They were scouting in New York this week and they threw a party down in Brooklyn last night. I had a great time; dancing, drinking, flashing, stripping, kissing girls, kissing boys, screwing against the walls, on the bar, in the bathrooms. They taped everything for the show . . ."

"Taped? For the show?" Frankie said faintly.

"Don't worry, I signed a release."

"You mean . . . all that could be on TV?"

"I didn't do anything much—kissed a girl, showed my boobs. Oh, wait, I think they caught me humping a guy at the bar . . ."

Jesus. She was speechless.

"Not great sex, but I love it when they're looking, you know? Or filming. Anyway . . ." She blasted off the stool. "We're having a massage this morning. I need some special attention, and so do you."

"But—"

"No buts. The point is, you're not supposed to get in the way of my fun. Massages are a great release when you've had a tough night. I mean, Rob all night, and then dealing with Dax. I probably shouldn't have fired him. He just needs to be taken down a notch sometimes. I'll call him later this week and reinstate him. Anyway, the massage guys are super-special. Come on, time to get naked. They'll be here any minute."

She'd spent the night bumping, banging, and baring her breasts, and she was ready for more action? Or maybe—Frankie hoped, prayed—just maybe, these guys *were* coming to give them a massage.

She changed into a short, light robe and returned to the living room just as Marianne opened the door to admit the men. They were each carrying a portable table and a huge bag . . . of tricks? They were tall, tanned, muscular, dressed in tight white tees and trousers.

They briskly set everything up in the living room, side by side, with a small table each to hold their potions and soft jazzy music in the CD.

Marianne disrobed and mounted the table, impatiently motioning for Frankie to do the same. Frankie wondered about her hesitation. It wasn't because she was shy about getting naked in daylight with strangers.

But. Now . . . they were waiting—

She let her robe slip to the floor and swung onto the table. Her masseur covered her with a tissue-thin silk drape.

She closed her eyes and let herself sink into the sumptuous stroking of his hands. Nothing sexual here. This guy was an expert, kneading, rubbing, and manipulating her muscles and tension points from her head down to her toes, with no stops in between.

Maybe she needed this, another touch, another sensation all over her body to wipe away the memory of *his* touch, the sensation of his skin against hers, his body covering hers, her body buttery with surrender . . . and now succumbing to the dark magic of another stranger handling her body.

There are consequences for fulfilling your fantasies . . .

One of them was you couldn't have what you wanted.

But she could have this, whatever *this* turned out to be. She could have anything, as long as she didn't wish, long, yearn, or surrender again to *that.*

Definitely a win-win situation, if you looked at it that way.

Her masseur motioned for her to turn on her stomach.

This was the best part—the hard massaging of her shoulders, her spine, her back, deep into the small hollow at the curve of her buttocks. Her thighs, her legs.

She melted into the expert hands moving over her body, stroking, pushing, pulling, lifting—lifting?—her onto her knees, her chest on the table, her ass skyward, her cunt exposed.

And then—he began stroking her. With his tongue. Just the bare nakedness of her, licking her cleft with the hard tip of his tongue, inserting it into her soft, moist labia, wriggling and wiggling it into her hole, and then sucking and lapping at her cunt like it was dessert. Her orgasm exploded out of nowhere and everywhere, from the relentless thrust of his tongue.

But he wasn't yet done: he inserted his fingers next, slowly opening her up, little by torturous little, pushing apart her labia and going deeper, spreading her tender-to-the-touch inner flesh and penetrating deeper still, stretching her to accommodate his invasive fingers, how many fingers . . . how wide could he spread her cunt . . . how deep could he penetrate her jangling body with just his fingers . . .

She could just see him bent intently over her ass, could

only feel him twisting deeper and deeper into her hole. It was too much after orgasm, and it wasn't enough. Fingers were not thick and filling, it wasn't enough . . .

She heard Marianne moan, she felt her masseur suddenly pull her forward to the edge of the table, felt his fingers slide from the wet creaminess of her hole, and the bulbous head of his penis pushed emphatically between her legs just before he thrust deep.

She felt breathless at the heft of him inside her, and at the strength with which he lifted her then, back to front, his penis embedded tight inside her, and sank to the floor with her on her knees.

His body covered her, forcing her onto her elbows so that his penis was angled into her cunt, penetrating to the hilt. He eased up and she could feel his hips tight against her ass, his hands hot on the curve of her cheeks, his penis thick and throbbing, his body moving in a dance all its own until the first piston-like thrust that would take her to orgasm oblivion.

He rode her hard, taking her hard, his hands rough on her body, slapping her, goading her, pinching her butt, playing on his sole connection to her body and her lust for his tireless penis.

And when she spasmed and convulsed in the consuming pleasure, he withdrew his instrument, turned her over, and, still on his knees, he canted her body and penetrated her still-quivering cunt again.

There was no conversation, no pretense that this was anything more than raw, unequivocal sex from experts who never let up, who never stopped caressing, massaging, arousing, and fucking. They were machines. Or they were on something.

On her—again. So like the Boutique, changing partners to dance. No difference between them. Penises the same size, hands the same touch, the same expert pressure, the same caressing strokes. The same kind of arousing, coarse sex, front, back, mouth, upside down, inside out. Naked and available instantly for coupling at the mere touch of a finger.

They were the slaves to the hired penises, and that *was* different. And they were coming for her again, both of them this time. One of them—they were interchangeable by now—bent her over so he could push himself into her anal bud, the other presented his penis for her to suck until his partner was embedded, and then he spread her legs, and inserted himself into her cunt all while she was upright.

And there she was, penetrated front and back, taking them both mindlessly, heedlessly, while Marianne watched, sprawled on the couch.

Cunt rider came first with barely a half dozen thrusts of his penis. Anal guy took a little longer, was a little gentler in his possession of her most private part; he bent her over, he held her buttocks and he rode her tight and controlled, until he seized and spewed. And then he gently lowered her to the floor while his partner attended to Marianne.

Now her turn to play voyeur. While they recovered their vigor, they played with Marianne's breasts and cunt, taking turns caressing, kissing, and sucking, as she lay there like Cleopatra, taking her due.

They ended the day in Marianne's bed. Frankie didn't know quite when she dozed off, but when she woke up it was six in the evening, everyone was gone, and Marianne was in the living room watching TV.

"Hey. About time you woke up. I'm hungry as hell and raring to go. I ordered dinner already, so we can eat while we decide what to do for sex tonight."

Marianne couldn't sit still for ten minutes at night if she knew there were places to go, to be seen, to find men, or to dip into the forbidden, the dangerous, or the unknown.

"Well, why not? Who's stopping me? Actually, you do try. It's one of the reasons I wanted you with me. I listen to you—"

"For about thirty seconds," Frankie said wryly. "You really don't have to go out *every* night."

"Yes, Mom, I know. Except, I do—because I can."

"The massage men weren't enough?"

"Oh, pooh. Everyone calls them because you know exactly what you're going to get. They're the Plan B fuck when there's no one else. But what about the unknown guy who's out there? The one with that look in his eyes, the one who knows you in a glance better than you ever knew yourself? The one who'll ride you to a lather, and not give a damn, except you know he does? I want to fuck *that* man, Frankie. Tonight."

"Odds are," Frankie said with compunction to be kind, "that man lives only in your imagination."

"You have no faith. Honestly, you'd think after almost

107

four months with me, you'd believe. Did you ever know you were such a bad girl? Have you ever had such sex in your life? Would you have if you'd continued working and then gone back home?

"Well, we'll be looking for Mr. Gleamy Eyes tonight. I have a great idea where we could find him, and get some hard head along the way."

Her great idea was a quick trip to Maine over the Memorial Day weekend.

"I've been thinking about all those brawny truck drivers on the road all those hours. They have to be horny as hell when they make a pit stop. We could get a man sample on the way up to Portland. God, I'm creaming just thinking about all those underused penises."

All those penises? Frankie was faintly appalled, but she said, "Ah—I hate to be practical, but . . . car?"

"Oh, the limo of course. We have to be comfortable on a five-hundred-mile trip. You didn't think we were going to do the driving, did you? The only thing I want to drive is a hard shaft between my legs."

"Oh."

"It'll be fun, different."

"The Diva Dick Drive? The Pack in the Penis Package Tour?"

"The Bad Girls Bed and Bang Tour?" Marianne countered. "Yeah, it's all about the package, Frankie. We'll take a Bad Girl break and do the nasty. Just you and me. I'll check on the house, you'll see your mom, and we'll do a dozen dirty guys along the way. Tell me that doesn't sound like heaven."

"When in God's name did you dream this up?"

Marianne waved it off. "I think from some music video. But I love the idea, so let's figure out the timing. And a list of possible no-tell motels along some scenic back routes. It pays to be prepared. What if they don't want a fuck in a truck?"

"Good point." How could she argue? She'd be interfering with Marianne's fun.

"And clothes," Marianne went on. "We want tight, hot, obvious. Forget underwear. Figure one bag, birth control, diaphragms, jelly. We're going to give our pussies a good workout."

They left midday the Friday of the holiday weekend to avoid the getaway traffic. Or rather, Marianne's driver, Rollie, drove them. The route, up I-95, was smooth, unhampered.

Riding in the limo was like being in a living room. There was a TV, a mini-fridge stocked with drinks and snacks, a banquette against one side for napping. Or, to listen to music—there were three iPod docking stations. Or to go online—a notebook Wi-Fi computer tucked into one of the many cubbyholes. Or you could look out the tinted windows at the scenery.

They were just crossing into Connecticut. "We'll stop up-state, in Manchester," Marianne decided. "It's about two hours from here. That's a likely place to find men. Not too crowded, the way it would be at the Sturbridge stopover. If a guy wanted some fast service, some downtime, he'd probably stop somewhere the others don't. And there we'll be . . ."

109

This was weird. Marianne had put this road trip into motion so fast, Frankie hadn't had three minutes to really figure out what was going on. It couldn't be that she simply wanted to get out of Manhattan.

Or maybe it could be. Marianne was such a chameleon, always in search of novel sensation. Maybe smoky clubs and useless hookups had paled and she wanted fresh air and fresh men . . . for this weekend at least.

And Marianne was right about one thing: she would never have had such sex in her life if she hadn't met Marianne. This was the stuff of fantasies, and she had decided practically from day one that it was worth anything she had to do, any price she had to pay, to be part of Marianne's impervious inner circle.

"Didn't I tell you a tight, white, thin-knit tank was the perfect thing to wear? If you could just see how it shows your breasts and emphasizes your nipples."

"I can *feel* how it emphasizes my nipples," Frankie said tartly.

"Oh, they'll be salivating all over you. You won't be wearing that tank for long. Or those skinny pants either, so aren't we smart to have brought along a dozen of each."

They were tight black capri pants that hugged her calves and accentuated her black stiletto gladiator-style sandals. She'd applied her makeup rather forcefully for this trip, and she'd tousled her hair into messy bed-head curls.

Marianne was similarly dressed, except that her white tank had a deep vee neck front and back, and it revealed her midriff as well as her breasts. Her skinny pants were siren red, her shoes sparkly gold stiletto mules. Her blonde hair was pinned in a topknot, and her makeup emphasized her mouth particularly.

But as the miles crept by, it seemed like it was taking forever and Marianne was getting antsy.

Finally, she said exasperatedly, "Oh, let's just stop *somewhere*," and tapped the window to indicate to Rollie he should veer off the highway and look for a restaurant. "A diner would be good. Where are we? Is there a motel somewhere near here? I swear," she started reapplying lipstick, "I'm going to jump the first guy who looks at my nipples."

"That's way too subtle," Frankie said. "Wait—I see a neon sign."

"That we're going to see some men?"

"No, for the Nu-Way Thru-Way Diner. A few trucks. Some cars. Let's get some coffee and scout out the action."

"There couldn't possibly be any. This is too one-horse for me."

"Someone I know who's always hot and horny told me to have faith."

"Oh yeah? Who was that?"

"Everyone's looking out the window. They figure we're celebrities or rich bitches or something."

"Come on," Marianne said. "Let's see what the local talent looks like."

Every eye followed them as they came into the diner. There was an empty table at the far end and a lot of staring and whispering as they settled themselves in. A waitress took their order: coffee and toast, and Frankie surreptitiously looked around.

"No one likely here."

"Shit. Okay," as the waitress brought their order, "let's just eat and leave."

They stopped after that at a gas station/convenience store to fill up before going back on the highway, and were just about to leave when a huge cement truck turned in, heading for the convenience store parking area.

Marianne, who had one leg out the door, reversed course. "Rollie—*GO!!*" Rollie gunned the engine and drove toward the truck, stopping almost nose to nose just as the driver was about to turn into a space.

Marianne popped out at the same time the driver looked out the window to see whose car was obstructing him.

"Hey!"

"Hey yourself."

The guy was in his forties, maybe, decent looking in a grizzled, weary way, and eyeing Marianne like she was cream cake as he jumped down from the cab.

How could she tell from that far away that he wasn't paunchy or fat or not desirable? God, Marianne had to have some kind of sex sonar; the guy looked about ready to eat her up.

"I'll have my driver back up—" and she motioned to Rollie. "Sorry." She looked up at him. "Hi."

"Hi, yourself." He spoke to her breasts, his groin visually bulging as he saw she was naked under the tee-shirt. "Could I buy you a cup of coffee?"

"You could give me a fast hot fuck in the men's room."

His face hardened. "How much?"

"I'll pay *you* for your penis," Marianne retorted. "Yes or no?"

"You got a friend or something?"

"As it happens, I do, and she's as horny to fuck as I am."

It sounded like bad porn movie dialogue, but the guys were real, ready, and willing. Marianne motioned to the car and Frankie got out just as his driving companion came around the far side of the truck. Younger, more muscular, a little more rawboned, and glued to every bounce of her nipples as she came toward him.

There was nothing like that crude, lustful look of pure raw male anticipation.

"You take the ladies' room. You—come with me." Marianne was in charge; Frankie could only follow her lead, pulling the young driver into the ladies' room, locking the door, pulling down her capris, and pushing up her tee to find he'd already popped his penis. It was real long and super hard, and he couldn't wait to shove it between her legs.

Neither could she.

He held her tight against the wall, his hands shackling hers, his hips tight against hers as he filled her to the hilt and let her feel the power of his penis up inside her as he pushed himself deeper and tighter. "You like that, huh? You like a young hot penis. You like it rough. You take it hot and hard, don't you, baby? Yeah. It's gotta be real long and hard for you . . . yeah. I can tell . . ."

Yeah . . .

He rotated his hips, pushing deeper, holding her immo-

bile. She arched her body, begging for more. Hip to hip, connected by only the length and strength of his young avid
penis, it was so good, too good, she loved it too much—this
hot raunchy coupling with a strange penis . . .

"It can't be long and hard enough for you, can it? You just
love fucking any penis, every penis . . ."

"Yes. Oh yes," she sighed.

"You'll probably fuck ten more stiffs today."

He withdrew slightly and then drove himself into her.

"More," she said.

"Am I your first today?"

"Yes . . ."

"Then I'm gonna make sure you remember *mine* and nobody else's." He took her like a piston, pumping, pounding,
driving her body hard against the wall, filling her, fighting
her, undulating and pushing her to a hard, ruthless, bone-
crackling orgasm.

"*My* penis, baby," he growled as he took his shot and
heaved and spewed himself into her. "*Mine*," as he eased
himself out of her, tucked himself away, and zipped up. "You
are some piece of tail, lady."

"You, too," she murmured.

"Call me any time you need a hard five-minute fuck.
Rocky's Cement Company. I do lunch." And he wheeled
away, unlocked the door, and sauntered out.

When she finally got herself to rights and left the ladies'
room, the truck was gone.

She climbed into the rear of the limo. Marianne was on
the banquette, a coy little smile grazing her lips. "So?"

"That was one hard-driving boy stallion. You were right. This is a great idea. How was your penis?"

"So, the bad girl likes hot, dirty sex on the fly, too. I knew it. My guy was adequate. Sometimes when they're older, they get more complacent and put the burden on you, especially when you ask for it. So I need a really hot bed buddy tonight. Maybe we'll find one in Massachusetts."

She told Marianne everything as they continued northward. How could she not, when Marianne was so eager to know—what his penis looked like, felt like, how he'd fucked her, how long it took, how hard he was, all the details of a fly-by in a bathroom.

They passed an inordinate number of trucks during the afternoon. After a while, Marianne said speculatively, "You know, I think we're missing something here. All those trucks, all those guys. We gotta get some and I can't wait."

She rolled down the windows and kept watch for a couple of miles, noting that there was a lot of curiosity about the limo, its occupants, and the fact the windows were wide open.

Trucks were slowing down, especially those with a high seat where the driver could see down into the limo.

"So," Marianne mused, "what if we flashed them?"

"Just any old driver?"

Marianne ruminated some more. "What if I sat in the front seat and flashed them? Rollie could drive down the center lane. We'd get a lot of truckers because they seem to tend to be on the right. They've got to be bored by now. A little naked pussy could be delightfully arousing. What do you think? Damn, I wish we'd packed skirts. Where's there a scissors?"

She rummaged around and came up with a small pair of utility scissors, which she used to cut off the legs and open up the crotch of her hot red pants.

She slipped them on and had Rollie pull over onto the shoulder so she could get into the front seat. "Don't look," she cautioned him, then told Frankie, "Rollie's about a hundred years old, and he's as proper as a dowager duchess. Okay, now you pull down the utility seat behind me. I want them to know there are two of us."

"And the plan is?"

"I'll just open the window, pull up my skirt, play with my pussy, and see if someone's interested."

It didn't take long. A big semi drove up alongside them, the driver ogling Marianne, but he didn't evince interest in finding out more.

"He's jacking off," Marianne said in disgust. "Screw him."

Rollie accelerated and they left him far behind.

"Let's do a twofer," Marianne called out after a while. "Roll down that window and flash your nipples."

"You think?"

"Go on. You know you want to."

The odd thing was, she did. She wanted every last erotic thrill on this trip, no matter what she had to do. Baring her breasts was the least of it. Fucking a young hot penis was the best of it.

"The minute you—or I—rope our stallion, Rollie will get us somewhere private."

Frankie rolled down the window and took off her tee-shirt. Traffic slowed down. SUVs honked. Truckers slowed down on both sides of them.

She made certain her naked nipples were wholly visible and that they were pointy hard with excitement. She could see Marianne in the front seat, her legs spread wide, and the shadow of a truck riding side by side. She felt the limo swerve suddenly and slow down purposefully, heading up toward a weighing station that was no longer in use.

Perfect privacy. The truck parked far to the back and the limo drew up beside it. She heard the truck driver growl, "Come on up, Miss Pussy," and the sound of the door opening, Marianne's shadow moving, the door slamming.

"Tell your friend to come up, too," the gravelly voice invited. Frankie needed no further urging; she slipped out of the limo and around to the driver's side of the truck just in time to see Marianne settling herself onto the driver's penis. "Ah, nipples. Come here, you. Nothin' I like better than pussy and nipples."

She moved closer, holding Marianne's gaze for a moment, then cupping her breasts to give him better access. He sucked off her nipples one at a time as Marianne rode him hard and high, her arms braced against the back of the cab, her hips drilling him tirelessly into her body until he couldn't hold it back, and he convulsed and spewed.

Marianne sat back and looked at Frankie. "He's still bone hard. It's your nipples. He can't get enough of us. You want his rod now? He can suck my nipples."

She opened the door so she could climb off his penis without interfering with Frankie's removing her pants. As she made her way to take Frankie's place on the driver's side, Frankie mounted the guy's slick, cream-coated shaft.

"Oohhhh . . . ah . . . that feels so good, so insanely hard . . ." She braced her arms above him as Marianne had done. Her breasts swung erotically near his mouth and he fastened his lips and tongue around her right nipple.

Her body constricted, a combination of the throbbing hard thickness of him filling her hole, his hot saliva on her taut nipple, and his lips avidly sucking on it. She moved, she undulated, she did a belly dance on his penis as he sucked each nipple and Marianne avidly watched.

She couldn't wait to come, she didn't want to come. Truck guy had stamina to spare. She didn't even care what he looked like. Just let him fuck her and suck her until she exploded. Until her body went into rocketing unconstrained spasms of pleasure. Until she couldn't bear one more thrust, one more suck, one more anything except the thought that soon he'd be up to fucking her again.

"You're the best pussy I've fucked in weeks."

"Want more?" Marianne asked coyly.

"Big boy's raring to go. Come and get him." He ran his hands over Frankie's haunches and she shivered.

"We want a night of hard-driving dirty sex. You up for it?"

"How much?"

"This isn't about money. It's damned hard to find man meat that can handle us. We should pay *you*."

"There's a motel down the road."

"I was hoping you knew where one was," Marianne murmured. "Why don't you drive us there? That is, if you can handle the truck as well as two horny pussies."

"I can handle all of it," he growled. "You get into the passenger's seat. Pussy pie and I are going to slide over and drive this baby to orgasmic heaven."

Frankie sat on his penis for the short trip to the motel. Rollie made the arrangements. Marianne paid. They took a room at the far end of the complex and only then did Frankie remove herself from his throbbing shaft.

No thinking allowed. Just feel. The thrill. The risk. The danger. The anonymity. The mind-bending, body-sapping pleasure.

They got naked and crawled into bed. He was so long, thick, and rigid, the bedspread tented over his tall muscular body. Immediately, he began fingering each of them between their legs simultaneously.

"Warming you up."

"I don't need warming up, I need fucking," Marianne said plainly. "Who goes first?"

"The one in heat. You—really need a penis right now." He rolled over onto her. "Here he comes . . ." and he swooped over her and she gasped as he drove hard between her legs. "That's what you need. A good hard pounding from a man who knows what he's doing. I'm bringing you home."

And when he'd brought her to orgasm, he turned her over, and fucked her again from the rear. And then he took

Frankie, from the rear first and then on her back. And then Marianne again, alternating the two of them through the night, in different positions, different approaches, unbelievable vigor in his iron man penis.

He did rest. And he licked and sucked and got them off by mouth. He did them simultaneously, by penis and by hand. Marianne blew him once, amazed he still had any cream to spare.

They fell asleep early in the morning, but not before he awakened Frankie for one more round of fucking on the chair as Marianne slept. After, he pulled her onto his lap, sucked on her nipples, and whispered all kinds of dirty things in her ear. And, "You're the one I'd keep."

He left her with that as he crept out at dawn. Not even the roar of the semi's engine awakened Marianne.

Frankie watched him back out of the lot, expertly maneuvering the truck around to exit, make a right turn, and disappear from sight.

Just for a breath of a moment, she wished he'd asked her to go with him.

She let Marianne sleep while she rooted out coffee and pastries, the easiest thing to have for breakfast.

They were on the road by ten, Marianne languid with satiation for the first time since Frankie had known her.

"*That* was a penis," Marianne sighed. "Now we're coming to Route 495. There's nothing interesting there. It goes about an hour and then we're in New Hampshire for about ten seconds. Still, waiting increases anticipation, don't you think? I bet you're hot for more."

"I wouldn't mind more—with that guy."

"You think he was as good as your bathroom banger?"

"Oh yeah. Better. Bathroom boy was a fly-by. We had trucker fucker all night. That man had some serious *cream*."

"God, yes," Marianne said. "Well, we just have to find another one, that's all there is to it."

"Are we getting naked in New Hampshire?"

"I think we're going to find a bar . . . it's time for some bar banging."

They got off at Portsmouth. It was about two o'clock then, and they drove around downtown a bit, and then, at Marianne's direction, headed away from the city.

"We don't want the corporate crowd bar. Those guys are married with kids and benefits; they don't spend Saturdays telling sex stories over a mug of draft. We want the billiard bar."

"What, real guys play pool?"

"Real penises are good at getting their balls in your pocket . . ."

"I like the sound of that." Frankie was squirming already. Just the thought of enticing another vigorous penis between her legs made her soft and succulent with anticipation. She was prepared, she was ripe and ready.

It didn't matter what place: it only mattered that there were men there, hot, horny men who wanted to fuck two gorgeous, juicy young women in tight, sexy clothes.

They sat at the end of the bar closest to the door, aware of the intense scrutiny of the few customers already there as they made a show of getting comfortable.

The bartender looked at them skeptically. "No soliciting."

Marianne smiled at him. "I wouldn't mind meeting a guy here. I'd love to meet a guy here, actually. So . . ."

"What's your pleasure?"

A thick slab of hot, hard penis, thank you.

Marianne ordered a beer, Frankie a screwdriver.

"There's a menu," the bartender said.

"What's on the menu?" Marianne asked with a touch of coyness.

"Anyone you want," someone called out. All eyes were riveted on them.

"I'm Marianne," Marianne said in reponse. "This is Frankie."

"Buy you a drink?" the same voice. The bartender made a disgusted sound and stalked away.

"Sure," Marianne invited. "Come on over."

He was at one of the tables at the rear of the bar. He came out of the shadows, a middle-aged guy with a pleasant face and an eager-to-please manner.

"Sit." Marianne made room for him between her and Frankie. He motioned to the bartender to refill their drinks and tossed a twenty on the counter.

"So. You're obviously not from around here."

"No. We're just traveling through." Marianne caught Frankie's eye; she wanted this guy, if she could hook him.

"In a limo?"

Oh, so they'd gotten that. She leaned into him, and told him confidentially, "It's a road trip. We call it the Dirty Girls Road Trip."

He looked down into her tee, at her full, taut-tipped breasts. "How dirty?"

"As dirty as you think. What"—she brushed her covered nipple against his bare forearm—"do you have in mind?"

"What do you need?" He put his arms around her shoulders as she leaned even closer.

"There's lots of room in the limo. You feel like going outside and . . . talking?"

He pulled her closer so he could whisper in her ear, "I feel like going outside and feeling something."

"I want to feel something, too."

"Let's get another round." He motioned again for a refill. "Miss Marianne's gonna show me that old limousine of hers."

They took their drinks and ambled outside. Thank heaven, Rollie had parked behind the bar; no one could see what they were up to.

Frankie nursed her second screwdriver and let the third one sit.

"Your friend is a piece of work," the bartender said. "You don't come sashaying into a bar with your nipples on display and your ass waggling from the tight end of a pair of spandex pants unless you're selling your body—"

"Or giving it away," Frankie countered.

"Are you?"

"I'd love to meet a guy here," she answered. "You never know where the evening can end."

"Okay," the bartender said. "I'm Barney."

"Hey, Barney." He was hotter than the guy Marianne had

gone with and he had the same country-bred look as her bathroom banger. He was heavier, fleshier, his eyes were hotter, his mouth fuller. He knew about bar girls and a quick pick in the bathroom, she was certain of it.

"You planning to stay in town?"

"I might, for a night. Depends."

He turned and called behind him, "Hey, Frank, you wanna take over for an hour? I want to show Miss Frankie our town before she leaves."

Frank came to replace him and Barney came around, took her elbow, and propelled her out the door. "My car's over here."

"Please don't tell me we're doing a backseat fuck."

"I've got a room on reserve. You don't think you're the first chick who's ever come on to me?"

"God, I hope not. I hope you're really experienced in quick fucking."

"I hope you're ready to strip naked and spread your legs the minute we walk in the door."

It was a quick drive to his motel. Another anonymous room. He called it his tryout room. She liked that; a man prepared for the spontaneous moment.

She was half undressed before the door closed. He was already out of his pants, his penis jutting a full nine inches in front of him, flushed with arousal, thick and mighty, throbbing with lust.

She mounted him as he stood, no easy task to get his bulbous penis head aligned with her cleft. Playing with it, stroking it, kissing it aroused her all the more, made her hot and thick with wet, so that when she finally mounted him, his penis just slipped into the thick slickness of her hole.

So deep. She felt him stretching her inner walls, he was so thick and long and she reveled in it. She wound herself around him and let him pin her to the wall, so he could push even deeper now that his penis was properly angled.

She murmured sexy words in his ear as he undulated and shimmied his shaft deeper. There was no end to the depths of her. She couldn't take enough of him. She had never had a penis this big, this filling.

"Aren't you glad I came to play?"

"You're one bad girl."

"I love being a bad girl. I love fucking every guy I meet. So fuck me, Barney. And then maybe I'll fuck the other guys at the bar. You think they're lining up to fuck me? A dozen penises one after the other, hot, thick, luscious . . ." She made a slurping sound, and it was too much for him—he groaned and shifted and with a hard thrust, spent his cum. "Oh, Barney . . . I was really looking forward to a good screw job."

"I'm not done yet," he growled, and she could feel him flexing and that his penis had not diminished its size or power.

"Then let me feel it. Let me taste it. Let me have it . . ."

He let loose then, driving into her with a lustful fury, pounding her ass against the door until her body convulsed all over his shaft.

She stayed with him all afternoon. He took her on the bed, on the floor, in the bathroom, on her back, her knees, orally as she sucked him off, and anally just for a fast jack-off. It was pure lust, fueled by his size and his writhing contempt of the kind of woman who would fuck anyone who was willing.

And finally, he couldn't think of another thing to do to her or with her, and he took her back to the bar.

Marianne was nursing a drink inside. "Oh God, the bartender?"

"Yeah, and let me tell you, the operative word is *bar*."

"Shit. How big?"

"Nine inches at least."

"Wow. Big Spender spent his wad, all right . . . All over me, and not much else. Why do I get all the nuts?"

"You are always too much in a hurry. You grab the first piece of candy you see and you bite before you even know what's in your hand."

"Damn. I want truck guy. I let him go too fast. He was really big and really built. He had that look."

"Truck guy is probably in Canada already."

"So I guess we'll stay over tonight, huh?"

"Sure. We'll get some dinner and maybe we'll run into a couple of other guys. If we do, I know a nearby motel."

Chapter Six

They dressed for the evening a little less explicitly than for bar hopping: they were wearing underwear for one thing, and a dressier knit top that wasn't quite so tight. Toned down makeup.

They drove back into Portsmouth to find a good place to eat. But the best surprise was, it wasn't hard to find men at the best restaurant in town.

Within ten minutes of their being seated at the long, old-fashioned bar to wait for a table, Marianne had hooked up with a well-dressed guy who liked to talk, flirt, and kiss. A guy who looked bedazzled enough to pay for dinner, if not more.

Frankie moved a little further away to give Marianne enough room to play. This was definitely Bonus Guy; they hadn't really been *looking* to hook up tonight. Marianne's mind was focused on truck guy, who'd assumed the sexual proportions of a raging bull in her mind.

God, if he walked through the door . . .

Not.

She told the waitress that she would need a separate table.

Let them have the meal to themselves; it was rather fun watching Bonus Guy operate on Marianne. He was good. He touched, he whispered, he made her laugh, he had that look, especially when he focused on her mouth, and invariably he followed it with a little kiss that with each one grew more and more intimate.

He was really good. A study in contrasts: their day of hard immediate fucking, and this guy's cool leisurely approach. He had worked up to squeezing her arm, patting her thigh, putting his arm around her, pulling her into a deeper kiss, his tongue in her mouth this time . . .

So when their table was called, Marianne was already ripe for an evening of unfettered lust. They had arranged that if one of them got lucky, they would meet later at Barney's motel, but this guy didn't look like a motel mooch. It would be interesting to see how the evening played out.

Meantime, she was set to dine alone . . . not a terrific prospect, and no prospects for company in sight. Maybe it was a good thing. Maybe she needed some breathing room. Two nonstop days of anonymous sex was enough to give anyone pause.

And she'd gotten the best of that random lot, so she didn't begrudge Marianne Bonus Guy.

She just wasn't certain they were going to make Bar Harbor by tomorrow. But what did it matter? They were on Marianne Time, and that stretched to eternity when sex was involved.

Her name was called, and she was shown to a table on the opposite side of the room from Marianne and Bonus Guy. She deliberately sat with her back to them. She deliberately refused offers of company. She had a seafood salad, a glass of wine, coffee, devoured as quickly as she could reasonably swallow.

She was aware of the low hum of conversation behind her. She didn't know if Marianne and Bonus Guy were still there—she didn't want to know—but eventually she had to leave, and there they were, nuzzling over coffee.

A night alone would not be a bad thing.

A hand grasped her arm as she was passing the bar and she stopped, startled and just a little put out by such aggressiveness.

"Hey," he said

Truck guy! And he cleaned up really, really well.

"Hey yourself. What are you doing here?"

"I had an off-load about fifty miles east of here, and I'm on my way back south. You?"

"Pit stop. Here for the night."

"Your friend?"

"Busy in there." She motioned to the restaurant.

"Good." His gaze grazed her body. "I liked you the best."

"How best?" she asked brashly.

"I'd like to make a standing date to fuck you whenever I'm in town."

She hid a smile of deep female satisfaction. "A very tempting offer. Too bad this isn't my town."

"No shit. Let me buy you a drink."

"No, thanks. I'm on my way out."

"Hell, not all by yourself? *You?*"

"You have any better ideas?" she asked coyly.

"At least one," he murmured, rubbing his knuckles against her arm.

"I'm open . . . to hear it," she countered—and froze. Marianne and Bonus Guy were on their way out and headed in their direction. There was no time to regroup or pretend that she and truck guy weren't having the conversation they were having. Marianne could tell at a hundred feet when sex talk was involved.

She arched a brow as she saw them. "Well, hello you."

"And you," truck guy said coolly.

"Nice to see you again," she said to him. "I'll see you soon," she told Frankie, and let Bonus Guy lead her out of the bar.

"Brrrr," truck guy said. "Is this a problem for you?"

"Which this?"

"Us, here, talking, together."

"Not if he lives up to his come-on."

"Good, I'm up for fucking you tonight. Now. All night. And whenever I'm in *your* town. Wherever the fuck it is."

He took her hand surreptitiously and pressed it against his ferocious erection.

She made a sound of pure female lust. "Where?"

"I don't care," he whispered. "Let's get the fuck out of here before I fuck you on the floor."

He took her on the floor of his truck instead, the closest private place to the restaurant. Didn't take off his clothes, just whipped out his penis, pushed down her pants, and loaded his heft into her.

Her body spasmed instantly; her body remembered him big-time. Truck guy was huge, thick, tasty. Maintained that erection like a flagpole. Liked to do it hard and fast to start—or maybe he was so engorged, it was all he could do to contain his cream when he was deep inside her.

She liked that idea, too.

"I have a room," she whispered after her second orgasm.

"I'm not moving my penis from your cunt. Just so you know."

"No one wants your penis crammed inside me more than I do."

"Good. I'm not moving."

"Even for a little comfort? Even for the ten minutes it takes to get there?"

He gave it a moment's thought. "Only if you fondle my penis while I drive there."

"Sounds like a luscious idea to me."

She did more than that. As he drove, she played with his shaft, stroking and fondling it, and kissing and sucking his penis head. He was almost ready to blow when he turned into the motel parking lot, and he was containing it master-fully.

"Better strip before you get in that room or I'll tear off your clothes."

She was naked before they reached the door.

He pushed her onto her knees, pushed his penis in from the rear until his hips butted up against her bottom. "I'm liking this."

She felt his hands on her butt and she canted herself

upward to take him deeper, and he began to ride, his penis hot and heavy inside her. Huge and thick inside her, the axis on which her world revolved.

Until the streaming pleasure pooled between her legs and exploded all over him. But he held back, eased her up onto his lap, and dropped into a nearby chair with his penis still embedded in her, then he cupped her breasts and felt for her nipples.

"I remember these beauties . . ."

He knew just how to finger the hard tips, just how to stroke and tweak them, just the right pressure to squeeze them. Her whole body convulsed again, catching her unawares.

He rode the orgasm with her until it eddied away.

"Where did you say you live?"

"I didn't," she murmured.

"Guess I have to work harder to convince you."

"Of what?"

"To give me that invitation. You are one hot cunt. I don't get why you're out fucking strangers."

"I like variety. A lot of penises. A lot of men. A lot of fun. A lot of fucking. Where would we have hooked up long enough for me to fuck *you*—twice now."

"My pleasure," he growled, running his hands from her breasts down to her thighs. "Every man you meet probably wants to fuck you. I want a permanent place in that line."

He couldn't see her kitten smile.

"Maybe," she gasped as he heaved his hips and his penis up into her. He drove into her again. "Maybe you can be in line . . ." And again. "Okay, okay—you made your point."

"So how can I reach you? When can we fuck again?"

He kept thrusting into her, short, sharp strokes in tandem with his fingering her nipples in that seductive erotic way. Her nipples were his secret weapon. She felt them too much; her orgasm broke over her again in long spasmic ripples and she rode him hard to the end.

"How many men?"

"Oh don't . . . how do I know?"

"How many penises—*memorable* penises?"

"Yours, for sure."

"How many?"

"Don't go jealous lover on me, after such a lovely orgasm."

"Just want that place in line."

"You'll be number one with your stamina. I don't think anyone had the staying power you have."

"I practice with random cunts."

"Don't get nasty. *Do* the nasty."

"No, I just want to sit here with my penis hard in *your* cunt."

"So—how many cunts?"

"Too many, and none as orgasmic as yours."

"And we have the whole night."

"Exactly."

Truck guy didn't give up. She liked that about him, and she didn't. On the other hand, a go-to fuck with a vigorous proven penis ought not be rejected out of hand. It was something to consider. Something to look forward to. Who knew what truck guy's schedule was, or even whether, for all his insistence on a standing date, he'd ever be anywhere near Manhattan in the course of his work anyway.

So that should make it an easy *yes*. And if he did for some reason come through New York, she'd have a night of fabulous fucking.

Except—

Marianne.

God, why was Marianne always in her bedroom? Forget Marianne. Or maybe truck guy would be up for a threesome now and again.

Forget that.

He rolled over, mounted, and covered her, nearly in his sleep. "You there?"

"I'm here."

"Me, too."

"Can't miss you."

"Hope not." He began pumping, his penis half asleep, waking up with a jolt as her wet and heat enfolded it and took it deep. He shoved himself tight, hip to hip, to the hilt. "That feels real good."

"It's better than good." A night of stellar sex with a virile penis that held its charge. Couldn't ask for more than that. It was almost enough to give up anyone else.

But no. They had a long trip yet to go, and truck guy was heading south. It was four a.m. His penis was heading south, too.

Almost time to go.

By the time she peeked out the door he was sound asleep, wholly exhausted by her—something she hadn't thought could happen.

She was shocked to see the limo was actually there. It didn't bode well if Marianne didn't stay the course with Bonus Guy.

Stealthily, she packed up her clothes and wrote truck guy a message: *standing fuck ok. e/m ok,* and she put down Marianne's business email address.

One last look at truck guy, deep asleep, looking faintly vulnerable as men did when they were naked, his penis at half staff, but still interested . . . she had only to stroke it once, twice, and it would bloom hard for her, ripe for her—too necessary for her to take the time this morning when the car was waiting.

She wanted to lick it, to kiss it all over, to . . . stop it!

She slipped out of the room and resolutely opened the limo door.

"So you got truck guy," Marianne said with a tinge of bitterness, as she climbed in.

"No, truck guy got *me*. How could I have known he'd be there last night? What about you? How was your night?"

"We know how *your* night went," Marianne said testily. "He was okay. All show, not much substance."

Or was that the case with every man she met, and about every man she wanted but couldn't have?

"Look. The truck guy—wanted to get in touch again. I gave him your business email address, so—he's all yours."

"Why does he suddenly want to get in touch?" Marianne asked suspiciously.

"He wants a harem honey whenever he's in town. It's kind of a sexy idea. I wouldn't sit around waiting, but it's a guaranteed twelve hours of vigorous fucking with a dick that knows how to stay bone hard and feels a yard long."

"You should know," Marianne muttered. "All right. I'll try him on again and see if he fits. Meantime, no more tight pants. They're too hard to get out of when you need to, and too in the way when you don't need them. We got the best action with pussy power, so we're going for breakfast, then we're going shopping for thigh-high skirts. Easy in, easy out. And then we're heading home. I can't deal with these country deadheads, so we're going to fuck some serious head on the way home."

It was best not to argue when Marianne was displeased. And she was seriously displeased, and obviously didn't think the penis potential was any better further north.

"Okay—coffee and shopping it is."

"You didn't call your mother?"

"No, I actually thought I would when we actually got to Kittery."

"Well, we almost made it. But—God, another three hours . . . I need some seriously dirty, hard ass to do me— soon."

They found an all-night restaurant on the highway and ignored the stares and the tentative come-ons, because Marianne wanted the details about truck guy's new interest.

"He said we were the best cunt he's ever had, how about that?" Frankie lied, just a little.

"You should have gotten me away from my guy."

"Well, who knew where you were?"

"I'll leave a text message next time," she said caustically. But still, the idea somewhat mollified her. "Tell you what—we'll entice another truck guy on the way back."

Oh God—what if they ran across original truck guy? Shit. He was going south, he was traveling I-95—damn damn damn—and in all probability, he hadn't left yet . . . Jesus. Stupid, telling her he wanted her, too. But maybe, if her worst nightmare happened, maybe he wouldn't mind boning them both. The damn truck was big enough . . . fucking one while the other waited? Not so hot.

"We don't have to do designer duds, either," Marianne went on. "I'm fine with whatever box store we come across."

So, maybe she could delay things a little at Wal-Mart. C'mon, truck guy, get up and get gone!

She felt like a teenager as they tried on clothes in the tiny dressing area in the store. Short, flippy skirts that weren't quite as short as Marianne was envisioning. "We'll buy some tape, hem them up to *easy in* length. And we're on our way."

They chose half a dozen skirts, and Marianne found the sewing department, where they found fabric glue and pins. "Well, now . . . this is way cool," she said as they made the purchases and her excitement escalated.

In the limo, in the parking lot, they removed the price tags and tried on the skirts to take an accurate measure of how high the hems should go, and then pinned and glued them. "Perfect," Marianne pronounced. "Now we'll see some fast action with nothing to get in the way."

It was ten o'clock. They had bought some tea and snacks

to restock the fridge, and Marianne directed Rollie to head toward the highway. Frankie crossed her fingers that truck guy was a hundred miles south of there already.

With her luck, not likely. She needed another delaying tactic—now.

"Hey—wait. Over there."

"What's over there? Ohhh . . . I see. Lumber and hardware. Rollie! We're going to find us some big screwdrivers."

Of course, the two of them, dressed in their tight shirts, short skirts, and high heels got some heavy stares in a store full of jeans and chambray. Marianne found someone to show them the screwdrivers, and she chose a repair kit for the car. Then she asked directions to the automotive section—she needed some jumper cables and highway emergency things.

They tripped through the store, reveling in the overt attention, picked up sundry objects of interest along the way, found the highway emergency kit they needed, and finally checked out.

"One of those hunky guys will follow us," Marianne predicted as she pushed the cart to the parking lot. She'd had Rollie park far from the entrance, so they had a chance of meeting a tool guy coming or going. "I get first dibs."

"Hey, need some help?"

One of the guys they'd seen in passing. Tall, beefy, open face, not too old. Snug jeans. Tee-shirt. Gimme cap. Marianne flashed Frankie a telling look.

"Sure. My car's over there."

He helped her load her purchases into the small trunk. "Nice car."

"Would you like to go for a ride? My friend can stay here or come, what's your preference?"

"To ride you," he growled.

Marianne climbed in, showing a fair amount of ass, and he followed, unzipping himself before he even settled on the seat. Frankie closed the door as Marianne climbed onto his rampaging penis and Rollie drove away.

Easy in, easy out. What a genius idea this was, a place swarming with men!

"Excuse me." A nice strong voice. She turned. He wasn't so bad on the eyes, either. Or maybe she only cared about what his tools looked like. "Did that dumb dick just leave you here?"

"I guess you could see he did."

"I'd be happy to offer to . . . service you."

The morning sun was hot on her body, her face; it made her feel juicy and sexed up. "Do I look like I need servicing?"

"You look like you're creamy all the time."

"Do I look like I want it?"

He gave her a hard knowing look that rested on the outline of her nipples pushing out from her shirt. "You want it."

"You up for servicing me?"

"I've got all the tools, lady."

"Where do we go?"

He motioned. "Van over there."

"Perfect." A twenty-minute energizer. He slid open the side door and she climbed in to find a mattress already in place.

"I guess you use your tools a lot, huh?" she murmured coyly as she wriggled onto her back.

"I guess you don't wear a skirt that short and no underwear unless you're always hot for a man tool between your legs. I got a good look at that creamy crotch and I decided to get me some." He ripped open his zipper as he closed the door behind him, pulled down his pants, shoved up her skirt, and drove between her legs.

She took him hard and high, his strokes long and firm, so it was easy to undulate her hips in rhythm with him.

But she was too hot for him, her body too responsive; he pulsed and throbbed, valiantly trying to contain his cream. "Sonuvabitch," he gasped as he poured himself into her. "I was so right about you."

"How?"

"You gotta have a man between your legs all the time."

"All the time, tool man. So don't move. I want more."

"Oh, believe it, there's more."

There was much more. Tool guy loved his tool, and he loved getting it off a half dozen times before he ran out of steam.

"Cunt for lunch." He liked sucking her off too, even saturated with his musk. She was lush with it, her body spongy with the pleasure of him lapping at her and digging his hot tongue into her swollen cunt lips.

And then back on top of her, covering her, mounting her. "What about your friend?"

"She'll be back—when she's had enough."

He nuzzled her nipples. "You ever get enough? Or do you just want it all the time?"

"All the time."

That jolted a spurt out of him. "You like what I've got?"

She arched her body to pull him in more. "I like what you've got."

He had hot, hard, brisk strokes, banging her body emphatically as she canted her hips upward to take him still deeper. This time, the orgasmic wave caught them both and they came roaring down to climax together.

He collapsed on top of her, an unwelcome weight now that simultaneous pleasure had been achieved.

She wondered if Marianne had returned. She wondered if enough time had elapsed that she wouldn't have to travel in fear they'd meet truck guy. She wondered if tool guy would ever get off her body.

"Hey—" she said.

"Yeah?" He shifted and she rolled out from under him. "Don't go."

"Not yet." She crawled to the front seat, liking the fact that just by pulling down her skirt and shirt, she was already dressed. The limo was parked exactly where it had been, as if it had never left.

"Tool guy . . ."

"Yeah?"

Lord, Frankie thought, he was bone dry and sapped as a maple tree. "Gotta go."

He reached out, futilely, because she had climbed into the

front seat so she could exit by the passenger door. "When—again?"

"Dream about me, tool guy." This was *so* the ideal ending to the morning. "I won't forget that penis very soon . . ."

And she opened the door and left him.

There was just no satisfying Marianne. The horny hardware guy helped himself to plenty of pussy, but Marianne refused second helpings.

"How come you get all the great sex?" she complained.

Frankie decided to downplay the infinite pleasures of tool guy.

"Well, first, you were right about the skirts. Much better access. And they're looking. But tool guy just wanted me to sit and do all the work. I got rid of him quick. What's the point of fucking if the guy won't even mount you?"

"Exactly," Marianne agreed peevishly. "Stupid bulls. They think cunts like ours come along every day? They think they can fuck bodies like this every day?" She made a disgusted sound. "Those idiots fall short every time. I really thought we'd have great hot sex on this trip. I didn't think the guys at the pit stops would turn out to be the pits."

"Well, it's not over, is it? We've got a day or two to find that great fuck."

"Truck guy was a great fuck."

"And he's got your number, so he and his dick are coming at some point."

"There's a fantasy. Truck guy awash in cum."

"You, stuffed with his cum."

"Ummm—oh, I like that . . ."

"Maybe we could find some cool place to find guys in Massachusetts. Maybe find a place to go dancing. Minimum, we get a guy's arms around us. If we're lucky, he'll cop a feel and a whole lot more."

It was a karaoke bar, with canned dance music and a DJ. There was food, a smoky ambience, booths, a bar, a nice big dance floor. It was what it was. And it was crowded. Lots of guys, a fair amount of women. It was five o'clock on a holiday weekend and they were there to celebrate.

"No competition," Marianne whispered as they entered and scanned the crowd. She was hungry, for food *and* sex by that time.

"Grab a seat at the bar, then. I see they're handing out buffalo wings and bull."

"I need the ladies' room."

"Okay, I'll get the seats." She forged forward. Not easy. Every seat at the bar was taken. But then, there were gentlemen in this town. A half dozen of them offered her theirs. Easy to be cynical about the reason why. She took one close to the entrance so Marianne would see her, and immediately was inundated with offers to buy her a drink.

She waved them off. "I'm waiting for my friend."

"Everybody's waiting for a friend. How about a dance?"

"Gotta wait for my friend—she's in the ladies' room and she'd love to have you all buy her a drink."

But Marianne wasn't in the ladies' room. Marianne was

engaged in conversation with someone at the door. Oh, God, truck guy! How the hell did he get here?

Crap, it was like he had sonar or something.

He saw her a moment later and pushed his way over to her. "Well, hell."

"Truck guy," she said brightly.

"Going south, your friend tells me."

"Not fast enough, apparently. I left an email address."

"Yeah, but I've got the real thing now."

"No, you've got two real things, and if you want to even talk to me, you had better make my friend real happy—real soon."

He gave her a smoking look. "You don't mean what I think you mean?"

"You've got a real big truck. Use it."

He looked at her again, from head to toe, particularly noting that she wore a skirt. "She wasn't that good."

"She thought you were king of the cowboys. So you have to do her, if you have any hope of doing me." She gave him a simmering look from under her eyelashes, and he turned on his heel and stalked away.

How odd to think she had the power to command him to do anything, let alone demand he have sex with someone he didn't particularly want. But that couldn't be a hardship for a guy with his staying power, to get it up and in someone as beautiful and endlessly horny as Marianne.

Of course, now that he was here, her interest diminished in anyone else.

She nursed a glass of wine. She picked at the buffalo

wings, and answered all the obvious heat-seeking questions with good humor.

An hour went by. Two. Goddamn, he had walked out on her! He was gone in his big old truck with his big old honking penis, and she was stuck with whoever was available tonight.

But then, where was Marianne? Hell. A stupid idea, a place like this.

And if they went off together . . . well, she had a buffet of men from which to pick and choose. Except—she wanted *his* penis, which was probably fucking Marianne right now.

A pair of hands clamped down on her shoulders and her breath caught. Truck guy. "How *do* you do?" he murmured. "Care to dance?"

"Love to dance."

He put his arms around her and jammed his steaming erection against her hips. "We need to be naked and alone."

"That sounds good to me."

He maneuvered her into a far corner away from the crowd.

"This is what I was thinking about out there." He ran his hands down her back to cup her buttocks. "And this . . ." He worked his fingers under her skirt and into her crease. "And this ." into her honeyed cunt lips from the reverse position. "Like that . . ." They swayed to the music while he penetrated deeper and harder. "And that . . ." as she arched forward to give him a better angle. "Yeah . . ."

His fingers were so deep, she had to stand on her toes as they swayed to the music. "We could do this a better way . . ."

"I need to punish you for making me do that."

"Punish me? Because I demanded you fuck my friend? Poor truck guy. What a hard job I gave you."

"Big-time punishment for that." He squeezed her buttock. "You feel like getting spanked?"

"Finger fucking is a good punishment for me."

"Or I can ease my penis up under your skirt."

"Awful punishment." In public. Among all these customers. Fucking her on the dance floor. Which he was doing already. She couldn't be more aroused. "Why don't you whip it out and give it to me?"

And then she felt his penis head nudging her between her legs. She spread herself and he pushed his penis further into her cleft. She shimmied against him, working his shaft into her cunt. And then, when the angle was achieved, he just thrust and he was there.

"I hate that I can't mount you properly, that you're not naked under my body, and that I can't have every inch of my penis tightly packed into your cunt. And I can't suck your nipples into hard points the way I want to. But I *can* fuck you, and I'm doing you right here and now as my reward for doing your bidding."

He held her hips as they rocked together in rhythm. No one was watching, and since he was taller than she, no one could see her face, just her arms wrapped around his neck and the slow somnolent movement of their bodies.

He pinned her to the wall, his hips undulating and thrusting in rhythm to the slow beat of the music. She was barely on her feet, totally supported by the strength of his hips and his penis, and she rode on a pillow of voluptuous sensation, not even caring if she had an orgasm. Just let him continue the luscious pleasure of his hard rhythmic thrusts. Just let him . . .

The orgasm came coiling downward from nowhere, right between her legs, and spilling all over the thick bulbous head of his penis on an out-thrust, and exploding as he drove into her one more time and spent his cream.

She barely heard the music as he pulled himself from her. "I need you naked."

"Me too." She could barely get the words out. Everything seemed at a distance, as if they were moving outside what was happening in the bar, as if they were ghosts.

One ghost was waving at her. "Hey—we gotta get moving."

Oh shit. Marianne.

She swallowed hard and looked up at truck guy. "No nipple sucking tonight."

"Son of a bitch. Why can't you stay?"

"It's not my dime."

"She's not your bitch?"

"No. Just my friend. Email me."

"But where are you?"

"New York."

"That's a goddamned big place," he called after her as she went to join Marianne.

"Maybe not," she shouted back.

Into the limousine, and Rollie pulled hard and fast out of the parking lot. Marianne lounged back on the banquette and looked at Frankie thoughtfully.

"The reality is never as good as the fantasy. Was it good for you?"

Just lie. "It was okay. I mean—standing up, in the rear of the dance floor, people all around us. Guy couldn't get us privacy?"

"He really just wanted to bang you," Marianne said.

"Yeah, well—lucky me."

"Even after two hours of fucking me. He came after you with *my* juices on his shaft."

The thought actually made Frankie hot.

"Anyway, I don't want him anymore. He wasn't that great. He's all yours," Marianne said.

"I doubt it. He's the kind that says he'll email and then he never does."

Marianne held her gaze, her expression tight. "What if he did? Would you fuck him again?"

"That's what *he'd* want. That might not be what I want when the time comes."

"That's exactly what you want," Marianne said, "all the time."

"That's what tool guy said. And so do you."

Marianne's lips thinned. "But you're getting it."

"I'm not so much getting *it.*" *Liar.* She didn't know it was possible to get so much *it,* from so many random penises.

She was ripe for *it* now, more specifically for everything truck guy had offered. Her nipples were stiff with arousal, the musky wet from their sex seeping between her legs, the residue of his thick semen mixing with the lush honey of her body.

She could smell it, it was so intoxicatingly arousing.

"Try on one more guy," she said coaxingly. "Come on. You see how many guys there are just willing to drop trou for a free fuck."

Marianne thought about it a minute, as if she would actually consider putting a limit on her excesses, but obviously the thought of the next man over the horizon was too seductive for her. And maybe always would be.

"Why not? You can't wind up a Dirty Girls Road Trip without some final down-and-dirty sex."

Now Marianne wanted it fast, hot, and raw. She was thick with it, desperate for it. Around midnight, Rollie pulled into a gas station that was just about to close.

Marianne emerged from the backseat, long bare legs first, short skirt, braless in her tight top. "Can I get you to fill me up?" she asked the attendant coaxingly.

He was young, eager, and erect the instant he eyed her nipples pushing tight against her top. "Come into the office to sign the credit slip."

She came in the office, her back against the door to the garage, his long, slippery penis pumping heat and sex fumes into her jangling body, his hot tongue swiping her nipples and sucking hard on the tips.

"*That's* what I'm talking about," Marianne said as she climbed back into the car. "I want more of that."

Speed sex. Anonymous. Primal. Momentary relief and then on to the next hot penis. Marianne was like a heat-seeking guided missile.

They pulled up to a tollbooth just as there was a change of toll taker. This guy was younger, too. Maybe a college student. Devilishly good-looking. And he had a look that said he knew just what they were up to.

He looked at Marianne, he looked down her shirt at her naked breasts and the dusky shadow of her nipples, and he said, "I know a place." She opened the door for him and he directed Rollie just off the shoulder, behind the highway department building, into a small discreet parking area.

Frankie slipped out of the limo. Ten minutes later, Marianne opened the door. "You want some?"

She did, but this was Marianne's show. "No. I'm good."

The guy was still sucking Marianne's nipples; she slammed the door and took him between her legs again. Ten minutes later: "This guy's good. Come on, Frankie. He's still hard."

She wanted some really bad, but he was Marianne's.

A half hour later. "Okay. Enough." She was naked, still hot with lust as she climbed out of the car. He came after her, naked too, wrenched her around, pushed her over the hood, and forcefully humped her from behind.

"*You* . . ." Now he was in control, grasping Frankie's arm and pushing her into the limo. "You want?"

In the dim light, he was still massively erect, his penis slick with wet from Marianne, throbbing with the primitive lust to fuck. She leaned back in the seat, hiked up her skirt, and invited him to root between her legs.

Ahhhh . . . did she moan, did he, at the luscious feel of her body being penetrated by something hard and hot.

The angle was perfect, he was on his knees above her, she was canted upward on the seat, her legs bent, her cleft tilted to accommodate the driving angle of his slick, hot penis.

He ripped off her shirt to look at her breasts, he fingered her nipples, rolling each between his thumb and forefinger. He pushed his shaft deeper with a shimmy of his hips, knowing she felt every inch of him.

Move, don't move . . . little sexy movements, her nipples molten with feeling. He loomed above her, rolling her nipples to stiff points, his expertly undulating hips rolling tight against her hips, not too much movement, just enough to make her billowy with lust.

Marianne watching . . . this one's a keeper, email me for sex anytime, I do lunch, I lunch on penises . . . a tasting party just with that penis . . . and truck guy—and that Rocky's Cement bathroom guy . . . he's torturing my tits . . .

And she came, a long smooth rippling flow of glowing satin, ribboning right down between her legs.

He pulled his penis out of her ruthlessly, and turned to Marianne. "Ready for more?"

She cupped his balls. "I'm naked, aren't I? What do you think I'm here for?"

"I know *exactly* what you're here for." He pulled her onto the floor of the limo, on her back, and shoved his penis into her. "The naked lady wants hard, cunt-busting cock. And I'm here to give it to you." He got her off with five minutes of hard thrusting and left her panting on the floor.

"Now—Miss Nipples here . . ." He climbed onto the backseat with Frankie. "I can't decide whether to suck you or fuck you."

"How about you do neither," Marianne snapped, ending it suddenly. "How about I pay you off and you get out of here?"

"Yeah, sure. Don't be mad. You're a hot piece. You got what you wanted."

She threw some money at him. "So did you."

She was angry again. "The son of a bitch wanted you. They *always* want you. Next guy, I do alone."

"Fine." Damn. She shouldn't have gotten in the limo. She should never have let him fuck her. "Speed sex isn't my thing."

"Yeah, I could tell. He took his time with you."

Best not to comment on that. Best just to lay there naked and let Marianne sulk. She couldn't help it if she was orgasmic. Or that the guy's penis turned her on. Or that her breasts were so enticing to him.

The hell with it. They were almost home anyway, and for all she knew, Marianne was going to fire her.

How nuts was that?

They made a bathroom stop that took twenty minutes, and when Marianne returned, she was flushed and bright-eyed. "Got my morning fuck. Guy coming out of the bath-room gave me the *she's naked, hot, and I want to fuck her now* look. So I stopped him and he did. I love speed fucks. Easy in, easy out."

Maybe early in the morning was the key. There weren't

many people around. There were a lot of cars scattered all over the parking lots with people asleep or just taking a break from a long drive.

When they stopped for a break again, Marianne got out of the car and wandered around the parking lot until someone came to talk to her. Five minutes later, she went off with him into the darkness.

Marianne fucked. Marianne had to have all the action.

Frankie wondered why she hadn't realized it before.

Chapter Seven

The week following their return, Marianne was a bitch, standoffish, fault-finding, moody, and disinterested in everything.

"So you got sex the whole hundred miles home, and you're still ticked? I don't get it." Frankie had to say something; Marianne in a continuing snit was not a pleasant prospect.

"That was then, this is now."

"You weren't expecting any of them to . . ."

"What about truck guy?"

"I wrote him off a hundred miles ago. C'mon, Marianne. That was a thing. Guys like that don't follow up. It's too much effort. It didn't take any exertion on his part to get us to bed."

"You fell into his lap, he fell for you."

"Well, he's over. And your last three speed bumps were massively good. So . . ."

"Yep. But that's over now."

And, Frankie thought, so was the excitement, the danger, the risk. Obviously nothing in Marianne's everyday life could equal the adrenaline rush of having random sex with a dozen strange men in three states.

Or was Marianne going a little over the edge, endlessly searching for the guy with the glint in his eye, the guy who existed only in her imagination?

Why even want him? A lifestyle of casual coupling meant all the sex you could eat. And when you took it out of town, it became even more alluring, seductive, thrilling, and dangerous. Everything that ratcheted up the goal of getting some guy with a hefty penis to fuck you. The one-shot guy. Seduced by your body, your come-on, your scent, your sex . . .

Powerful, making a man instantly in lust with you.

Not that those guys needed much of a come-on. They were always looking for easy sex—backseat, front seat, motel, no tell.

The best thing about one-shot sex was no emotional investment. It was grab and go. Bang and bolt. Fuck and flee. Why Marianne seemed to want something more was beyond her. It was as if for her, the trip had been a quest for the holy penis.

And damn, truck guy *was* good. If he ever did contact her, if he ever was in New York, she'd get naked with him in a heartbeat.

And never tell Marianne.

Oh damn. Disloyal over a random penis. How low could she go?

"Hey, Frankie—" Marianne was at the computer. "Come and look at this. Oh, damn—maybe not. What do you think?"

Frankie read the blog entry over her shoulder:

What bed-hopping socialite just spent a week on her back on a sex-spree trip? You have to wonder how many lucky stallions got two insertions for the price of one.

"Oh God. *The Diva's Daybook—Divine Dish Daily.* Who on earth leaked that?"

"I don't know. Who knows where they find these things out?" Marianne didn't sound particularly upset. "It's such an insular world. Everyone knows everything, always. Well, this is a wake-up call if ever there was one. I've been moping around here; I need an afternoon out. Spa time, I think. Are you coming?"

She needed some time away from Marianne.

"No. I'd just love to take a nap."

That answer didn't set Marianne off, as it sometimes did. "You know what. I'm glad they printed that blind item. It's sexy. It's a call to action. We haven't had sex for a week. So gird yourself for tonight—I have an idea."

Her ideas were exhausting. Frankie climbed back into bed, but felt too restive to sleep. She went onto the computer, clicking on the business email folder.

And there was the message she'd hoped would be there—and wouldn't.

In Manhattan, have two hours—is this where you are? Come to the Skyway by two p.m. Room 15. My penis is stoked . . .

She felt her whole body flush. It was two-thirty, it was too late. She couldn't call; didn't know his name. She could make it by three if there was no traffic, no detours, a cab out front. No time to change, damn damn damn—

She raced for a cab and pushed him to get to Tenth Avenue, her heart racing. She got there at three-fifteen, ripping open her buttons, her jeans as she flew down the hall to Room 15 and knocked. The door opened to truck guy, his penis jutting out at her through the tails of his shirt. He slammed the door, she kicked off her jeans, and he pushed her against the door.

"That's better."

She just let him slip and slide in and out of her honey wet. There was nothing like a good hard penis . . . she needed to get one in-house—permanently.

Meantime, truck guy knew all the right moves: in and out, slick and slow; then he blew.

He lifted her, still embedded in her, and carried her to the bed, where he laid her down and covered her with his body.

"And I expected you to keep your promise to soak my nipples . . ."

He made a sound and lifted himself enough to cover the nearest nipple with his hot tongue before he sucked it, hard. Her body jolted under his; his penis elongated.

"Just stay that way."

"You don't want much," she whispered. "You have to leave in forty minutes."

"Then we'll see how many times I can fuck you in forty minutes."

It was forty minutes of straight-on missionary, as if he wanted to mark her body with his. Forty minutes of inventive sucking of her breasts, and explosive orgasms even in this most ordinary of positions.

The clock was the enemy. Even he was watching it surreptitiously and he couldn't push his time any more forward. He had to let her up, let her go.

"You lucked out, truck guy."

"Big time."

"Big penis. I like a big, long, hard penis."

"It fits you like a glove."

"Real tight and hard, the way I like it."

"So fuck me again if you like the way my penis fits so much . . ."

She climbed onto his lap, undulated her body down onto his shaft, and worked it, belly dancing up and down, her breasts bobbing and enticing his mouth, pushing away time until he spewed an explosion of semen that caught her orgasm in the backwash of his pleasure.

"Shit, I gotta go."

"You know where to email me."

"Hell—no names, no address, no . . ."

"You asked for a standing date, you've got it. It's better this way."

Even this was too dangerous, seeing him without telling Marianne.

She patted his still-erect penis, kissed it, and she left him standing naked in the doorway.

*   *   *

Then she could sleep. She slept, knowing Marianne had something obscenely sexual and dirty planned for tonight, and she had to be juiced up for anything. Knowing she had to shower and dress within hours to become a plaything again, to get in Marianne's game.

But at least Marianne was smiling.

"I'm calling the Insatiables. Have them meet us here and we'll implement my idea. It's been too long since we all had sex together. I'm up for something different tonight."

Every time she said that, Frankie cringed a little.

When the Insatiables all arrived, dressed easy in–easy out for clubbing, Marianne handed out drinks and made the big announcement:

"We're going to a strip club. I want to see how those naked women entice their customers to fork over big bucks for a dance and a show."

"Love it," Nina said immediately, and started to strut her stuff across the dining room and down the steps into the living room.

"Ooo, she's good." Marianne applauded. "Get her onstage. Get *me* onstage. Okay, everyone—diaphragms and spermicide tonight. I don't care what birth control you're on. There'll be lots of men, and if they can't have the strippers after hours, they can have us. So let's be cautious and prepared."

"I have a feeling you've researched this," Becca said as they crowded into the elevator fifteen minutes later.

"Oh yeah. We don't do the sleazy side of town, ladies. We

go where the big-time business managers go—East Side and top drawer all the way."

Corporate East Side—right in the mid-fifties off of Third Avenue. Very discreet. It seemed more like the entrance to a chic apartment building than to a strip club. Up an elegant carpeted staircase and into a reception area where there were comfortable club chairs arranged in a conversational setting, side tables to hold a drink, muted paintings on the wall, the doorway to paradise with a discreet sign: *Gentlemen's Lounge, please wait to be seated.*

"Well," Nina murmured. "Isn't this the experience?"

Becca said, "I have a feeling this isn't Marianne's first time."

Marianne slanted a coy look at her. "Oh, I don't know . . . there's first times and then there's first times. Ah, the hostess . . ." as the elegant double doors opened and a beautiful blonde gowned in couture elegance came to greet them.

"Ladies. If I may, we prefer to take your payment method first."

Marianne flipped her black Amex card; the hostess took the card, disappeared for a moment, returned, and motioned them to follow her inside.

On the intimate stage, spotlighted so it was what you saw on entering, an exotic redhead, naked but for a veil that she manipulated expertly and suggestively, was shimmying her hips to Middle Eastern music, and, as they watched, sliding her veil between her legs, lowering herself in supplication to the guests in the front row, her legs spread wide apart to give them ample view of her shorn mound as she caressed herself using the veil like a lover's touch, arching her back to the floor, shaking her breasts in a paroxysm of desire.

The acrobatics were breathtaking; the view erotic as she parted her cunt lips with the expert manipulation of the veil and then slowly raised herself upright to enhance the experience with her fingers.

This was a girl who didn't need to wrap her body around a pole. She had every man's eyes riveted on what she was doing between her legs and every one of them wrapped around her questing fingers as she revealed all the naked mysteries of her cunt.

She knew what they wanted to see, to feel, and she gave it to them, the spotlight following her hands as she spread wide her most intimate part for them with a coy little smile that invited them to pay tribute to her sex, which finally ended with an orgasmic spasm and the darkness of surcease.

The hostess led them to a banquette right at the foot of the stage.

"I don't know that I want to be this up-close-and-personal with a stripper's genitals," Frankie muttered.

"Oh, for God's sake—don't be a prude," Marianne scolded, and ordered a bottle of their best champagne cru for five hundred dollars. "Don't be surprised if one of us gets up there to perform. That was breathtaking, watching all those men lusting for her."

"Mr. Gleamy Eyes wasn't one of them," Frankie warned.

Marianne looked at her from under her eyelashes. "Thanks for the reminder, Mom. This is about head games. I love head games."

"Depending on who's giving head," Frankie tossed back.

"Shhh . . ." The lights had gone down again, the spotlight up, the next dancer waiting in the wings, the music hard driving and hot. Biker girl, slamming her way onstage, ripping off her helmet so her long black hair cascaded down to her waist, her leather vest, her studded belt, her crotch-high leather skirt to leave her dressed in a studded leather collar, a cut-out leather bra, and thigh-high leather boots.

This one was raucous, out there, swinging her hips, spreading her legs, sprawling, crawling, and displaying every inch of her body all around the stage to each of the front-row customers, commanding big bucks from them for the privilege of unhooking her bra as she swung her taut-tipped breasts close to their faces.

Then, naked but for the collar, she hoisted herself up on the pole, twisting her body around it sinuously, and vaulting it into an inverse position to give everyone full view between her legs before she slowly slid to the stage and lay there, her legs splayed around the pole until the lights went down.

There was a break. The girls who had performed came out into the lounge, minimally dressed now—biker girl had put on her bra and boots; the redhead was wrapped in her veil—and now the lights were brighter, they could see that along the periphery of the main lounge, there were alcoves in which other girls were entertaining guests—with drinks or with lap dances or both.

The two dancers they had just seen were introduced by the hostess to several gentlemen who had particularly expressed an interest in meeting them. A couple of bottles of champagne were ordered, and the girls cuddled up next to the gentlemen who poured them each a flute, and put their arms around them possessively.

Marianne whispered, "But they can't go home with those guys. At least that's club policy. Or maybe it's he'll ask, and she'll never tell. But if they can afford that kind of money for that kind of booze, they're my kind of guy." Her expression grew speculative. "How can we get those guys?"

"Marianne's already made up her mind what she's going to do. Don't let her fool you," Becca said. "She's going onstage."

Marianne arched her brow as she got up from the table. "You know me so well, Becca dear. Let's put it this way. It's something I have yet to experience."

She disappeared toward the rear of the club and Becca shrugged. Nina murmured, "This should be fun."

"This," Becca said to Frankie, as they both watched the biker girl and the exotic redhead, who had let her veil slip to the floor so that she was sitting there stark naked, playing up to their "dates," letting them touch, pat, stroke their arms, their backs, their buttocks, "this is what I meant about Marianne . . . she'll buy her way onstage just because she feels like it."

"The redhead bought herself a lap dance," Frankie observed as the woman got up with her date and led him to one of the alcoves.

There was a low drum roll. The lights flared and dimmed, and a stentorian voice came out of nowhere— "Gentlemen, ladies—welcome to the stage a new talent, the rich bitch you can never have—Miss Marianne!"

THEA DEVINE

An echoing drumbeat. Jazzy music. Marianne in the shadows, strutting her way into the spotlight in a tight hot dress, strapping heels, flowing hair, not much else. Running her hands all over her body, giving each man around the perimeter a heated come-get-me look, slowly slowly sliding off her dress and hitching herself onto the pole dressed only in her stilettos and a thin glittery chain wrapped around her hips.

How did she know how to work the pole? It was transfixing to watch her. She loved exposing herself. She loved all the men leaning forward to get a better look, to get a better fix on how they could have her because they would divine her secret.

She showed them everything and gave them nothing. And just when they thought she was about to bow down and bow out, she reached out from the stage and the spotlight followed her beckoning hand to where Becca, Nina, and Frankie were sitting.

"All of you," she mouthed, "up here—NOW!"

"No disobeying the queen," Nina muttered. "Come on. She won't let us off the hook. She planned this whole thing just to get us to do this."

"I'm game," Becca said, rising up. "Why not? Pretend it's part of her act."

Pure Marianne. Why not, when they were all superficially aroused by the heady male response to the gyrating female bodies that could have been them, and now were going to be them, because Marianne wanted it to be them.

They sashayed onstage to the rhythm of the music, acted

164

as if it had all been prearranged. "Don't embarrass me," Marianne whispered as she pushed them to dance. "Get naked—quick . . . it's not like you never did it in front of an audience before . . ."

But an audience of two or four was quite different from a roomful of unknowns with lust in their hearts.

Nevertheless, they caught the thick, viscous sexual mood of being onstage and in control of their bodies and the men avidly lusting for them.

It was powerful. They were so different in size, shape, coloring, and it didn't matter. They were living fantasies, on diverse levels, to every man in that audience.

Pick a man and play to him. It was obvious. It was arousing. In that arena, the aura of uncritical unfettered sexuality they exuded was the bargain they made with the audience. You can have me. I'm giving myself to you right now, every inch of my naked body is yours, and you don't have to do a thing except want me.

It was heady, all that concentrated male libido . . . the heat, the energy, it fogged up the room as their clothes came off, as they slowly bared their bodies to the rhythm of the music escalating in tandem with the blood-pounding excitement and arousal of being the object of desire of a roomful of male voyeurs.

Marianne buck naked, sitting on the edge of the stage, twenty-dollar bills flying all around her as she spread herself wide for the audience. Becca on the other side of the stage, nearly naked, gyrating for all she was worth; Nina on the pole, slowly and daintily removing her bra and tossing it into the audience; and Frankie, belly dancing her way around the stage, pausing now and again for a twenty, a fifty tossed at her feet.

This was insane. They were going to want more. Already she could feel the voluptuous thickening of the air. She could feel the sexual intensity. She could see the hostess taking cards from those who wanted an introduction.

That much male lust focused on her was so seductive, so tempting. The idea of half-hour dates with a variety of men every night, the big-time money, the exercise of the power of her naked body . . . It was so erotically alluring, she got creamy just imagining it.

She got down on her hands and knees and crawled inch by inch around the stage, flagrantly displaying herself in every way. The money rained all over her. She saw Marianne make a cutting motion. The music was about to end, their power was about to be short-circuited.

She swept the money under her body and rolled over to splay herself for the last final jazzy note before the lights went down. Then she gathered her money and picked up whatever clothes were left onstage as she made her way back to the curtain.

Marianne was already giving instructions. "Don't get dressed, the hostess has cards for everyone. New men. New challenge . . . can you say lap dance? Don't say no. These guys are loaded and they're ready to spend it—in every way you can think of—on you."

"I'm in," Nina said.

"Cool." Becca.

Frankie nodded. Why not? She still felt sky high from the dance. Didn't feel a thing about her nudity. No bra. Heels. Necklace, dangling earrings. Crazy. Why not?

The hostess approached. "I have a particular request for Miss Frankie. And for you three . . ." She fanned out a deck of business cards. "Take your pick."

"We want the wealthiest three," Marianne said immediately. "Whatever they want, since we're not bound by club regulations, are we?"

She shook her head. "No. So let me introduce you. I'll take you three first. Someone will see to your clothes; they'll be refreshed and hung for when you want to leave."

Frankie watched as she led Marianne, Becca, and Nina out into the main lounge, saw every man turn and watch their progression as the hostess brought them to their dates, Becca and Marianne at the one table, Nina at the other. And the sexual foreplay began. The conversation, the ordering of drinks, the coddling and cuddling, the sex-larded get-to-know-you questions which engendered enough intimacy that they would quickly feel free to stroke, touch, and get past the innuendos to straight sex talk.

Marianne's customer would start by saying, *You're new here.*

And Marianne would say, *Did you like what you saw?* which would cut to the chase instantly.

And the preordained dialogue would go:

I liked it so much, you're here with me now. And I like what I see even better in person, close to me where I can fondle whatever I want to.

I knew the minute the hostess introduced us that you were a masterful kind of guy. I like take-charge guys. Why don't you take charge of my naked body, right now?

Where can we go?

There are privacy alcoves behind us. Why don't you order some more champagne, and we'll go back there and see how take-charge you can be . . .

It wouldn't take long. Becca and Nina might prolong their conversations, but not Marianne. She was already naked and ready to party, and a well-heeled guy and no restrictions were just what she craved.

"Miss Frankie?" The hostess was back. "This way."

To the opposite side of the room from where Marianne was cozying up to Mr. Gleaming Moneybags, letting him play with her breasts as she leaned into his chest and sipped champagne.

"Let me introduce you to . . ."

She stiffened; she wanted to die.

"Mr. Cordrey. Miss Frankie."

Dax's expression was perfectly benign, as if he'd never seen her before, didn't know her, hadn't ever made love to her. "Have a seat. Have some champagne." He poured. "Play it out, Frankie."

She sat, wrapping the shreds of her pride around her, leaning into him slightly so it looked as if they were having an intimate conversation. "What the hell are you doing here?"

"You think Marianne could put on a show without her audience? The group's all here, scattered around, wondering why they wasted all that time pretending they didn't want to boff the untouchables."

"What do *you* want?"

"Right now? A hot shower to scrub off the dirt. But I'll settle for obscenely expensive, too-cold champagne. And only for you, Frankie, because we're going all the way tonight. You're going to treat this big spender just as if I were the stranger at the next table."

His icy contempt stiffened her backbone. This was all about fantasy anyway. He had paid for her, he was the customer, and she was the commodity. The only measure of her power now was how much more she could get him to spend before—

Before *what*?

"Drink your champagne, Frankie. Tell me what you think I want to hear."

"I hate you."

"Now, that's not the hot sex talk I paid for. It would shrivel any man's intentions. Or his wallet. Just play the game."

"I don't have the stomach for—champagne—tonight."

"Not from what I hear," Dax said matter-of-factly, holding her gaze with a disingenuous look. "About the having stomach for *it*, I mean. By all accounts, it's been champagne nearly every night for the past couple of weeks."

If it was a war of nerves, she was going down. But damn it, he had no exclusive rights, and she had just as much right to her fun as he did his. For all she knew, he frequented strip clubs every night.

"When do we get to the lap dance part?" Dax asked.

The hell with him. She would not let him intimidate her. Could not let anything personal get in the way, because there was nothing between them.

Nothing.

"I'm ready now," she whispered in her sexiest voice, startling him. Oh, he'd expected her to repent? Well, she meant to go ahead full bore, play the game, act the role, and do the nasty. "Oh—here comes Marianne," she added, her tone just a shade too disingenuous.

And there she was, holding her customer's arm and leading him to the privacy alcoves just beyond where Frankie and Dax were sitting.

Her step faltered as she caught sight of them and her face hardened, but she had no choice but to stay with her customer. And then Becca, steps behind her, her eyes widening as she saw Dax, and throwing Frankie a warning look as she passed.

"Ready?" Dax asked, rising and pulling her out of her chair.

She smiled up at him and took his hand. "I am so looking forward to this."

Now his gaze was shuttered in that way he blanked out all emotion. He was now the guy on the town looking for a little passive action and she was the instrument. That was the fantasy, wasn't it? That some naked lusty young woman wanted him and made him feel like a pasha.

She led him to an empty alcove sumptuously carpeted and furnished with a wide club chair that could accommodate two, some strategically placed tables, and the requisite low lights.

"Take off your jacket, make yourself comfortable. We want more champagne, don't we?" She motioned to a passing waitress and gave the order and then returned to climb onto the chair and straddle his hips.

She braced her arms against the back of the chair, and sank back on her knees just enough so that her nakedness was an inch over his groin, her hips swaying suggestively in rhythm with the music.

"So," she murmured, "tell me what you like. Tell me what you want me to do to you. Tell me . . ." And she spiraled her hips downward to sit tightly on his iron bar of an erection. "Tell me . . ." She leaned over him, swinging her breasts temptingly close to his mouth. "You don't have to do anything. I'll do everything. Tell me your secrets. Tell me anything you ever wanted and I'll do it . . ."

She stole a covert look at the adjacent alcoves to see what the other dancers were doing. Sinuous movements, long sensual stroking, pressing their bodies tight against the customer. Stroking his hair, his chest, wriggling their fingers into his pants.

Anything overtly sexual to arouse the customer. Anything she felt like, only with him, it went so far beyond.

She pushed the feelings away. He was a stranger who had come for his hour of sensual ego-inflating attention, and her job was to pump him up and make him feel like the sex king of the world.

She eased herself off of him just enough so that she could cover his body with hers, and run her hands over his chest, his arms . . . *silk tie, expensive oxford shirt, hard muscles, oh*

God, stop stop . . . her hips grinding down hard on his erection in time with the music, her body up and down in a
slithering motion against him.

Up again, her breasts bouncing slightly, working her
hands down to his hips, his stomach, between his
legs . . . testing his power on all levels . . .

. . . *just a guy, just a stranger out for sex.*

But—a stranger she knew, whose every pleasure point
she knew, whose hands, body, every expression she
knew . . . damn damn damn—

She heaved herself upright and straddled his thighs, her
hands grasping his hips tightly, and she leaned toward him.
"Touch me. I'm under no constraints. Touch me . . ." She
cupped her breasts and he explosively grabbed her hands.

"You're too good at this. Stop it. We're getting out of here."

"No."

He was adamant. "Get dressed. Five minutes, or I come
get you and carry you out."

She believed him. There was just that look in his eyes,
laser cold and slicing her to ribbons.

She fled. She felt Marianne's eyes on her as she made her
way back to the stage entrance. Everyone was watching,
everyone envious of Dax. The girls wishing their date was
him—tall, elegant, icy-eyed, stone-faced him.

The hostess was in the dressing room.

"He asked for a date," Frankie murmured.

"They always do," the hostess said. "Your clothes are
there." She gestured to a rack at the back of the room. "And
they're always in a hurry. I'll tend to him."

She had worn a gold jersey dress with a draped bodice that showed a lot of skin. No bra, no panties, no excuses. She ran a perfunctory brush through her hair, then checked her makeup. What was she thinking? What was Dax thinking?

He was waiting at the stage door. There was a limo parked in the No Parking zone just by the rear of the building. He helped her into the backseat, spoke to the driver, and they took off toward First Avenue.

"You should go back home to Maine, Frankie," he said at length.

"Are you crazy? I'm having a fabulous time."

"You're having lots of irresponsible sex."

"Don't big brother me."

"That's not nearly what I'm doing."

The car turned north on Second Avenue.

"What *are* you doing?"

"Whatever I want, tonight."

A tremor of anticipation slithered through her body. *Whatever he wanted* . . . the thought took her breath away.

"Don't say a word. I bought your services tonight. All you have to do is keep quiet and spread your legs."

"I can do that."

"So I've heard," he murmured.

More ice water. She kept quiet and carelessly splayed her legs as she focused her attention out the window. The man was paying. All she had to do was *anything he wanted*.

They were at Sixth Avenue and Fifty-seventh Street, and the car slowed down in front of the Parker Meridien Hotel.

He wasn't taking her home. Her disappointment went

deep. But then, she *was* the hired help; this was the fantasy—
the big spender springing for the big-bucks hotel and permission to do *anything he wanted.*

The driver opened her door. "Miss."

Miss. Missed by a mile. A thousand miles.

He'd already checked in and needed only to whisk her up
to the room on the top floor, so flagrantly luxurious she
couldn't stand it.

If he'd do that for her, what would he do for any stranger
he picked up?

But the sexual tension simmered, and just a touch of fire
would send it blasting like a furnace. She felt it. He knew it.

He tossed the room key on the console by the door. "Get
on the bed." His tone was implacable. He pulled back the
floor-to-ceiling curtain to stare for a moment at the night-lit
view of the park. When he turned to her, there was something in his usually reserved expression that was different,
determined.

He ripped off his jacket and tossed it on a chair, pulled
open his tie.

"There's really no point to fucking you, Frankie." He
climbed onto the bed, pushed her on her back, and straddled her thighs. "You don't need rescuing. You know
damned well what you're doing all the time."

"I'm having the time of my life," she said testily. Just like
him to go all moral on her, instead of getting between her legs.

"Pretending to be a stripper? Going on road trips and
sleeping with truckers?"

Her heart stopped. He knew about all that?

He went on inexorably, "Getting laid by masseurs, for God's sake? Sure you know exactly what you're doing. So let's do it. Take off your dress. Oh, and don't forget the show. I paid for the show." He sat back on his knees and unbuckled his belt.

"You shit."

"You're not being nice, Frankie. Call me Mr. Moneybags. And take off your clothes. Although"—he eyed her with that cold blue look she hated—"you can't have much on under that dress. Take it off."

She could have, for any other guy. But not him. Not like this. Not after this afternoon . . .

Sleeping with truckers.

"You're a lousy cock tease, Frankie. You get a man up, you let him pay exorbitant money for the night, for the hope, for the sex, and then you freeze him out. I'm not a slab of meat, I'm a guy with feelings who thought a gorgeous thing like you might want to spend some time in my company if I paid enough for you."

The club guy line.

"You don't do things like that," she said explosively.

"Don't I?" he murmured. "Your dress, Miss Frankie. Or we can leave things right here. The room is paid for. You can stay. I'll go."

Oh God, yet another choice. A night with Dax, a punishment in its own right, or a night alone, a punishment for her sins.

She felt a hot desperation. Not only for his sex, but for *him*, the indefinable essence of him that knew her, that was irrevocably and mystically connected to her. It was lightning in a bottle; she couldn't catch it, couldn't contain it, and yet it crackled and glowed, in spite of everything she'd done to try to exorcise it.

And all she could say was, "Don't go."

His face softened for an instant, and her knees went weak: it was just how she imagined he would look at someone he loved.

Then he said, "By the way, Frankie, we don't marry strippers. Not to make babies and a family."

His tone was even, neutral, but the words struck her like a lightning bolt. "You didn't have to say that," she said stiffly. "Marianne warned me about that a long time ago."

"Did she? When did she say that?"

"That first summer, when she nearly drowned."

Dax made a sound. "Marianne corrupts everything she touches. You'd do well to remember that, Frankie."

"She's been wonderful to me."

Dax shook his head. "But the fact remains you're still not naked, which is a damned waste of my time and money."

No softness now. Just pure hard-edged fuck-ready male with the same up-and-at-'em penis as any guy when a naked body was in play.

"Fine," she spat, and shrugged out of her dress and threw it at him. "Here I am." She lay back against the pillows, her legs splayed. "Come and get it."

His eyes took on a speculative glow as he stripped away his clothes and positioned himself above her, bracing himself so he could fully look down at her.

She turned her head away from that intense all-knowing gaze.

He's just another guy. Just another roving penis looking for a place to root, just another—

He breached her quickly, emphatically, and just so that her cunt lips enclosed his penis head only to the bulbous ridge. And then he stopped—everything stopped. Her heart stopped, the sensation was so exquisite. He was there, and not there, within and without both, and joined with her, and yet not wholly connected—yet.

And he could see clearly what she couldn't: the length of his penis not enfolded in her, and that luscious erotic part that was.

She couldn't breathe, the sensation of him there, not moving, just her naked awareness that he was there, within her, within . . . imagining how it looked to him, what he was feeling . . .

This had gone way beyond the game.

He flexed his hips, and she felt his power, his control, his masterful restraint. She grabbed his arms and arched upward, mutely seeking, begging for full hard-core penetration.

He held her eyes with his dark blue sensual gaze as he pushed into her, one torturous inch at a time, her body convulsing with each thrust until the ultimate erotic sensation of finally enfolding all of him.

She wanted to say a thousand things to him as she lay suspended in the pure sumptuous pleasure of holding him so nakedly, so intimately, in such a gorgeous perfect fit. But it was a moment to just let herself be engulfed by the potent coupling of her body with his, and what it meant.

Not a game. Too real.

She held on tight as he took her, as she rocketed under him, with him, fighting him, seducing him, and ultimately surrendering to him, as a bolt of cataclysmic pleasure jolted her whole body and his orgasm erupted simultaneously with hers.

So fast, couldn't-stop-it fast; she would pay a huge price for playing this game, and she was running out of time.

No words now. Just his body covering hers and the ineffable sensual joy of holding him tight in her arms, in her heart, and hard between her legs.

Nothing existed outside this moment, this room. She was Rapunzel, locked away forever in a tower with her lover, where the past did not exist.

Hours crept by as he used her body precisely as a man would who had paid for the privilege. Precisely as she would have expected after the initial shock of that whole body carnal fusion that stunned them both.

He took her every way possible, imprinting himself on her sexually as if he were branding her, and in the end, after the final glorious orgasm, pushing her away.

Words were unnecessary now. He had said everything to her in every way possible with his body as he fucked her through the night. And it *was* fucking. After that first, breath-stealing, soul-searing coupling, he became an automaton, going at her body relentlessly, his hunger for her warring with his contempt for everything he knew she'd done.

This might be all of him she would ever have. Nothing could salve over any of it. It was what it was. And he was right: she knew exactly what she was doing, and there were always consequences for fulfilling the fantasy.

Very early in the morning, she heard him in the shower, listened to the soft sounds of him dressing, and kept her eyes closed against the reality of last night.

Everything paid for. Even her.

Men like him didn't marry strippers to make babies and a family. Or sluts.

Her breath caught tight in her chest.

This is the last time ever, with him.

He'd marry someone else and make babies with her . . . oh dear God. She would die. She couldn't bear to watch him, couldn't bear to see that fantasy irrevocably walk out the door.

She heard the door closing softly behind him, to the steady tick of the clock. The game was over.

Time's up.

We're done.

Chapter Eight

The Insatiables were all at the apartment when she came back that afternoon, lounging around the living room, drinking margaritas, and comparing notes on their customers.

"Whoa, Frankie—the whole night? Some Dax-tion," Nina said coyly. "Isn't he the stud? Who would have thought? You did sleep with him?"

"Wasn't that the point?"

"It was supposed to be. *We* didn't get an all-night fuck-fest. We were lucky if we got five minutes of boning at a time. Those guys were boneheads. Marianne was telling us you all hooked up with some real fucksome guys on your road trip this week."

"We did."

"Tollbooth guy?"

"Oh yeah. You heard about him?"

"And the others. So-o . . . how did Dax compare?"

Wasn't Nina the nosy bitch today. And why hadn't Marianne said one word yet? She did not look amused.

"Let's just say he got what he paid for."

"And what was that?" Marianne now. Of course. No detail was too minute for Marianne's eager eagle eye.

"A cunt," she retorted. "You invited him. You didn't think he's just like any other horny guy in a strip joint?"

"He chose you," Marianne said silkily. "Why do you suppose?"

Damn, Becca had warned her. She had to downplay this. "Maybe he knows you guys too well. I wish he hadn't chosen me, because it wasn't fun." *Liar.* "It was servicing."

Not enough for Marianne. "Where did he take you?"

"Where did you guys go?"

"Somewhere elegant," Becca said, shooting Frankie one of those looks. "Dax never does anything by half. Even when he's going down and dirty, he wants Egyptian cotton sheets. Where? The Waldorf? The Carlyle? The Parker Meridien? Nice to have money."

"Last night was a flat bust," Marianne said grimly. "The best part was shaking my boobs onstage and all those men salivating over them. There's lots of money in voyeurism; they tossed about five hundred dollars on that stage. If you perform a couple of shows, four or five nights a week? Take the money—forget the sex. Who wants sex with those guys?"

"You do," said Becca, the only one who could have said that to her face.

"Because I want sex with every guy. But anonymous penises on the road fuck way better than anonymous penises at high-end strip clubs. So—so much for that social experiment." Marianne slanted an opaque look at Frankie. "Frankie still got the best end of it. She slept with Dax."

"Tell us everything," Nina said. "Dax doesn't sleep around with our crowd, so we want the details. How big, how long, what about the body, what did he do, what did he say . . ."

Frankie was speechless. Quicksand here. She had the feeling Nina's pointed questions weren't idle curiosity.

She looked at Becca, who raised her eyebrows, and then at Marianne, who was staring at her skeptically.

"What, you think he's got a body far and above mortal men? He's a guy. Not as built as some, not as muscular as some—"

"Frankie, Frankie, Frankie—get to the penis. We want penis dish. Length, width, feel . . ."

"Hell, I didn't measure the guy."

"Did he fit good and tight?" Marianne asked. "Like—oh, like truck guy, for instance."

Why did she bring up truck guy? Sinking now. "About on a par."

"You really fell for truck guy." Marianne looked at the others. "She even gave him the business email when he told her he was interested in a fuck date whenever he's in town."

"Like I'm waiting," Frankie murmured caustically. God, what if Marianne had seen the email—didn't she delete it? Even so . . . shit. It would be in the trash. Perfect. She'd just waded into the quagmire hip deep.

"That good?" Nina asked, her eyes alight with interest. "A fuck date? You know we don't do booty calls."

"A *standing* fuck date," Marianne amplified insinuatingly. "Nothing personal, just cunt."

Frankie regrouped. "Marianne didn't like him a lot."

"Sure, because the second time we ran into him, he had me for two hours and it felt like a damn pity fuck. Then he fucked Frankie against the back wall of the restaurant we were at, which *I* would've infinitely preferred."

"So was he better than Dax?" Nina again, dripping with malicious curiosity. The incisive writer getting the dirt.

"It's been—" Frankie almost said two weeks, but now she couldn't be certain Marianne hadn't seen that email and she amended it to "a while. Truck guy is raw, rough, brawny. You know what he wants—and he sure as hell wanted Marianne's pussy when she flashed him on the road. He did us both all night, alternating. So let's not pretend Marianne didn't get some from this guy."

"Dax," Nina goaded her. "Compared to Dax."

"I don't know. Different. How do you calculate the differences?"

"Well," Marianne said, her tone offhanded, "since you fucked them both in one day . . ."

Dead. She closed her eyes and drowned. She heard Becca say, "Holy hot shit." She heard Nina's faint whistle.

She opened her eyes. Marianne raised her eyebrows.

"God, I saw him for forty minutes."

"Eight times at least, at five minutes a pop," Becca calculated. "And Dax, too?"

"*You're* this week's booty queen," Nina said. "You come back from that doing-the-nasty road trip and a week later, you're in bed with a guy you fucked on the road, dancing naked in a strip club, and then you get it on with the unobtainable and ever aloof Dax Cordrey. That is some record. And you refuse to give us the details. Hell."

"I have a better chance of fucking truck guy again than ever doing Dax again."

"But—does he talk? Does he moan? Did he get naked? Did he really get between your legs?"

"No, no, yes, yes," Frankie answered tersely.

"Okay," Nina said, "now we're getting somewhere. Did you undress him or did he strip? Did he take your dress off? Did he want you to strip for him? What about underwear? Was he hot by the time you got there, or did you have to arouse him?"

"Nina!"

"Well, okay. Then truck guy—"

"Was naked when I got there, and I didn't have time to strip before he stuffed his penis into me."

"So he did it standing up. Okay. We'd all like to think Dax isn't quite so primal."

"Who knows how he would be with any of you guys?"

"The question on the floor is, how was he with you?"

"Hot." An all-purpose answer, one they were not going to accept, either.

Nina asked, "Hot how? Body hot, penis hot? Sweet-dirty-nothings-in-your-ear hot? Technique-in-bed hot? Did he rush the bush or did he take his time? Does he suck tit, or what? C'mon, Frankie. This is good stuff."

"I'm already exhausted, and what you guys are doing to me is a marathon fuck. Look, this was Marianne's show." She turned to Marianne, who just raised her eyebrows, but she could see Marianne was simmering way below the skin. "You invited him to the exhibitionism for some reason, and whatever it was, it didn't work the way you planned. So Dax is a dead issue. And truck guy is hot and kicking, has a penis that fits, and just *loves* fucking me. So I'm going to go see if maybe he stayed in town and wants more sex. Maybe you all would like to join me."

"How big is he?" Nina asked, willing to be distracted since she was getting nowhere baiting her.

"*Big.*" Frankie held out her hands.

"Yet you don't know how big Dax is?"

"I was with truck guy a half dozen times. I know how big he is."

"I think you just want to keep all the goodies about Dax to yourself," Nina said. "Well, Frankie darling, *we* fuck and tell. You have to give, because if you don't want to, there's a reason. And it really looks like you don't want to."

It was mean-girls talk. It meant it was time for her to take sides: with them or against them? Inclusion or ostracism?

"I'd rather talk about truck guy," she hedged.

"Sure you would," Nina said, "but we don't know truck guy. We want to know—hell, we *need* to know—everything about Dax."

"And," Marianne added, her voice silky, her face hard, "don't leave out a single detail."

Time for true confessions. *Edited* confessions.

Tell them what they want to hear. Didn't people who fictionalized memoirs get on the best-seller lists? A girl has to protect her interests, after all.

And her secrets.

But with Becca looking at her that way . . . no, no. No one was getting that piece of her night with Dax. They got too much as it was.

The questions continued, all of them insanely intimate: Was he strictly missionary? What other positions did he like? What about foreplay? How long did it last, how many times, what did he do, how many orgasms, what did *she* do to him, did she suck him off, did she suck him at all, did he taste good, did he like to eat pussy, did he like how she tasted, did he kiss her tasting of pussy, did he, did he—?

With Marianne sitting there, stone-faced, absorbing every last word, boulders sinking in bottomless pond.

Nina was so rabid for the details, Frankie almost thought she was Marianne's mouthpiece.

Becca wasn't much help either. "So *how* many times that night?"

She made up a number. "Eight times, minimum."

"Did you get off each time?"

"I sure as hell tried."

"Did he?"

"I think he saved himself once or twice."

"Did he talk dirty?"

"*Dax?*"

"Yeah, our Dax."

"Maybe . . ." Just to rile them up. Now she was getting a little pissed. It was too tempting to embroider to get them even more hot and bothered.

186

"What'd he say?"

They were absolutely salivating. Did Nina and Becca also have a thing for Dax?

Omigod . . . deep shit here.

"So here's the real, deep, true, absolutely want-to-know question," Nina said. "Did you really want to fuck him all along?"

Real, absolute, deep shit. How could she answer that? "Maybe *he* really wanted to fuck *me*."

It shut them up, as if that thought never had occurred to them. They had to chew it up, digest it, maybe gag on it, because how could that be possible? They married their *own*.

"Good job," Becca whispered on her way out. "If I were you, I'd make truck guy my cover. Take my advice."

Was it then a coincidence that truck guy was suddenly in Manhattan twice a week, and he was demanding those dates she'd promised him?

"Hey, I work, too." But she had a sneaking suspicion he might have altered his hours just for the pleasure of doing her. "This was a good idea, seeing you when you're in town. Only, you're in town a lot suddenly."

"I rearranged my schedule to accommodate this hot, juicy woman I met."

"I hope you're talking about me."

"You're the best I've ever had. I'm willing to stick around to stick my penis into you as often as you let me."

But she actually didn't know how she felt about it being *that* often. They were still on a no-names basis, and she liked it that way. The thing was not to get proprietary about a random coupling. Not to let any emotion or feelings seep in. Because then things got complicated.

And things were going to be tricky enough as it was, juggling dates with him, Marianne's schedule, and Becca's ongoing curiosity about her night with Dax.

"Oh, you can tell me the real story. I'm the champion of true love and soul mates."

"Are you nuts? Marianne's furious enough already that her scheme backfired, and she blames me as if I somehow induced Dax to request me. I didn't even know he was there, for God's sake!"

"You could've refused to go with him."

"He made it perfectly plain that he expected me to play the game all the way. I think he was teaching me—us? Marianne?—a lesson."

"That's fine. But how big *is* his penis?"

The next morning, Marianne announced she was not going to Maine for the summer. "Too deadly up there this year. Everyone's staying here or going to Europe, so there won't be any interesting men. And besides, nobody will write about us if we're in the boondocks. And someone is writing about one of us . . ."

She turned the computer and Frankie saw it was the *Diva's Daybook* blog.

What new on the scene humping honey has a hideaway horn stashed in a cozy couples cave so she can indulge herself bonking in broad daylight whenever she feels the urge?

"It's you and Dax, isn't it?" Marianne's voice was neutral, but there was something icy in her tone.

Oh God, even before coffee. Frankie took a running dive into the truth. "No-o-o—that's me and truck guy."

"I don't believe you. You never mentioned you'd seen truck guy again."

"It's truck guy. We meet in a West Side motel, far from prying eyes."

Marianne snorted. "You chose truck guy over Dax?"

"I'd take a no-brainer fuck over a smug sanctimonious bastard any day."

"I don't believe you. Not after what you told us."

God, she was going to be hung out to dry on her own lies.

"Fine. Don't believe me. I'm not the one who set up that whole strip club fiasco. Or his buying me for a night."

"You know what? Don't shovel shit. You know damned well you loved showing off your naked body onstage. And I really believe you love showing your naked body to Dax twice a week in some tawdry rut roost."

"It's truck guy. And I'm not going to beg you to believe me."

"That's because you know the Diva doesn't dish about unknown humping honeys and their hot-body *nobodies*. You're someone if you're mentioned in that blog. So, no— it's Dax, and you're a conniving bitch." She turned and stalked into her bedroom.

Damn.

Frankie called Becca.

"Oh, she'll forget about it in an hour," Becca said cheerfully. "Just stay away from Dax."

"I haven't gone ten miles *near* him. You think I'm stupid?"

"I think you tried valiantly to sideswipe two issues—"

Frankie sighed. Obviously there was no getting around the Insatiables' curiosity about Dax in sex. "Which issues?"

"How big is his penis, and Marianne's one-track mind where he's concerned. And you failed. You made too good a case that *he* might want *you*."

"Shit. So what *was* that night about? Humiliating me?"

"It was about her desperation. She'll get over it."

"Sure—she'll fire him again."

"No, he's too deeply involved in her daily concerns now. Knows where the bodies are."

"And you know this? How?"

"Dear girl, don't be naïve. Marianne tells me everything."

But Marianne didn't tell Becca or Frankie where she was going that day.

After Frankie showered and dressed, she checked to see if Marianne wanted some breakfast only to find Marianne gone. All she left was a note to remind Frankie that Friday was the ASPCA event and to call Saks to send over some dresses.

Frankie put off making the call. She spent the day doing everything she could not to think about her disturbing run-in with Marianne. Not to think about the marathon of sex she'd been indulging in. Not to think about Dax, or the past, the future, or anything that would mar the perfect memory of her night with him.

It was a long, empty, awful day. Marianne was obviously pissed; she hadn't returned by the time the clock struck three, five, six, eight.

Frankie called Becca, Rob, and Nina. "Have you seen or heard from Marianne?"

No one had since the previous day.

Becca immediately mobilized everyone. Andy and Rob launched a search of her usual haunts, to no avail. Becca contacted the tasty boys and the masseurs. Nothing. Nina volunteered to inquire at the sex clubs.

"Meaning," Becca said acidly, having come to stay with Frankie, "she wants some action while she takes action." But there were no leads there, either.

Marianne's crowd gathered at the apartment near midnight and the consensus was that this was weird, not like Marianne at all.

"Did you search her room?" Rob asked.

"Gingerly," Frankie said.

"Topically," Becca amplified. "I mean, it *is* an invasion of privacy."

"Look," Rob said practically, "if we call the police—and technically we can't because it hasn't been twenty-four hours yet—they're going to come in and tear this place apart. So if there's anything in that room that might be a clue, we need to know before anyone else does."

They swarmed into Marianne's bedroom, carefully pulling apart her bed, her closet, her dresser drawers.

"Hell." Rob again. "It just occurred to me we should've used rubber gloves."

191

"We should have called Dax," Becca said.

"Not bloody likely," Rob growled. "He's not a criminal lawyer. And there's nothing here anyway."

Nothing to suggest why Marianne had not come home. Just mountains of clothes, jewelry, magazines, shoes. Nothing personal, no computer, no journal, no books, no bills, letters, notes, notations—Marianne unwrapped seemed to have very little substance at all.

No one said a word as they reconvened in the living room.

"What else? Where else?" Nina fretted.

"There's Bar Harbor," Frankie said tentatively. "But she told me this morning she wasn't planning to go there this year."

Nina said, "We could call and have someone check . . ."

"And raise questions," Rob pointed out. "And for all we know, she's rolling around naked in some horny guy's Park Avenue penthouse right now."

"But she's never gone out without coming back here to dress for the evening," Nina pointed out. "She wouldn't go out without being in full battle regalia. And she rarely goes out by herself."

"I think we should give it till morning," Rob said. "We don't know that she didn't meet someone somewhere—"

"Or maybe she's lying in an alley somewhere," Becca interjected sharply. "Why the hell are we so scared of the police?"

"We're not," Rob snapped. "We're scared of the details."

That silenced everyone.

"Okay," Becca said, "I vote that we scour every club we haven't visited yet, anyplace you think she might have tried out for kicks. And I'm going see if I can finesse information out of someone's cottage caretaker in Maine."

"What about my mom?" Frankie asked.

Becca clapped her forehead. "Frankie! You're a genius."

"I'm a local," Frankie said dryly. "But Marianne said she wasn't going there this summer."

But it turned out she did.

Becca woke Frankie late the next morning, tripping over the others sprawled out asleep in the living room.

"Shhh—come with me."

She knew the news was bad, just looking at Becca's face.

They went into the kitchen and Becca told her. "She went to Bar Harbor, although no one knows why or how. Your mom tried to get in—there were lights on, and the neighbors thought she was in residence, even though no one had seen her.

"Anyway, it was reason enough for your mom to contact the police. They found her—in a bedroom closet. They think it's suicide."

Frankie was shaking, "How?"

"She hanged herself."

"Oh, God."

Becca put a hand on Frankie's shoulder. "Brace yourself. It gets worse."

"How could it?"

"They're bringing the body back here. The estate will make the funeral arrangements. But what you need to know—the really shocking thing, and the thing that's already been leaked to the press—is that you're the sole heir to her estate."

Chapter Nine

Wealth came at a price. Suspicion. Envy. Notoriety. Disdain. Rejection. Unless you could trace your monetary roots back to the founding fathers, you were locked out. Pedigree was power.

And gossip was gospel.

A nobody from nowhere inheriting hundreds of millions out of the blue on the apparent suicide of an heiress was the stuff of tabloid titillation.

And the details just got better and better. The party girl millionairess. The poor working girl who grew up in a trailer park. The pity hire who turned into a conniving bitch. The wild nights and wilder parties. The drinking. The men. The sex.

Of course, it would all come out—everyone loved to dish, as long as they weren't the ones being trashed. The *Diva's Daybook* had a field day.

And then, the contents of Marianne's will were leaked, when allegedly only one person in the law firm had knowledge of what it contained. The investigation of Marianne's death, which eliminated any suspicion of murder, brought in a verdict of suicide.

For two months, reporters hung outside the apartment, waiting to pounce on the beleaguered and mysterious heiress.

Cinderella, they dubbed her. The mystery millionairess. The nobody from nowhere who had conned a wealthy heiress, they said. Or maybe they were more than friends. No, wait. I saw her partying at . . . fill in the name of the club. Witnesses saw her naked dancing on tables, saw her drunk and making out with every guy in sight, saw them both at a sex club, saw both of them flying first class on Air France the weekend before Marianne died . . .

Frankie couldn't stem the speculation or the fictions, couldn't prevent publication of the photographs of her in black, a hat and veil obscuring her face every time she ventured out of the apartment. On the advice of the lawyers, she had *no comment* to every question, every goading comment, every hypothetical supposition.

And no comment about or from Marianne's friends, all holding her at arm's length to see how the story played out.

Even at the cemetery, a week after her death, they stood slightly to one side when cameras were rolling, as if to be seen mourning with the gold-digging intruder tainted them somehow. But they were proper as Emily Post in conveying their condolences for public display.

The cameras and paparazzi hovered outside the apartment day and night, waiting for a glimpse, while Frankie secluded herself in the apartment, floored by the uproar that Marianne's untimely death had wrought.

Millions and millions of dollars, tightly invested.

Who cares? I can afford it . . . How many times had Marianne tossed off that comment as lightly as a silk shawl?

Frankie couldn't conceive of what *millions* meant until it was spelled out in writing with all the zeros and all the fine print. And it was all hers, vetted every way possible by the lawyers. She who'd never had more than ten dollars in her pocket.

Dear God. It was so unbelievable.

Dax delivered the paperwork, casually dressed in jeans and a leather jacket to distract any reporter or cameraman who might take him for a friend of the reclusive heiress.

He was the last person Frankie wanted to see; she looked like hell, felt like hell, and everything was going to hell. Dax, in cold lawyer mode, wholly disregarding the torrid connection between them, was another kind of hell layered over that.

But there were the papers, reams of paper spread out before her, blocks of printed text with endless *wherefores* and *party of*s.

"Did you know she did this?" Frankie asked.

"Just sign the damned papers," Dax growled.

She signed. "You knew."

"I'm not your lawyer, Frankie. You're not entitled to know what I know. Your safest bet is not to ask questions and take what you've been given with some grace and dignity."

"Dax . . . help me here."

He shook his head. "I'm helping with the legalities. The senior partner, who was Marianne's advisor, will be in touch tomorrow to explain whatever you don't understand. The funds should be transferred to your name within a couple of days, and her financial advisor will then call or meet with you to discuss what comes next."

"That's what *I* want to know—what comes next?"

"I don't know, Frankie. Everything goes to you, and you're clear of any suspicion that her death was anything but a tragic suicide. If other people, if her friends, don't understand Marianne's choices, well, they don't have to."

"But *I* don't understand. None of this makes any sense."

"It doesn't have to make sense. She had no family. She was capricious, erratic, and empty. That would be enough to motivate anything she did—from jumping off a yacht to jumping off a chair and choking herself to death. You happened to be there—twice. You lucked out."

That look was in his eyes again. He didn't know, wasn't sure, couldn't read who she was anymore, because of this insane turn of events.

"Right—except even *you're* wondering why and how, what I did, what kind of scheming con artist I am."

"Actually, I'm not thinking about you at all."

That stung.

"I'm just the messenger. The legal stuff needs to be done as quickly and quietly as possible. It was bad enough that the terms of her will came out before her body was even cold. Hopefully, the curiosity factor about the rest will peter out before the next news cycle, and you'll be free to walk the streets again."

She froze. He couldn't mean that the way it sounded.

Or did he?

Somehow she found her voice and said with as much dignity as she could pull together, "That is so reassuring. Thank you so much, Dax."

He gave her a guarded look. Wary.

Don't let him impoverish you in any way. Play the diva. Be a queen.

She felt like a mouse. "Are we done?"

"We're done."

It sounded so final. She felt a crash of loneliness so bottomless, she didn't know how she would climb out.

She couldn't even manage to stand to escort him to the door.

He closed it gently behind him.

We're done.

Becca bustled in later that morning. "Omigod, you have no idea what's doing out there. The news trucks, the cameras . . . have you been reading the papers? The blogs? They're going nuts. Thank God Marianne went into seclusion after her parents died. They don't know the half about her at all—or her friends. Every news item, apart from the two social mentions and those spewing voyeurs, is two years old. Hey—how are you doing?"

"I don't know a lot about her friends, either," Frankie said coldly. "You need to give me back the key."

Becca stopped short, obviously stunned. "You're angry?"

"I've been effectively abandoned by everyone. So you just can't come waltzing in here as if it were still Marianne's apartment and you're still her best friend. Or mine."

"No, of course not," Becca said slowly, handing her the key. "I thought I *was* your friend."

"You sure ducked for cover when the shit hit."

"No one thought you did anything that could have resulted in Marianne's death, Frankie. And let me clue you in on lesson one in the Millionaire's Manual: it's protect, preserve, and pretend. You protect your ass, preserve the social order, and pretend the shit never happened. You never get in the way of shit."

"Or of pretenders," Frankie said bitterly. She felt betrayed by all of them.

"Well, I'll tell you. You can sulk and wallow, or you can decide to get ahead of the heat. I actually came here this morning to help you strategize."

"Don't waste your breath."

Becca's eyebrows shot up. "Honest to God, Frankie, stop being a stiff ass! Just agree you want my help."

"Do I?"

"You'll never navigate around these sharks without advice. Mine is just as good as anyone else's. Maybe better because I'm pretty clear-sighted, levelheaded, and not wholly distracted by all the sex all the time."

"And someone else might be?"

"Um—*you*?"

"No. No more sex."

"Right. Okay, even without the sex, it'll be fun."

"Really?" Frankie said, mimicking Becca's tone. "Fun? How fun?"

"Look. Let's agree there'll always be a shadow over Marianne's death and your inheriting all that money."

"Will there?"

"I think it's just that kind of story, and there are people who are not going to leave it alone," Becca said cautiously. "Even with the verdict. It's a mystery why she took her life. Why you wound up inheriting it all. So you might just as well have fun with it. Get out in front of the story, because there's going to be speculation no matter what you do.

"So hell, become even more famous. The tabloids already got a bead on all the sex parties and wild-child stuff. You're always going to be a dirty girl to them, so keep doing the bad-girl diva thing. Except, be classier about it. Anything you do—you do the biggest and the best. When you have sex—the biggest and the best. And for God's sake, choose a husband for his publicity and prenup value. It's not about love."

Frankie blinked. "Whoa."

"The reporters are not going to leave you alone, so make yourself into somebody," Becca said. "Make them love you. That'll make their job harder."

Why did she have the feeling Becca was trying to tell her something?

"Now, do you want me to leave, or should we start having fun?"

Becca, in her chic Burberry suit and Fekkai-coiffed hair with the light of battle in her green eyes, was something to behold. She wanted to join this battle, and probably for reasons that had nothing to do with altruism.

She needed Becca and Becca knew it. Frankie said, "I'm game—let's have some fun."

First on the docket, clothes, a great haircut, and some lessons.

Becca was firm about it. "The other *P* in the Millionaire's Manual is Presentation. We'll take a week and get you camera-ready. You are going to morph into Publicity Princess."

Which meant a flurry of phone calls and an army of hair designers, masseuses, aestheticians, and wardrobe consultants smuggled into the building, and everyone vetted to be certain no one was a reporter.

It meant spa treatments in the commodious bathroom; massages that were light-years from anything sexual or salacious; facials; a designer haircut; a week of trying on clothes from the ateliers of the city's cutting-edge designers. It meant hiring a runway consultant and a stylist to teach her how to dress, make up, walk, and present herself: that certain way you turned your body, the angle at which you looked the thinnest on camera, how to do the kitten smile over your shoulder and make them beg for more.

"You can afford this now," Becca told her when Frankie looked horrified at the cost. "Get rid of that sale-rack mentality."

But Frankie couldn't look at those price tags without thinking about all the years her mother worked and scrimped to provide for them, and now was hiding from photographers snapping those horrendous where-the-nobody-came-from photos of her double-wide childhood home.

"I'm going to buy my mother a house," she said a couple of mornings later when she was at the mercy of a cadre of seamstresses who were madly fitting and altering a rack full of clothing.

"As you should," Becca said, eyeing her critically as she pirouetted in front of a portable triple mirror.

"And arrange it so she doesn't have to work if she doesn't want to."

"The trustees can make that happen."

"Good." She slipped on a pair of outrageously expensive pumps to match the outfit that was being tucked and tweaked. *How can I even think about indulging myself with four-hundred-dollar, four-inch heels, when that's how much my mother nets in salary for a week?*

It was so surreal.

Becca broke into her thoughts. "Don't feel guilty about your good fortune. The ferrets smell guilt like garbage. The only way to deal with them is to sail out like the *Queen Mary*—flamboyant, magnificent, and unsinkable."

"Not feeling so magnificent here."

"It'll become second nature before you know it. Just don't get too comfortable, and watch out for the snappers who'll take a piece of you when you're not looking. Now, about what's left of the summer . . ."

Frankie shook her head. "I have too much to do here. I'm thinking it's a good time to go house shopping."

"You're kidding. When did you decide that?"

"Yesterday. I can't stay . . . I can't *live* here."

Becca, to her credit, didn't pursue the reason why. "So what are you thinking? Fifth Avenue? Sutton Place? Riverside Drive?"

"No. The East Side maybe." She held up her hand, forestalling Becca's objections. "I know. I know. DUMBO is the trendy investment. LoMa is hot. TriBeCa is chic . . . I don't know. I don't care. I want a town house somewhere on the East Side."

"Not an apartment? You're going to sell this?"

"I suppose I could rent it. Or turn the profit into the town house I'm going to buy. But this is the point: I'm launching the public me this week, right? So I thought if I go house hunting, Page Six will get hold of it—and mention my name *not* in conjunction with wild parties and wanton sex for a change."

"Damn, that's brilliant." Becca applauded. "Unless they think you're setting up a brothel or something. No, that's fabulous. Of course they'll print it. Someone will tip them off. I love it. What else are you thinking?"

"Marianne always talked about writing a blog. I'm going to do it. Something like *My Cinderella Life*. And I have to make certain that whenever I get that media mention, they keep referring to me as the *whatever* heiress, because for a certain amount of time, they'll have to explain what it means, which gives me more press."

"You're going to become public property doing that," Becca warned. "I don't think you have a clue what that means."

"Gee, and I was thinking of hiring my own photographer and party promoter, too."

"Whoa, Frankie. Slow down. What little black book have you been reading?"

"Just thinking about how to do it right, as you said."

"How about you just buy the house and go on from there? It's only been a couple of months. Part of the mourning protocol is to observe proper decorum. You're still grieving. So just go house hunting and see what happens."

She began by sailing into the phalanx of reporters and photographers camped outside the apartment, never speaking, never answering questions—this at Becca's advice—always precisely dressed in designer black and always gracefully ducking into the long black stretch limousine with a friendly wave . . . Marianne's limousine, always parked and waiting in the building garage when Marianne was alive.

She always emerged baring one long leg in dark hose and dark pumps. She always acknowledged them. She never got angry at the questions that she never answered; she just showed a face of sad resignation when she greeted them.

And they began to write about the Heartbroken Heiress, the mysterious and elusive woman who had secluded herself in the apartment on the park, still in deep mourning for her friend and benefactor.

Then she started house hunting.

It didn't take a week for the first item to appear on Page Six in early September:

> *We hear the Heartbroken Heiress is actively house hunting. No word of what will happen with the stunning two-bedroom Central Park view apartment she inherited from Marianne Nyland, who died tragically and mysteriously three months ago by her own hand. Little is known about Frankie Luttrell, Nyland's legatee, except she was born and raised in Maine and now has the bucks to buy the state if she wanted to.*

Perfect.

She hired her own photographer to follow her discreetly and make sure pictures of her were posted to a variety of local gossip columns.

Things were now also in the works for her mother to buy a house in Bar Harbor and to retire from her job.

It was just a matter of finding the right house for herself.

She had already decided it wouldn't be an immediate decision. That would dry up the mention of her name, which was slowly seeping into the public consciousness in media where the hard-partying days were not referred to.

They were treating her like a legitimate heiress.

She kept looking, seeing more than a dozen town houses the first weeks—some cramped Federals, some more roomy brownstones, wandering up and down the tree-lined East

Side streets, trailed by her photographer, feeling as if it were home already.

Then Becca alerted her to an item in the online *Gawker*, reading it to her in a neutral tone with no inflection whatsoever.

Steamy hot item for a steamy September weekend: what unknown heiress wasn't so heartbroken during a recent spring fling in Paris, when she got down, dirty, debauched—and naked? A tape exists to prove it—a blockbuster of a ballbuster—we've seen it—and we know that what this girl puts out, money can't buy.

"What are they talking about?"

"Someone taped our Boutique getaway."

Her whole body went cold. "How? Where?"

"I don't know. But brace yourself, Frankie, the only one on the tape is you."

"WHAT?!"

"And that's not the end of it—it got blitzed everywhere."

I'm going to die.

Oh God—Dax . . . She felt faint.

"And worse," Becca went on inexorably, "The *Daily News* gossip column says,

"Well, *my dears. If you thought the rich were different, you were right. If you have enough money, you can jet to France for a weekend of hedonistic humping. If you put your estate into the hands of a stranger, strange things start to happen—like X-rated tapes suddenly appearing with all the naked details, up close and personal. If I were that unknown heiress, I'd be heartbroken that my true nature is on full frontal display."*

"Omigod—omigod . . ." Horror washed through her. Dax would hear, Dax would see . . . Her life was over. She felt paralyzed; her voice shook. "How is it only me on that tape?"

"I haven't seen it, so I don't know. But I know this—you can't let it bury you. Are you listening, Frankie? Right now, you *have* to turn it to your advantage somehow. You can't hide. You have to attack *now*. You have to be shocked, disgusted, and offended that some pervert is trying to disgrace and dishonor you.

"Because *that's not you* on that tape. Do you hear me? It's not *you*. And you have to get that message out there *today*. So call the lawyers. Now."

"Yes," she murmured, still in shock. *That* was what Marianne was paying for that weekend? A tape? Of only her? How was it possible?

Don't be stupid. Of course, it was possible. Anyone could edit a tape. But *who* would have edited a tape to showcase only her?

"Listen, I'm going to find a copy and we're going to watch it together."

"I don't think so . . ." Oh God, was it being sold everywhere?

"No, you have to know what you're up against. Hold tight. I'll be there as soon as I can."

Soon wasn't all that soon. Becca returned two hours later, with Rob, which made it even worse.

"I don't want to see you," she said, pushing him back out the door.

"Hey, come on. That tape is smokin'."

"Oh God, you've seen it?"

"Ohh, *yeah.*"

She let him in. Becca popped her copy into the tape deck. "Ready?"

"No." Not ready to see herself bare naked and winding, twining, and fucking with a quartet of strange men—

And it *was* only her, stark naked, with strangers fondling and sucking every opening on her body, every inch of her, with the finale, the virgin hold-down where four pairs of unidentifiable hands immobilized her while everyone took their turn mounting her one way or another.

She couldn't speak as the tape ended. It might have been fifteen or twenty minutes' worth of fully articulated nonstop action altogether, but the sole focus was her, the invasion of her body, her sex, her mindless pleasure at being handled and penetrated everywhere.

She heard Rob say, "God, that is hot—Lord have mercy," but she was absolutely speechless, her heart pounding, her breath sucked so tight back into her lungs that she couldn't breathe.

"Where is everyone else?" she managed to whisper. "Where are *you?*" to Becca. But it didn't matter. This would destroy her life and effectively take away everything she ever wanted, hoped for, or dreamt about.

Even the impossible and unobtainable. Dax. She felt sick.

"I don't know," Becca said slowly. "I have no idea where this came from or why we were edited out. Maybe Nina knows."

"Maybe Nina did it," Rob said and they both turned to stare at him.

"Someone did it," Frankie said, her voice trembling.

"Maybe . . ." Rob said, and then stopped.

"Marianne," Becca finished for him.

She had no choice but to wade into the swill. There was nothing else she could do; the lawyers told her so.

And she had to do it quickly, to control the spin, to get her side of the story into the news stream before the end of that day, just as Becca had advised.

She called for the limo, even though she had nowhere in particular to go. The minute she stepped out of the building, she was attacked by the aggressive questioning of the reporters camped out there. All about the tape. All about the multiple-partner kinky-hinky sex. All about her nakedness on every level.

She spoke into the nearest microphone, her voice shaking, still.

"I'm appalled, shocked, and deeply offended that some pervert would edit a disgusting sex tape to make it appear as if I participated in some kind of orgy, and then release it for public consumption. I've initiated legal action to suppress and remove the tape from every venue, and I will find and prosecute the guilty party if it takes every last cent I have."

"You're saying that's not you on the tape?" one reporter shouted at her.

"I'm saying someone is trying to discredit and humiliate me." That was skirting the reality while cherry-picking the truth. "I'm saying I won't rest until that person is arrested and admits what he—or she—did, and pays for it."

"Do you mean to sue?"

She slipped into the limo, her heart pounding. She and Becca had decided she would drive around Central Park for a couple of hours, and then return to the apartment and give another out-of-the-limo statement to the press.

She needed time away from the apartment anyway, distance from the reporters' pointed questions, and their glee that the heartbroken Cinderella heiress had fallen into the mud so quickly.

They'd say she was fucking away her inheritance. They'd say she was a porn queen and con artist who'd cleverly wormed her way into Marianne's confidence, and then the whole question of Marianne's death and the legitimacy of her will might come to the fore again.

Her nightmare. And it didn't begin to assess the ripples in the pool—she couldn't prevent strangers copying the tape, burning DVDs, or any underground distribution through auctions or websites.

The thing could haunt her for the rest of her life.

Oh God, oh God, oh God—

No, she had to present herself as strong, in control, and deny everything emphatically. If she did that repeatedly and often, people would believe. And meantime, the lawyers had their detectives on the case, the best money could buy.

It *was* all about the money.

She girded herself for the next go-round of reporters when the limo returned her to the apartment.

"I've just come from my lawyer's office." She projected a calmer demeanor now. "They are doing everything possible to track down the deviant who concocted that lie and made it public. He *will* be prosecuted. I can barely bring myself to talk about it, I'm so disgusted by the nauseating content. We are using every legal means to get that tape out of circulation and to destroy every copy. Thank you."

She forestalled any questions by ducking into the lobby, where the doorman held an elevator for her.

"Sorry, Miss Luttrell," he murmured.

"Thank you," she whispered.

Becca was waiting for her with comfort food. "I got rid of Rob. Don't worry—he's nothing if not loyal. He won't spread the dirt."

"My God, Becca, he was nearly ejaculating in his pants, watching it. And who's to say *he* wasn't involved somehow? He as good as blackmailed me into sex by threatening to make the details of that weekend public."

"But where would he have gotten the tape? Screwing and telling is strictly forbidden in that place. That thing didn't come from Rob, and it wasn't the staff at the Boutique.

Come on, I got us some food. It is definitely a cheeseburger and cheesecake night."

"It's the night of the living dead, as far as I'm concerned."

"This little detour won't kill you. Everyone knows who you are now. Think of it as your fifteen minutes of fame. See if you can make it last. Just keep telling them, it's not you, it's not you, and it's not you—and make sure the photographers are right there every time."

"What if someone goes to France and—and . . ."

"The Boutique would be out of business in thirty seconds if anyone ever came forward. Trust me. There have been other . . . moments, shall we say? . . . where even more prurient things have been leaked, or people have been followed, or somebody told tales out of the bedroom. The perps were done and gone as if they never existed within days. It will be taken care of. I suspect the lawyers were well aware of Marianne's proclivities, and that there have been other incidents they've had to take a hand in. So just keep telling them it's not you.

"It'll blow over. Probably not soon, but it will. And meantime, you live your rich girl's life. Clubs are off limits for a while. No drinking, no flashing, no tasting parties. No *out there* sex, so no Plumb, no Mound."

"Oh great. So what am I going to do? Call the tasty boys?"

"No tasty boys, no penises." Becca's eyes glazed over for a moment. "But God, we did have fun . . ."

"*You'll* be having fun," Frankie said mournfully, swiping cheese from her burger and licking it off her fingers. "I'll be getting fat."

"Keep house hunting. That'll get you out on the streets so they'll follow you around. And you know what—write that blog. That's a good second way to get your story out there."

Becca hunkered down on the couch with her burger. "Let's concoct a title—something like *Cinderella's Confessions*. Or *Sins of Cinderella.* You go right on the offensive. This is what you've heard. This isn't true. Here are the *real* details of my freaking fabulous heiress life . . . and don't you wish it was you? Hell, no one could make this stuff up, and you're living it! And they will damn well wish they were living your life, sex tape and all."

Becca was right. All she had to do was keep bulldozing her way out of the shit.

Becca tapped her arm. "Hey—this is fun."

"Not so fun." And why was Becca so into it with her, when all of Marianne's other friends had backed off? "You're a fountain of advice and information. What's in it for you?"

"For the first time in years, I'm not bored, and I'm not using sex as a distraction. That's *something*, Frankie."

Something she wouldn't know about, since she was never bored.

And, okay, so the tape had utterly rocked her off her feet. But so what? It might be a *cause célèbre* for a week, maybe a month, which meant she'd still be in the spotlight. Maybe not for reasons she'd planned, but she had nothing to lose—really.

"I'm sure it is," she murmured, in answer to Becca's response. "Okay . . . I'll live the life of a nun while we have all this fun."

"Good," Becca murmured. "Meantime—the blog."

Starting a blog was easy. Becca brought up a choice of host sites from the search engine, picked one, filled in some basic information, agreed to the terms in Frankie's name, created a password and a name for the blog.

"Invite comments, too. Okay. Write."

She typed:

Confessions of the Cinderella Heiress

Call me anything you want, but in my wildest dreams, I never thought I'd be living this fabulous life under these incredible circumstances. They've called me Cinderella, the Mystery Millionairess, the Libidinous Legatee. But I'm really none of those things. I'm just a plainspoken girl from a small town in Maine, and how I got here is a fairy tale to be told on some leisurely rainy day.

The story today is that nasty humiliating sex tape, edited to look as if I had been a participant in a swinging orgy, that's all over the tabloids and being distributed everywhere.

The story is, it's not me. It's NOT me, plain and simple. And I'm taking active steps to get the tape suppressed and destroyed, and to be certain the culprit is apprehended and pays for what he/she did.

But let me assure you—that scurrilous tape hasn't stopped me for one minute from my usual activities. I'm actually out right now shopping for a town house. So for more juicy details of my fabulous life, come back and visit me tomorrow.

"How's that?"

"Short and sweet, unapologetic and aggressive. Perfect. Now we have to post it, get it listed on the various search engines, and see what happens."

"In other words, hope it doesn't explode in my face."

"Don't think about it. Press send, and—ladies and gentlemen, the heiress's daily diary shoots into the ether. Congratulations! This is a true cheesecake moment. Where the hell are those forks?"

"Hold it—I'm checking email. I don't think I've looked in the business box for two weeks." She clicked into the server and brought up the mail.

BOOM. Truck guy. She'd forgotten all about him. Oh God. Oh shit . . .

Hello, Gorgeous. Well, now I know who you really are and I'm really hot to fuck you again. Get back to me soon. But of course, now I also know where to find you . . .

Chapter Ten

Unapologetic and unafraid. Her new mantra. *Never let them see you sweat, deal with truck guy somehow, sometime—later.*

Time to appear in public again, to make those denials. To be seen out and about, cultivating normalcy. Or as normal as anyone could be with people shouting personal questions at you and with lights constantly flashing in your eyes. And hope that truck guy hadn't turned into a stalker.

No problem.

There were no new houses on the market, so she called her broker and arranged to revisit one she'd at first thought too small.

She decided to take a new tack with the press, as well. Get them on her side in case she needed them, in case truck guy turned ugly.

So this time out, she was in no hurry to evade them. She sashayed out of the apartment dressed in a muted raspberry silk dress, beige wedge-heeled shoes, big sunglasses, and a big Tod's leather tote bag. The cameras flashed and she struck her best kittenish poses as they shouted out questions:

"What about the tape? What's the latest on the tape?"

"My lawyers are handling it; there are private investigators on the case. I reiterate that I will not have my name and reputation sullied in any way, shape, or form by that filthy piece of garbage. Now—I'm going house hunting today. Care to come along?"

They didn't need much of an invitation to jump into cabs as she climbed into her limousine and made her way to meet her realtor at the four-story town house she'd seen the previous week.

It was a triplex with a basement floor-through apartment. On the first floor, the galley kitchen was tucked behind the main staircase, adjacent to the rear parlor which was the dining room now, with French doors opening to a deck. The second and third floors each had two bedrooms and a bath. Fireplace in every room. Original parquet floors, plaster moldings on the ceilings. Wonderful floor-to-ceiling windows in the front parlor overlooking the street. A great location, nice ground-floor apartment that could be her office.

Not that she needed the money. Technically, price was no object. Nor did she need any more space than the triplex. And she loved the location.

More than that, she loved the photographers snapping away out front.

It felt like *her* house. She nodded to the realtor. "I'll call you."

Out on the street, she posed on the steps, and as she gracefully entered the limo, showed a lot of leg.

Up to Madison Avenue now, to implement another strategy that had occurred to her—a red-carpet invite to Fashion Week. It was barely a week away, a definite place for an heiress coming out of mourning to be seen and photographed.

She dropped thousands of dollars at the shops of three on-trend Madison Avenue designers and dropped hints she'd love to attend their runway show, as the photographers snapped photos of each store, and of her emerging with a half dozen shopping bags, designer logos prominent, hanging on her arms.

The pictures appeared the next day; the caption read: *Mansions, Manolos and Missoni—Frankie Luttrell, the libidinous legatee on a spending spree along Madison Avenue, and (photo 2) contemplating a town house on the Upper East Side.*

Perfect. Nice shots, actually. She called the broker and made an offer on the house, and then she updated her blog:

Today was the best day. I spent the morning shopping on Madison Avenue and bought scads of clothes that I'll be wearing to the various fall charity events, for which you will have a front-row seat each time you come back to visit me.

But better than that, I made an offer on that town house after I went back for a second look and just fell in love. More luscious details tomorrow.

It didn't take long for invitations to start pouring in after the pictures appeared. She hadn't thought the photos would bear results that quickly, but obviously everyone wanted a piece of the *man eater* of the moment. Even the designer whose storefront was featured in the photo the previous day sent her a note and a coveted invitation for a seat at her show.

And the crowd, Marianne's crowd, suddenly appeared out of nowhere—calling her and making play dates.

And truck guy. Truck guy *really* wanted to play.

I'm in town, lusting for some of that luscious booty. When can I see you?

Words to strike terror in her heart. Good God, what had she unleashed?

Busy now, as you can imagine. Lots of details. Contact you soon.

That wouldn't hold him for five minutes, let alone forever.

And then Rob actually asked her out to dinner.

"Real dinner? No sex?"

"Real dinner *and* sex," Rob countered.

"Well, the dinner's a nice change," she murmured. And it was Rob, comfortable, good-looking Rob, a known commodity. She hadn't had sex in forever, and sex with Rob could only make things better.

They went to Café des Artistes, with its suggestive murals that perhaps Rob thought would put her in the mood.

He'd shown admirable restraint, not asking her anything about the tape until they were seated and had ordered.

And then, "Are you okay?"

"I'm buying a house," she said. "I'm writing a blog. I

bought new clothes. I don't know if I'm okay. I'm pretending to be okay, because that's the only thing I can do."

"You're doing a good job, but I'm thinking people are waiting for you to get naked on the table right now."

She looked around. Everyone was blissfully unaware of them, of her. "That's not funny."

"The libidinous legatee? Come on. That's a mouthful."

"Let me tell you, a nasty public outing suppresses your libido like a nuclear bomb."

"Are the lawyers really investigating?"

"They really are." Better not to comment further that they were deeply familiar with the prurient side of an heiress's life and knew just what to do.

"Yeah, I think I remember Marianne had a couple of incidents that had to be *handled,* actually," Rob commented. "Listen, you know every time they talk about you, they're going to raise the question of Marianne's death."

"It hasn't been so bad lately. I counted only three references in the last couple of days."

"But that kind of thing comes in waves. You get an investigative reporter who thinks you're dribbling away all that money, and the thing comes right at you again like a bad tennis serve. I'm just saying—"

"Don't get comfortable?"

"Hey, you're buying a house. That's huge. And since you're not working, you're probably paying cash. Which will be splashed all over the real estate sections of the *Times* and the gossip columns. Just one example."

"Okay. What am I supposed to do? Take on a mortgage? I

suppose I could . . . but it is what it is. I didn't coerce Marianne, I had no idea of her intentions, and now everyone's telling me to pretend I'm not in this position, in case someone tries to prove I coerced her and I knew exactly what she intended."

"Yeah, something like that," Rob muttered.

"I'm supposed to wear sackcloth and ashes just in case I really did what some people think I *might* have done?"

"Kind of. Sort of."

"Like penitence in reverse? Why would I do that—even if it were remotely the case?"

Rob made a face. "I don't know."

"This is so off-the-wall thinking, even for you," she said.

"I hope so," Rob muttered. "I don't know. There are a lot of crazies out there. Your lawyers have probably fielded hundreds of requests for money since you came into it. You probably don't even know about any of it. Why wouldn't envy push them even further: like come forward and try to claim some of the estate? Or accuse you of conning her out of it somehow."

"Oh yeah, me conning Marianne," Frankie said wryly. "Not likely."

"But to people who didn't know her? I'm a little concerned something like that could come back to haunt you."

"So not like you," Frankie murmured. "Dinner. Concern. Honestly, Rob, what's got into you?"

"Maybe . . . Oh shit, guess what's on its way to our table? Dinner and Dax, and not in that order. Looks like the old-boy network is dining out. Dax—what a coincidence."

God, he looked so tall and formidable.

"Rob. Frankie. Where's the Scooby crowd?"

"It's dinner for two tonight," Rob said, prickling.

Dax gave him a look and turned to Frankie. "Odd, isn't it?"

"What?" she whispered. *Go away. Leave me alone. I can't bear to look at you when I know you've probably seen that tape.*

"Dinner, suddenly. I'd be concerned."

"Suddenly everyone's concerned," she snapped.

"That happens when a boatload of money is involved, Frankie. People get romantic. And concerned."

"Or jealous," Rob put in snidely.

"Familiarity doesn't breed suitability," Dax said. "In any event, Frankie isn't looking to get married. Yet."

"And you know this how?" Frankie asked tightly.

There was that knowing look again, tinged with pity. "Read the fine print, Frankie. The lawyers vet everything and everyone, just in case anyone has ideas about swooping in before he was aware there were prenups and legalities like that."

"No one had any of those ideas," Rob growled.

"Glad to hear it. In that case, enjoy your dinner." He left.

Rob let out his breath. "What a bastard. He was always a bastard, but never like this. Who the hell does he think he is?"

"My lawyer," Frankie said dryly.

"Uh-oh. I guess no sex tonight, huh. I didn't read the fine print."

"Neither did I," Frankie admitted.

Rob jabbed his steak with his fork. "And I'll tell you something else, Frankie. Mr. Holier-than-God over there is running his own agenda where you're concerned. I'd read that fine print, if I were you."

So there was no sex. It was a refreshing change, actually, to sit and really talk with Rob at dinner. And then to have him bring her home, share a drink, and a long sumptuous kiss that could have led to other things—but didn't. She forestalled it, her mind still occupied with Rob's suggestion that Dax was competition somehow.

Not bloody likely. Not after her pornographic tape.

It wouldn't matter to truck guy. Who had left another message: *Waiting to hear from you. We have a good thing. Don't let your millions get in the way.*

Oh God, he wasn't going to stop. And her millions *were* a brick wall.

Her offer on the house was accepted, and the funds were transferred for a quick closing.

She wrote in her blog:

My offer on that fabulous town house was accepted, and we are going to close in two weeks. I feel as if I'm clearing the slate and starting everything fresh and brand-new. I can entertain in the huge parlor and dining room, which leads out onto a lovely little deck through French doors in the back wall, that overlooks a garden. And I can have friends overnight in what will be a top-floor guest suite. I will cook gourmet meals in my lovely compact kitchen. I'll be able to walk everywhere and be close to everything. I couldn't be more excited.

Comments: 1

Of course you can buy any Manhattan real estate you want when you're living high off the hog on ill-gotten gains. You have to ask, What really happened to Marianne Nyland? And how did a piece of porn trash from a trailer park in nowhere inherit all that money? For more, read Sex-a-rella's Exploits.

Oh God. She had been warned, and here it was already: a war on two fronts.

"Don't respond to it," Becca said firmly. "You have to have a public face of positive—positive—positive. You did nothing wrong, ever."

"Okay." Not okay, but she'd made her bed, and what else could she do? "What about truck guy? He hasn't stopped, and you know what's going to happen."

"Maybe he's a decent guy, really."

"Maybe he wants to be paid off. Or to blackmail me."

"You don't do it, Frankie. You're going to have to confront this at some point, but you don't let him bulldoze you into anything. Even if he threatens to . . . what? Tell the world? Sell his story? Fine, let him do it."

"More shit for me to wade through?"

"It's all about the sex. So what?"

So what. Here was Becca, doing the mother thing, and all about sex was a *so what?* in her book of ethics. Why was she surprised? She was Marianne's friend.

She corrupts everything she touches. Dax had said that about Marianne, and the mess she was in with the tape and truck guy was proof.

"It could be worse," Becca added comfortingly. "Get rid of the putz. Ignore the Blog-a-rella bitch. Just be relentlessly positive and it'll all go away."

"Fine." Frankie sighed. "All right, forget about all that for the moment. What should I do with the furniture in this apartment?"

"You call the Salvation Army. Get the tax deduction. Offer the crowd their choice of Marianne mementos first. Trust me, they'll want something, if not everything. Did you decide to sell the apartment?"

"I think so."

"Give me first refusal?"

"Really?" That stunned her.

"Really. And don't be shocked if everyone else feels the same way. Oh, and by the way—in case I didn't mention it, *don't* read that bitch's blog ever again."

"How can I not?"

Becca gave her an exasperated look. "Believe me, you can skip the details. She's out to get you"—she sat down at Frankie's computer, pulled up the page, and skimmed the contents—"big time—and she's doing it anonymously, too. Okay, I'll be your buffer. Hang on to your hat and listen."

These are the exploits of a scheming social climbing piece of trash who wound her way into the good graces of a generous benefactor who not only introduced her to her friends, but took her in when she came to fat city, and gave her a home. What do you suppose the fairy-tale ending is to this story?

I'll tell you. Our conning cunning butter-wouldn't-melt-in-her-cunt whore wound up with everything when her benefactor mysteriously died. No one knows just how that happened. The verdict was suicide, but the benefactor had everything to live for, and the shit twit had everything to lose if some things had been found out about her.

Let me just caution you not to believe the lies our porn princess has been disseminating in her blog. The press has already pegged her, and now I will too—we're talking about the infamous Sex-a-rella Heiress. Here she is—and there she was, full-face frontal over Rob's shoulder—*dining out on a man as usual, so can you doubt how the evening will climax?*

"Omigod . . ." There were no words for that ferocious vindictive rant.

"Holy hot shit." Becca shook her head. "Where did that picture come from?"

"I'll get it removed. *And* the comment section. It's obviously too tempting to my enemies."

"I hope you can. God. But meantime, ignore it. Delete it from your brain."

Frankie sent her a cynical look. "I have to respond to it."

"You'll start a war. You're better off just doing what you're doing. Deny everything, act normal. Get the crowd up here this weekend and give them *carte blanche* to take any or all of Marianne's things. Let them do the work—less to haul away, and it'll distract you so *you* won't be tempted to do something stupid."

"I'm supposed to give them stuff even though they abandoned me?"

"They were Marianne's friends."

"How do I know one of them didn't post that garbage?"

Becca sighed. "You don't. You have to trust that none of them did."

"Well, I can't know that. I can't let that piece of shit get away with writing that. I *have* to do an entry tonight."

Becca shook her head. "Not a good idea, Frankie. The public loves a catfight, and I'm not sure you'd win this one. But—if you're going to be stubborn about it—at least let me edit what you want to post."

She peered over Frankie's shoulder as she typed:

By now you've read that obscene and vindictive diatribe on another blog, which I categorically refute and deny and have given to my lawyers for possible legal action. Meantime, I'm forging ahead with the purchase of my wonderful house. Papers have been signed, and I'll be taking possession in a week or so. I'm also excited to report I've received a much desired invitation to Fashion Week and I can't wait to give you all the red carpet details as I attend the shows!

"Okay, not bad. But will you? Bring in the lawyers?"

"You bet. Why do you think I have them? Or at least that's what Marianne used to say." Tears filled her eyes, and Frankie paused with her finger over the send key. "Oh shit. You'd think I'd cried enough over Marianne by now."

"Yeah, the grief just comes out of nowhere and hits you like a rock. That's fine, what you wrote, Frankie. Not too much, just enough. Go ahead, send it. You know, maybe you ought to get the lawyers involved with truck guy, too."

"One thing at a time. I want to know where that picture came from." She punched the send key.

"A cell phone probably," Becca said. "That's too easy."

"Then I want to know who's following me around, and who this effing bitch is."

She invited the crowd over for a Saturday brunch and memento party.

"You all know I bought a house and I'm going to be moving soon," she told them when she called, "so before I sort through Marianne's stuff to donate it, I thought you all would like to choose something to remember her by."

She invited everyone except Dax. She couldn't face him among Marianne's friends and with the spectre of truck guy hanging over her.

"Anything we want?" Nina asked, as they all descended like locusts.

"Anything and everything I haven't labeled," Frankie said. "Help yourself."

They buzzed through the apartment like experienced tag sale operators. *And* they'd arranged for trucking even before they arrived, which told her how many of Marianne's possessions were going to walk out the door that morning. She provided boxes and brought in a buffet brunch—trays of cold cuts, cold salads, rolls and bread, pastries, coffee cake— laid out in the dining room so that if anyone wanted the table, they'd have to come back for it. Coffee, tea, and cold drinks in the kitchen.

They ate, they tussled over who would take what, they shared memories of Marianne as they scavenged the apartment, and took the living room TV, the dual tape and DVD deck, the bed frame, and matching dressers. Nina wanted the china, the silver, and the serving accessories. Becca wanted the sofa and the club chairs. Both of them sorted through the clothes and shoes, which Frankie hadn't had the heart to look at before today.

And everyone wanted first dibs on the apartment when she was ready to sell.

"Where's Dax?" Rob asked at one point.

"He couldn't come today." Big fat lie. "He's coming tomorrow." Bigger fat lie.

"You shouldn't be here with him alone after what he said to you."

"Nonsense."

"I'll come over tomorrow."

"Don't, please."

He didn't say anything more, just went back to rooting through Marianne's books and CDs.

And that as good as committed her to calling Dax later and inviting him to pick at the bones of Marianne's possessions—if he wanted to. Maybe he wouldn't have wanted to. Dax didn't strike her as someone who was sentimental about things like that.

She was a little taken aback when he said he'd come.

Worse and worse. She wandered around the apartment, now stripped of most of the furniture, small appliances, and decorative accessories. Only her bedroom had been off limits. And the stupid coffee maker.

Maybe she was the sentimental one.

And maybe she was sadder to give up the apartment than she knew.

Keep moving. It was the only thing to do.

Rob arrived first the following day, bringing bagels and food.

"Really, Rob . . ."

"He's a snake, and after what he implied, I wouldn't trust my mother alone with him."

"Fine." She chomped on a bagel and cream cheese.

Ten minutes later, Dax came bearing pastries. Like they were trying to outdo each other. This was stupid. They were eyeing each other like pit bulls.

Dax was walking around. "The crowd pretty well tore this place apart."

She rubbed her face tiredly. "Actually, I'm glad they wanted it all. It would have been terribly distressing to just give it all away to strangers. There are still some things here and in the bedroom if anything interests you."

His benign blue gaze collided with hers. "The dining room table."

Whomp. That was the last thing she expected. "Not the coffee maker?"

"I notice it's hot and steaming. I'm inferring that's a message."

"You're so astute."

"Hey hey hey." Rob barreled into them. "How about let's all sit down and have a cup of that *hot* steamy joe. And those nice calorie-laden pastries that Dax so kindly provided."

He herded them into the kitchen. "Here you go." He poured the coffee as if he were accustomed to doing it every Sunday morning, as if he lived here. "So what's your choice memory of Marianne?"

Dax eyed him for a long moment. "I'm rather partial to the day she fell off the yacht. I never could decide whether it was an accident or she jumped. I'm leaning toward the latter."

"No," Frankie protested. "Why?"

"Because," Rob answered for him, "it would be just like Marianne to do something dramatic and destructive to attract attention."

"That's pretty drastic," Frankie said, but even before the thought was out, she knew she had known that. Everything Marianne did bordered on risky and dangerous on one level or another.

"That was Marianne," Rob said sadly. "Meantime, Dax, what says Marianne to you in all this leftover stuff?"

Frankie jumped in. "He's taking the dining room table."

"Interesting choice. I'll help you out with it."

The conversation came to a dead stop. Rob wanted Dax out, and Dax was in no hurry to leave.

"The closing is set for the week after next," Dax said at length, "but I assume Rob knows that."

"Rob's interested in the apartment," Frankie said. "But I assume *you* know that."

"I know everyone is interested," Dax corrected her. "A bidding war is good for you. But I wonder how many of Marianne's friends can swing it financially."

"What do you mean?"

He set down his mug. "Impending inheritances and trust funds notwithstanding, who really can afford to spend that kind of money for an apartment now? I guess we'll find out." He looked at Rob. "Rob? Ready for that table?"

"You sure?" she asked him as he and Rob were halfway out the door. "How will you get it home?"

"I've got a van. I'll see you at the closing."

The elevator door closed like a punctuation mark, everything tied up neat and tidy. *We're done.*

Sex-a-rella's Exploits

Sex-a-rella is buying a town house. Can my readers even conceive of the money involved—in CASH? And how does Sex-a-rella have all that money? Why, she inveigled it from her benefactor who named her sole legatee in her will. The waste and extravagance are beyond outrageous. If I could sue on be-

half of her benefactor, I would take her to court in a heartbeat. If I had the means to hire detectives, I would prove she was complicit in her benefactor's death. All I can do is sit and watch while a no-good little nobody heedlessly runs through a shocking amount of fabulous wealth, having humped already every available man in the city.

She wished. One thing about being held hostage by an anonymous blog was there were just some things you couldn't indulge in, no matter how much money you had. No, one thing: sex.

Only, sex kept posting on her email every couple of days.

Hey, heiress lady, it's been too long. That wasn't our agreement.

Her heart was going to explode if she didn't resolve this one way or another. No matter what he wanted.

Hey, truck guy, I'm a busy girl, in case you haven't noticed. And I didn't sign a contract.

It didn't deter him a bit.

Find some time.

That sounded dire.

She found time to go shopping instead. She felt no compunction about spending money, not a bit of guilt over the purchase of the town house, not a morsel of regret for wanting to sell the apartment. But to give Anonymous the satisfaction of being right about her sex life? To let truck guy stalk her like the heroine in a horror movie? She *had* to draw the line.

"So what do I do?" she asked Becca.

"Get married," Becca said.

Not good advice. No one wanted to touch a porn princess: couldn't bring her home to mother. Not even Rob would sacrifice himself on that altar, and he was importuning her to hook up all the time. It was an easy out, but who wanted good old Rob as a bed buddy forever?

On the other hand, being involved with a known commodity, when she was so publicly defiled, might not be a bad thing.

She didn't know what to do. Rob wanted too much, even insisting on going to the closing with her two weeks later.

"You know, I know how to sign my name," she told him gently.

"Moral support."

"The lawyers are there for that, and to make sure I dot my i's and cross my heart."

"I'm certain Dax will scrutinize every last word in every last clause."

"Exactly. So what can you do to help?"

"I can take you out to celebrate afterward."

"Rob, even though my virtual concierge provided a nice bed and temporary furniture, there's not much in the apartment that's conducive to romance."

"Yeah, but we're not talking romance, we're talking *sex*."

How right he was. Pure out-and-out elemental-body-parts sex, the plug-and-play kind that felt good in the afterglow and made you wonder what you were thinking an hour later.

Not today . . . I have a headache? A house ache? A truck stop?

Not that she wasn't hungry for some plug and play. But she couldn't be certain now that someone wasn't watching her every move.

She went to the closing alone. Signed the papers, signed the checks, made small talk with the former owners who were retiring to Arizona, shook everybody's hand cordially, and got trapped by Dax before she could leave the conference room gracefully.

Formidable, unobtainable Dax, the reproach always in his hard blue gaze. And knowledge, wariness, pity.

"I'm heading to the house," she said, hoping to deter him. No such luck. "Good. I'd like to see it."

They left the offices a back way and grabbed a cab, a refreshing moment where she didn't have to deal with cameras and reporters. Just Dax. Maybe the press was easier, she wasn't sure.

When the cab drew up in front of the house, there was Rob, with flowers.

"Goddamn," Dax muttered. "What the hell . . ."

"He's protecting me."

"Yeah, me too," Dax growled as he helped her out of the cab.

Frankie took the flowers, Dax said nothing, and they filed up the stoop and entered the front parlor which, empty of furniture, seemed cavernous. Rob wandered into the dining room, kitchen, out onto the deck, and down into the garden.

There was nothing to explore, really. Everything was whistle clean and move-in ready.

Maybe the blogger would leave her alone once she moved. Maybe truck guy would just give up and disappear.

Fat chance.

Her sins would follow her, every electronic way possible.

But here at least, for this five minutes, her life felt pristine, and as if she were on the verge of new and wonderful things.

She went onto the deck, leaned against the railing, and let the sun play on her face. Across the yard was a twin of her house and garden, one among a line of town houses marching up the adjacent block. There were no apartment buildings, which meant good light in the back of the house. Everything she could have wished for, except—

Rob joined them. "Nice. Great investment."

"Oh, you son of a CEO," Dax said, goading him. "Always thinking about the bottom line."

"For Christ's sake. Why the hell are you intruding on a private celebration?"

"Protecting my client's interests," Dax said smoothly.

"Shove it, Dax. You're protecting your own interests. Like you weren't privy to Marianne's will? Like you don't have an ulterior motive for your interest?"

"Unlike you," Dax put in dryly.

"Yeah, but you *knew* and you were just biding your time to make the move. The strip club, the night at the hotel, the nasty blog—tell me that isn't you and you're not trying to scare her into doing something rash and permanent—like marrying you."

"How Machiavellian of me," Dax murmured. "God, I'm devious."

"You're a goddamned lawyer; you *are* that devious. Frankie—don't let him get to you. Mr. Aloof and Elusive—all an act. We got him to a strip club, Frankie—by God, he *is* a mortal man."

Frankie closed her eyes in despair. "You were there, too?"

"Hell, yes."

And neither of them knew about truck guy. And she couldn't be certain Dax didn't know about or hadn't seen the scurrilous tape.

He had to know. It was heart stopping that he might know.

"Okay. I've had enough. Both of you—go."

"Come on, Frankie," Rob said, at his most boyish.

She wasn't moved. "*Go.*"

She turned to Dax. That soft look shadowed his eyes again because he thought she wasn't watching.

"I hope you're sane about him," he said abruptly. "That's about all I have to say."

"I'm going *in*sane here. *Did* you know about Marianne's will?"

"Pleading the fifth, Frankie. That's none of your business. And my business here is done."

He was in too much of a hurry suddenly. "Dax . . ."

"By the way," he said, ignoring her, "did you know there were photographers out in front of the house?"

"Dammit, no." She angled her way to the window to see. They'd caught Rob leaving then, and probably they would get a shot of Dax, and then her. Damn damn damn.

"As usual," Dax said, "you've left yourself no way out. They'll make a nice trashy fiction out of this, Frankie. But maybe, given your recent choices, that was what you intended. Whatever. I'm out of here."

"Dax, dammit . . ."

"Don't dammit me, Frankie. This cost a pretty piece of change, and there isn't anyone in the city who doesn't know it and that you paid cash for it. You'd have been better off staying at the apartment, because right now you have nothing between you and the rest of the world. They're going to dine on you for weeks, and you're going to keep coming back for more. Nothing's changed: you're still the heedless, exhibitionistic child. You're just doing it on a larger scale now. Thank God you have money and lawyers while you take your joyride to hell. Just keep denying everything. It'll get you in the headlines every time."

She felt flayed. And she hated that he was right when the photos appeared, one, two, three on Page Six, and in gossip blogs everywhere, with the damning caption:

How many lovers for the libertine lady who questionably inherited those millions? We counted two unidentified humpers in the space of two hours, sneaking out of her newly purchased (cash only) town house. Or did our licentious lady go for a tri-fecta?

And to terrorize her still more:

Hey, heiress lady. Getting it on with everyone but me? I've got a story to tell, too . . .

Chapter Eleven

Fashion Week! The crowds, the crush, the tents, the events. Socialites mingling with models. Reporters everywhere. Cameras snapping, film rolling. Not a minute to be missed. The beautiful people in beautiful clothes, mixing and matching. The diva do-si-dos. The air kisses. The stylists, the designers, the elegant private parties, dinners, receptions. All the excitement, buzz, gossip, madness . . .

It was marvelous, day to night, with crowds streaming into the tents, or cabbing downtown to showrooms for morning shows, or to luncheon charity events at the museum.

Frankie wrote in her blog:

So I went to the Luca Luca show first, which, fortunately for me, had been rescheduled. There were photographers everywhere. The excitement was contagious. During the show, a model lost her balance, but she waved it off with a smile. I'm not certain I could have been so gracious about it. Later, there was a movie screening, and then I went home and changed, because of course you can't be seen at one show

*wearing the outfit of a different designer. I went on to the
Charlotte Ronen show. What wonderful clothes, really, with
great colors, so easy to wear, a great favorite among the TV
stars and tabloid divas who populated the audience. There
were parties all day and all night long. I happened on one
held in a town house nearby my new home and I crashed it.
No matter. The Cinderella Heiress was known and welcomed.*

It had taken brazen boldness to walk into a house party
where she knew no one. But she found that too many knew
of her—as the new neighbor juggling handymen, the scan-
dalous Nyland heiress, the sex tape sensation.

And then the Fashion Week pictures were published—in
the *Post,* in *WWD,* on the 'net . . .

Notoriety made you valuable for the thirty seconds that
your name was emblazoned in light—it brought you the invitations, men, swag, the glitterati life—but it magnified
your accessibility, too.

Case in point: truck guy.

"This," she showed Becca his latest email, "is a threat."

"You've got to get rid of this guy; he's too down-market
for you. Unless he's got a couple mil stashed away somewhere. Or owns a company or two? No? Then he's just out
for what he can get."

"He *got* me."

"Well, that was pre-M, and now you have to pre-*empt*
him. Whatever exposure he threatens, slough it off, tell him
to go for it. He'll get a couple hundred thou from the *Star* or

whatever, and it'll be done. Whatever he has to say, it'll be landfill by the weekend."

Frankie sighed. "I should *pay* you to manage my publicity. You're so levelheaded, and I feel like I'm running around like a headless chicken."

Becca didn't say anything for a moment, and then, "I'll do that. I mean, I'll take over that role for real, if you want. Do you?"

"God, *Becca*! The sex tape is still a best-selling black market item, and now the gossip about those pictures of Rob and Dax, Dax hates me, Rob's constantly pestering me, and I'm not certain if he just wants to marry money, and truck guy is in my head like a crippling migraine . . . Do I *want* you to?"

"Okay. Look, there are lots of paths to resurrection, but we have to get the shit out of the way first. So—contact truck guy. Arrange to meet him somewhere high end and neutral—not that skeezy motel. And no mattress mambo."

"God, and he was soooo good. That's what's so freaking aggravating. You want to try him on?"

"Be the consolation prize? I don't think so. I think he's going to want to keep sexing you. You're going to say no. He'll probably try to blackmail you; you will say no. He'll tell you he's shopping his story around, and you'll tell him 'Be my guest.' He's over, Frankie. You will *not* tell him he is out of your league, not rich enough, good-looking enough, well-dressed enough, or whatever enough stupid things may come to mind in the heat of the moment. You will let him down easy, got it? Be nice. Let him do what he wants with his so-called *story*—it's publicity."

Frankie posted back to truck guy: *Time to parlay. Let's do lunch. Union Square Cafe, one p.m. tomorrow. I'll make the reservation.*

He came back quickly: *Rather dine on you. Here, eight p.m. tonight.*

She answered firmly: *I'll see you at the restaurant at one p.m. tomorrow.*

"That's all," Becca said, reading over her shoulder. "No arguments, no excuses, no demands. Another Millionaire Manual lesson: less is more, especially with explanations. He wants to see you, he'll come downtown. He'll hate that you blew him off, but we don't do booty calls. It gives them too much power once you get to liking the booty."

"Yeah, well, I really liked the booty at the time."

Becca slanted a look at her. "More than Dax?"

"Oh God. Dax is not remotely in the realm of booty possibility, in spite of that night."

"Which you refuse to talk about, so something titanic must have happened."

"Yeah. He realized how much he despised me."

"*Not,*" Becca murmured. "But that's a discussion for another day. You have to get rid of truck guy. And don't dress like a dirty girl, either."

"A suit okay?"

"With a knee-length skirt."

"Yes, ma'am."

She wore a black suit with a thin chalk stripe, very businesslike, the skirt kissing her knees, her hose off-black. She wore a silk tank to soften the severity of the outfit and not much jewelry—button earrings, a watch—mustn't look tempting on any level.

She was seated at the dot of one. As she scanned the menu, she wondered if he would show. Not easy to have a private conversation in a place like this, but that probably was why Becca recommended it.

"Hey . . ."

And there he was, tall, broad shouldered, dressed properly in a suit—a nice suit, and looking quite at home as he sat down opposite her.

She looked up. "Hi. Glad you came."

"Are you?" he asked. "Will *I* be?"

"Probably not," she said candidly, "but at least you'll have a good meal."

She handed him a menu.

"I need a drink."

"Who doesn't?" She motioned to the waiter. He wanted scotch on the rocks, she opted for a fruity wine. When the drinks arrived, he lifted his glass and asked, "What are we toasting?"

This was the moment for honesty. Maybe he thought she'd reconsidered, but she wasn't going to pretend that this was anything more than a sweet good-bye. There just wasn't any kind way to say it.

"Reaching the end of this road," she said finally.

"Not going to do that, Frankie. I'm seeing a limitless horizon."

She smiled tightly at his combative tone. "But I'm going to do that, truck guy."

"Still no names? That's insulting, after all that supernova sex."

"Fine, what's your name?"

"Carl—"

"Don't tell me any more," she interrupted him. "That's all I need to know."

"That and—"

"No. The *and* part is over," she said tersely. "So . . . let's order lunch and try to be civil."

"I don't want to end it."

She looked up from the menu. "I do."

"Well, as I said, I have a story, too."

"Do you?" She waited for the nasty part.

"So keep sexing me."

"Not going to do that, Carl," imitating his tone.

"What, needy millionaire nymphos don't need a go-to guy?"

"This one doesn't."

"Really. That's not what I understood from all those sweet nothings you whispered while I was giving you the good stuff."

"Things have changed, Carl."

"A hundred million times over. And that sex tape . . . that's one effing piece of pornography right there. It keeps me company the nights you're not keeping me company. And there's also the story I have to tell."

She put down the menu, her hands cold, her temper ratcheting up with the knots in her stomach.

"What story is that?" she asked, her tone silky with disdain.

"You know that segment they do sometimes on TV—where they show what stars looked like before they became famous? I got the one about the dirty whore before she became a rich bitch."

"Well, everyone likes a rags-to-riches story, Carl," she retorted, keeping her voice neutral with an effort. "I think you should go ahead and tell that story. I think it would be inspiring to a whole lot of people."

He gave her a tight look. "You're bluffing. You couldn't stand another sex scandal."

"Hey—I don't care."

A deep male voice came from behind her. "Frankie?"

Oh God, Dax, sweeping the two of them with his cool blue gaze and putting the worst interpretation on what he saw.

"Aren't you going to introduce me?"

"No need. This meeting is over."

"Are you ready to leave, then?" Dax asked.

"I'm ready."

"Yeah," Carl snapped. "She's always ready, if you know what I mean."

Dax arched an eyebrow and took Frankie's arm. She tossed a hundred-dollar bill on the table. "I think that's enough to cover everything—including your services today, Carl."

"Go to hell, slut."

She barely heard him, but everyone else did, as Dax whisked her out of the restaurant.

"That was a scene from a bad X-rated movie," he said

mildly when they were out on Sixteenth Street. He hailed a cab. "Home? Are you moved in yet?"

"You know everyone was eavesdropping," she fretted. "I bet Becca called you."

"I swear to God, I'm not going to rescue you every time someone tries to blackmail you."

"He had it both ways: do him and he won't; don't do him and he will. He's got a *story*."

"God, doesn't everyone?" Dax muttered as the cab drew up to the house. He paid the cabbie and followed her up the stoop and into the parlor, which was beautifully furnished by her virtual concierge.

"You're stepping right into Marianne's shoes. Do *not* tell me the estate has to pay him off."

"No. I told him to go ahead and do what he wants. Some magazine will pay him handsomely for the minimal details."

"Crap. Look, change your server, your email addresses, get a post office box somewhere far away from here. And maybe rethink living in this place alone."

"What do you mean? Like, get a roommate? Get married?"

"Son of a bitch. Did that idiot mention marriage to you?"

Oh good, he was angry. She feigned innocence. "Which idiot?"

"Either one—your bed buddy or rockin' Rob Gildred."

"What about you?" It came out without thinking—lightning on her tongue, if wishes were dreams and dreams weren't lies. And you didn't get caught and punished for your sins. And if you weren't the witless star of a pornographic foursome movie.

You couldn't erase that; couldn't pretend none of it happened. It was there in his shuttered expression and the way he tactfully moved toward the door.

"Not in ten lifetimes, Frankie."

He truly despised her. She had nothing to lose as she followed him and confronted him at the door.

"What about this lifetime?" Bold, brazen, stupid as shit.

His hand tensed on the doorknob. He turned and that look was there again, fleeting as a wish. And then it was gone, and he left.

Sex-a-rella's Exploits

Our Sex a rella can't keep a low profile. Look at this: a Fashion Week garden party . . . a picture of her in a Bryant Park tent . . . a Village happening party . . . a picture of her at the party she'd crashed . . . and then, the men . . . a replay of the photos of Rob and Dax leaving her town house, followed by a photo of her and truck guy at lunch, Dax hustling her out of the restaurant, the two of them outside the restaurant, entering her house, and Dax leaving. Let us count the men: did she not talk to a half dozen intrigued and possible bed-mates at the party? Money can buy anything, that's for certain, even for a nympho slut who's had a few too many brief encounters, like the one with restaurant man that apparently was the end of a torrid idyll. The wonder was he was so unhappy when he's getting a quarter of a mil

*for the X-rated details of his ménage à two with Sex-a-rella.
Of course, that isn't quite as titillating as that gangbanging
ménage à four . . .* captured picture from the sex tape, of
her held down by the four pairs of hands, her eyes closed
in what looked like ecstasy, her body parts appropriately
blurred out . . . *but maybe it will be. Ah, Sex-a-rella, you
never disappoint. And I bet all your men would say that,
too . . .*

Becca read this blistering entry over Frankie's shoulder.
"Number one, you shouldn't be reading this garbage. And
number two, deny everything."

"You can only do so much of that, and then it starts
sounding like you do have something to hide."

"This is true. Okay, don't say anything. In fact, why don't
we go out tonight just to prove there's nothing to any of this
garbage. I mean, how many people read it anyway? And we
haven't dined together, the crowd, I mean, since before
Marianne died. So let's do that."

But none of the crowd wanted to do that. Everyone Becca
called claimed to be busy.

"Uh-huh. They're circling the wagons again, so they don't
get hit with the shit."

"Yeah." Becca wasn't happy.

Frankie wasn't happy either. Marianne had been gone
now almost five months and things were too strange. All this
focus on her, her sex life, the money—God, the money. Well,
Becca had warned her that the circumstances of Marianne's
death would simmer under the surface for a while yet. Obvi-

ously the Sex-a-rella blogger was boiling under the surface, and maybe about to explode.

Truck guy did explode, and Page Six had it first: he didn't sign a book deal. He was doing a fast salaciously pornographic male confessional, every juicy detail, at $100,000 per installment in the *Star*, with the tantalizing tag line:

Her Infamous Sex Tape Isn't the Whole Story . . .

On a billboard. In sixteen-foot letters. In Times Square. Omigod.

"I should just stand in front of the goddamned thing and invite everyone to take a piece of me," Frankie spat. "The sons of bitches. *Why* are they doing this? Have we even analyzed all the garbage that's happened to me since Marianne died?"

"It's just speculation, fiction, and gossip," Becca said firmly. "So what? You've had insane sex. You can have any man you want now. You've got money. You're famous. Maybe not for the things you would have wanted, but file it under *this too shall pass* while you have fun."

"Unless truck guy takes me down."

"Please—the readership will find it insanely romantic."

"*Romantic?*"

"It's every woman's fantasy. It'll enhance your reputation."

"God, you're an optimist."

"And this is making you lose your bad-girl edge. Enjoy it, for God's sake! Ignore the anonymous hatchet job and revel in it. You're a sex goddess, and you have too much time on your hands. You know what you need? A good week-long shopping trip."

Frankie looked around the near empty parlor. "I think the priorities are clear. And you need a key."

"Good. Let's do Bloomie's and have some fun."

Except that Big Sister seemed always to be watching. A day at Bloomingdale's was a field day for cell phone photographers on the hunt for any celebrity sighting to surreptitiously snap away and make an instant submission under the daily deadline headline.

And make free use of the vulgar web log name with which Anonymous had christened her.

So much for the naïve idea that no one read that blog.

Sex-a-rella shopping. We all should be chauffeured to Bloomie's. A picture of one long leg as she prepared to slide out of the limo. A snap of her and Becca sitting on sofas in the furniture department. Another of her considering a piece of china. Another, with a piece of sterling silver in hand.

Oh, say it isn't so. Sex-a-rella looking at furniture, dishes, and silver? Is the oversexed siren engaged? Do men marry their sex machines? Read all the lusty inside secrets this week . . . Are you man enough to take her on?

The headline took up half the front page of the *Star: The Secret Life of the Sexually Insatiable Cinderella Heiress.*

The reporting became more intense after that first installment was published; it even made the TV tabloid *The Insider.*

In his explosive tell-all confession, Carl Moore, a self-employed trucker, tells his wild story of how the notorious Nyland heiress, Frankie Luttrell, picked him up at a highway convenience store for a night of blow-away anonymous sex. It's a story you have to read to believe, and even then, you still might think it's fiction. Luttrell, as you might recall, inherited millions on the death of heiress Marianne Nyland five months ago. Moore claims he had raw, rough, no-holds-barred sex with Luttrell multiple times before Nyland died, and that she demanded he service her by appointment several times a week. You can read the rest of the intimate juicy details in parts two and three of his bedroom revelation on stands Wednesday and Friday.

Service her by appointment, for God's sake! More like she serviced *him*. The exploitive son of a bitch. *She* should be telling tales out of the bedroom, like his attempt to blackmail *her*.

It was always about the money.

She sat down at the computer.

Aren't you just loving all the stories spewing out about my alleged sex life? I wish I had that life. But girls from small towns in Maine don't sleep around like that. And they don't pick up men like that. And when you're fortunate enough to be graced with a new and different life the way I was, you wouldn't ever want to screw it up like that.

Denial by nondenial. Clever.

But she needed to see what Anonymous had to say about it, now that the web sobriquet had become common usage.

Sex-a-rella's Exploits

Sex-a-rella never fails us. Not only did she con a smart, savvy, and wealthy socialite, she banged every ballbuster she could when she took her love out of town.

> *Sex-a-rella, dirty girl, where do you roam, outside, inside,*
> *Anywhere but home.*
> *Grab a guy, use his balls,*
> *Blow him off, troll the malls.*
> *Sex-a-rella, dirty girl, never gets enough*
> *Sex-a-rella sex machine likes it really rough . . .*

Okay, if that was how Anonymous wanted to handle it, Frankie was ready to play rough. She could run blind items, too. She could do mean girl. A bad girl never took things lying down, and she'd been too passive, letting this piece of garbage ride roughshod over her.

You couldn't be nice, civil, or even have good manners when someone used those tactics. People who acted anonymously were just begging to get slapped down. So be it.

She typed into her blog:

But our friend Anonymous never seems to stop taking great glee in blowing everything about my life out of proportion.

Anyone who hides behind a no-name web name and trashes someone as much in the public eye as I have been, deserves to have a lawsuit exploded on his or her head. So, I'm taking appropriate measures to out Anonymous, so you all will know who's slinging those muddy slurs, and I will make certain that no-name is tied up in court for the rest of (her) life. Because I can.

It felt good. You had to be proactive about these things. You couldn't let slime pull you into the muck with them.

Becca probably would have told her not to do it, but Becca wasn't imprisoned in her own life by two bottom-feeders who were looking for notoriety and money.

And Becca was right: She should go about her life, denying everything, being positive, positive, positive. Never let them see her sweat. Sweetness and light.

The thought surprised her. Maybe because it was the beginning of October and the start of the crisp fall, but she really could see, finally, how it all could be fun.

That didn't mean that the sex scandals went away. Truck guy was interviewed by every entertainment outlet, every single-girl fantasy magazine, and the *Wall Street Journal.* He posed for *Playgirl,* he did the rounds of the morning shows, he confessed to the on-air sex guru of the moment, and he was hot, happening, and he had groupies, too.

Anonymous backed off—a little.

Sex-a-rella's Exploits

We're so happy to report that Sex-a-rella must be on medica-tion, because she's calmed down considerably. Those at-home evenings. Alone? We don't think so; she's just not that type of girl. But then . . . maybe she got sober reading our reports. Maybe we got sobered up a little at the threat of a lawsuit, but then, that's what bullies do when they don't know what to do.

Anyway, I can report that Sex-a-rella isn't sleeping with any-one right now. New York can rest easy.

The press didn't.

"Is Carl Moore's story true?"

"Did you pick him up? Are you engaged? Are you sleep-ing with anyone now?"

"Is it true Carl Moore is really hung, and you hung him out to dry?"

She was going out more, appearing in places she knew there were crowds, reporters, photographers.

She particularly loved the *out of the limo* moment, that breathtaking instant before the reveal, when people were watching and wondering who, when, how famous. She'd take it slow too, stretching to reveal a good length of leg wearing sky-high heels. And then her thigh, her face still hidden by shadow inside the backseat. And then her arm, her shoulder, her other leg, a hand up, and she was out to the flash of digital cameras and shouted questions.

She dined out twice with Becca, once with Rob; she went to a couple of corporate-sponsored charity events; she attended a Broadway opening—all occasions where she would be seen and photographed but with the taint of her sex life following her like a bad scent.

"Hey, Frankie—Carl Moore is saying he was your service stud."

"Frankie, this way—is he *that* good in bed?"

"Frankie, Frankie—who's your new stallion?"

"Do you really like to get naked with just anyone?"

She flirted with them all. "Now, come on, a girl doesn't talk about her private life."

"Or her privates," someone shouted out.

Good for a laugh. "Or yours," she shot back.

"Have I slept with you?" the reporter asked.

"No, but I bet you wish you had," she retorted and got another laugh.

Make them laugh. Make them love you. Becca's advice, still good.

Marianne's crowd was still hanging back, watchful, waiting.

Rob finally made a bold move, escorting her to a fundraiser at the Central Park Boathouse, where there was dinner *en buffet* and live music playing softly in the background when they arrived.

"You've been great with the press," he told her over drinks. "You really shut up that blog-a-rella babe. And this bunch doesn't much care what they say about you, as long as your checkbook is wide open."

257

"Still, I bet there'll be an item tomorrow on her blog and in the papers about us tonight."

Rob gave her a hooded look. "If you really believe that, let's make it true."

"Did I mention I'm not having sex again before I die?"

He snorted. "Right. You not having sex is like, is like . . ."

She waited, amused.

"Well, you not having sex is inconceivable."

"Thank you—I think. Take my bet? I mean, look how the men are eyeing me. It's like I'm toxic or something. And Nina—it's like I dropped off the face of the earth. I haven't seen her in months. And Becca isn't even here. I bet you'll be the only one to talk to me tonight."

"No," Rob said resignedly. "Dax is here."

"Oh, he won't come ten feet near me. You're the only brave soul, so maybe you'll be rewarded for chivalry."

"I wish, but not. Brace yourself. Here comes Dax."

"Rob, Frankie." He lifted his goblet. "Good job with the press, Frankie. And Anonymous. Even I'm curious to know who the bitch is now."

As usual, Dax in formal wear struck her dumb.

"And we won't even mention Moore."

"No," she whispered. "Let's don't."

He looked over at the crowd. "They're not playing, are they?"

"You damned well know they're not," Rob answered for her.

"Good," Dax said, setting aside his drink. "Fewer distractions to deal with."

"Which means what?" Rob demanded.

"Fortune hunters," Dax said plainly. "Who will not be deterred by Frankie's sexuality—and greatly seduced by everything that comes with it. Know anyone like that?"

"You son of a bitch." Rob whipped around to Frankie. "I told you."

"No," Dax said, "*I* told her." He looked at Frankie. "Do *not* have sex with him tonight."

"And I need this caution—why?"

"Because you'll wind up doing something ill-considered and— Damn it, just don't do it."

"So what do you say?" Rob turned to her. "You look like you need a good hard tumble."

Dax looked as if he wanted to punch something. Maybe Rob. Maybe Rob was right about Dax.

"I'd like sex with Dax, actually," she said after a measured moment of consideration. "If I have any choice in the matter."

"Nonnegotiable, Frankie."

"He's pushing for the *everything that comes with it* part," Rob said nastily.

Dax tipped his glass. "Who wouldn't? Let's dance and call it sex."

Rob looked seriously irritated. Dax swung Frankie onto the dance floor before either she or Rob could protest.

She didn't see the flurry of women converging on Rob, or the covert whispering in corners. She felt a lightness inside for the first time in a long time, and secure in the firm way Dax held her.

She felt as if she were seventeen again, and this was the country club in Bar Harbor, and the night she was on the brink, and Dax had almost pulled her back.

Except in life, there were no do-overs. And Dax couldn't save her, then or now.

The buffet was set up by the time the dance ended, and Dax guided her over to the line.

Behind a flurry of voices that were just that little bit too loud, she heard:

"She has a nerve showing her face *here*."

"I wish someone would tell her to leave. She just contaminates everything. All anyone can talk about is—"

"Right—that Carl guy. God, is he full of himself."

"And she—"

"I know. And Rob is acting like—"

"She should leave. Just write the check and go."

"She just . . . *exudes* . . ."

"Right, and we can't have her exuding all over our men on the dance floor."

"Too obscene."

"Oh, as if *you* don't exude."

"At least I'm discreet about it. I just wish she'd—"

"Heard enough?" Dax asked.

"Oh, no. I'm staying right where I am," Frankie said. "I paid for that food and I paid for my right to be here, and a stupid bunch of mean girls isn't going to chase me away."

"Right."

She looked over toward Rob. "And why does Rob look so weird? Who are all those women?"

"Probably the moral minority, who don't admit to anything they do behind closed doors," Dax said wryly. "Fine. You'll eat dinner, then I'll take you home."

"Only one way you'll get me out of here in *this* lifetime," she murmured. Maybe it was the wine talking. She was all bravado tonight, wanting to stand her ground at a place she so obviously was not wanted. Why not stoke the fire?

"Fine. Food, Frankie. Take the plate . . ."

She didn't even know what she ate. She only remembered the succeeding confrontation—a half dozen society sisters descending on her all at once trying to be kind, cool, and not too condescending.

"We're going to ask if you wouldn't mind going home now," the one chosen to deliver the *coup* said, her voice gentle, conspiratorial.

"You need to go home," another said bluntly. "It's better that way."

Was Blog-a-rella secretly watching from the sidelines, relishing her fall from grace?

So unbelievable, so rude.

"Of course, you'll refund my contribution," Frankie said tightly. "I'm not feeling very charitable at the moment. I believe the amount was a thousand dollars, plus the tickets and the per-plate donation."

"Whatever." The ringleader shrugged. "Bad form, though."

"And telling me to leave isn't?" she asked belligerently. "I—"

"Frankie." Dax, commanding her to rein in her temper, holding her with his cool blue gaze until the mean girls retreated. "Time to go home."

He thought so, too? "Only if we have sex. I'm not going anywhere with you unless we have sex." Oh, God, where did that come from? Definitely the wine talking. And her impotent fury at the insolence of the bitches who'd just tossed her out.

"You're fried, Frankie."

"I'm . . . mellow. And I have other secret sources for sex," she said dreamily, not caring how that sounded. "So if you won't, I'll—I'll take Rob's offer."

"Fine. We'll have sex. Let's *go*."

"Really?"

"Really. Come." His voice was so soft as he held out his hand.

It didn't look like she was the pariah of the party. After all, people never stayed long at these events. There were always other places to go and be seen, and she could well have been on her way to one of them.

Everyone was cordial as they took their leave, and too polite; everyone said, *Good night. Thanks for coming. Thanks for your help.*

"What was *that* all about?" she demanded as he settled her into the limo.

"Just let's get you home."

"Getting me home doesn't sound like getting me in sex," Frankie retorted.

"Maybe it isn't."

"Rollie! We're going back to the party . . ."

Dax grasped her arm. "Home." And he meant it. And he meant no sex. He *thought* he meant no sex.

But they were a combustible combination. It didn't take much. Just a touch of his hand, of his lips, of his body molded to hers. He wanted it too, for all his denials and refusals; he might have wanted it even more than she, because it cost him so much to deny it.

And he fought it, he fought her, between his kisses. "Not happening, Frankie."

"It's happening," she whispered and she knew it *would* happen, because that softness glowed in his eyes again.

And because he took so much time to ready her, took endless time before he entered her, and most importantly, because the first torrid fusion of their naked bodies felt like he was claiming her forever.

In the morning, it wasn't quite that clear-cut. It felt more like . . . she didn't want to think what it felt like.

Or why he'd thrown every scruple out the window.

"Dax—"

He was on his back, staring at the ceiling. "What?"

Why *had* he? "Something's not right."

"Thanks. I enjoyed it that much, too."

She ignored the jibe. "Something stinks."

He turned on his side to look at her. *That* look. "Nonsense, Frankie. I *like* the scent of your sex in the morning."

She caught her breath. Still not right. Still—*off* . . . why? What?

"You were too easy," she said suddenly.

He shot her the more familiar, reserved, aloof look. The one that was harder, less giving.

Unlike the part of him that was still hard, and unreservedly giving. Distracting her. Just as he intended. Like this whole Sex-a-rella night. Even though she hated thinking it, her gut was telling her that he'd made love to her as a distraction.

"You wouldn't have just agreed to . . . Something's not right." She sat up. "This feels like a mercy fuck."

"It feels like an *I shouldn't have done it* fuck right now." He swung up off the bed and reached for his shirt. "It fact, it was an *I should've known better* fuck."

"What are you not telling me?"

"That I should have known better."

"Because—?" There was something about a naked woman confronting the half-dressed man with whom she'd just had a night of soul-shattering sex. He couldn't hide behind his clothes. He couldn't hide behind half-truths. The only weapon he had was silence, and the depths of that intimidating blue stare, and even that barrier was tenuous at best.

"The hell with you." She grabbed the chenille throw from the chaise longue by the window, wrapped it around herself, and stalked across the hall to her computer.

"There's one way to get answers. Thank God for the internet." She booted up *Sex-a-rella's Exploits*.

And there it was:

Well, kiddies, momma has been telling you all along that there was something rotten going on ever since our sex-a-lacious porn princess inherited the Nyland estate.

Here comes the perfect storm—a two-part investigative report in Vanity Fair *by one of the socialite's best friends. Who should know where the bodies are buried but a BFF? Only a BFF would bide her time and get the ducks in order, to pick off the horny heiress for good. I say bravo! It's about time to find out the truth about how and why Marianne Nyland died. And let the bodies fall where they may.*

She sat frozen, Dax standing behind her. He read the vituperative post over her shoulder but didn't say a word. He didn't have to, because everything was crystal clear except for one detail.

She asked, finally, "Who?"

But she knew even before she asked. She scrolled down and it was there: a scan of the magazine cover with the line: "*The Mysterious Death of the Man-Eating Millionairess*," subheaded: "*The Parties, the Men, the Sex, and the Friend*"—and the byline of betrayal: Nina.

Chapter Twelve

We marry our own.

She had been *so* warned.

And they protected their own, lied for their own, and defended their own . . . and an outsider was utterly doomed: judged, drawn, and quartered with no contest.

She couldn't believe it. Nina doing this to her. Nina, who had been witness to all Marianne's excesses. Nina, the tall elegant blonde fashion scribe with the roguish attitude, who was always the first to jump where Marianne led. Nina, who had been so silent, distant, and removed since Marianne's death, planning all the time to take the hatchet to *her*.

Sex-a-rella's Exploits—Nina?

All of it—Nina?

She felt heavy as a stone, as if she would never, could never, move again. *Nina . . .*

And if she pushed farther, to the place she didn't want to even consider . . . Becca.

Don't go there.

And Dax.

Dax was one of them.

I have to read it, I have to know what she wrote, what everyone will believe . . .

And refute everything.

No, that's what lawyers are for . . .

Dax was one of them—

Now the cold crept into her bones. She was near naked and realized she was still staring at the computer screen, at the cover scan.

And this is what alone feels like.

Dax was still immobile behind her, not saying a word.

She took a deep breath.

"So, you all knew about this last night?" Her voice was a croak, as another tumbler clicked into place. "Rob, too? . . . They all knew? And didn't want it rubbing off on them? And that's why they—?"

He didn't have to answer—it was all too obvious—that, and last night.

"It was a pity fuck," she spat. "You son of a bitch." She wrenched herself out of the chair. "Well, take a good long look, you lying shit, because this is the last time you'll ever see this body again. Now get out. *Get out!*"

She stood there like a naked fury as Dax walked out of the room.

Rob was complicit, too. And who knew about Becca?

Oh God, if Becca—

It was no use speculating about anything. The only thing she knew for certain was that Nina wrote the article.

And Anonymous was ecstatic.

First step: get dressed. No, first step—wipe every trace of Dax from her bed. Second step, wash every trace of Dax from her body.

And then she'd get dressed and get a copy of the effing magazine, and make a list of all the actionable lies for the lawyers.

The hardest thing to acknowledge was that Nina's reporting, at least in part one, was limited to just the facts. They were damning, and boiled down to these telling points: she had had a fight with Marianne that morning; she was the last person to see Marianne alive; she was the one who had alerted everyone that Marianne had gone missing late that evening; and she had no witnesses to her own whereabouts that entire day.

God, I look guilty as hell.

The facts. Dipped in poisonous innuendo, written with an *only she could have done it* slant.

The whitewashed portrait of Marianne was laughable, but the article held the ominous promise of more compelling details in the next installment.

Like virtually accusing her of murder wasn't compelling enough.

Well, there was only one thing to do about it. Deny everything.

She wasn't going to hide, she wasn't going to depend on anyone else. She'd find new people, new friends, new lovers to distract her, and she'd ignore the article and its implications altogether.

The best strategy: Be positive. Admit to nothing.

Next to the porn tape and truck guy's X-rated sex confessions, a slanted article insinuating a certain friend had had motive to commit murder didn't seem like a very big newsworthy thing.

Wrong.

The press were there in full force when she walked out the door later that evening.

"Did you do it?" Snap, snap, snap . . .

"Can you account for the time between when you last saw her and when she died?"

"Did you really save her life, or was that a con, too?"

She waved at them as she climbed into the limo. *Deny everything.* "Good morning, everyone. I have no idea what you're talking about."

"The article," someone shouted. "Read the *Times,* Metro section—"

"Sorry!" She waved again as she closed the window. Tonight was the opera, a new production of *Madame Butterfly.* A good place to meet people—or to hide.

Becca was waiting for her at the house when she returned from the opera, after fighting her way through the phalanx of cameras and paparazzi.

Snap!

Oh God, she needed a bodyguard; she couldn't handle this alone.

"Where the hell were you?"

She shrugged off her coat. "I'm stunned you had the nerve to use your key."

Becca's mouth thinned. "I didn't know. I thought something might be up when Nina went underground, but I never suspected this."

"Sure, I believe that. Well, I've had enough humiliation to last a lifetime—let alone a news cycle."

"You still need a friend," Becca interrupted her.

"But that's the thing, Becca. How do I know who's a friend?"

Becca went silent for a moment. "I'm your friend."

"But you were on the inside. How do I know all those details in the article didn't come from you? I distinctly remember you said Marianne told you everything."

"I thought she did."

Now Becca was feeling betrayed?

"Well, Nina's innuendos don't scare me," Frankie said. "I won't be intimidated, I did nothing wrong, and I'm going to ignore the whole thing."

"I'm with you on this, Frankie."

Did she believe her? There was something about Becca—the mother thing, maybe—only Becca had no reason to side with her at all.

Becca was well connected and well-to-do in her own right, so what did she gain? She surely couldn't be expecting Frankie to name her some kind of residual heir—everything went to her mother in the event anything happened to her.

So why was Becca determined to be her friend?

It might be interesting to find out.

Frankie closed the parlor window shutters to block out the continual camera flashing. "Okay, let's say I'm willing to believe that. Let's get some dinner and talk about it. And the hell with the paparazzi. The hell with everything. Let's just have some fun."

It was like Marianne all over again. Becca knew all the places, and beyond that, they discovered a few of their own. Mas, Le Gigot, Fish in the Village and Jean Georges on the Upper West Side, for dining.

Arthur's Tavern and West for hanging out, as well as Apt, Cielo, and Hell for kicking up. 119 Bar named a drink for Frankie after a wave of reporters followed them in one night, and then mentioned the place in a half dozen photo captions in the next morning's news.

Heiress au bar—she plays and she pays . . .

Frankie wrote in her blog:

I've decided not to kowtow to gossip and innuendo. In my life there's no room for hypocrisy, jealousy, betrayal, or deceit. Make what you want out of the article in Vanity Fair. *I'm leaving all that to my lawyers*

So—to continue the chronicle of my fabulous life, a friend and I went to the Broadway opening of A Chorus Line *this week. All I have to say is, singular and spectacular. And you might have seen the pictures of me at that club in the meatpacking district? Well, I swear I didn't bribe anyone to name that drink after me. They just liked the publicity. And I'd like to think they liked me, too. And the opening of that cosmetics salon in Midtown? Fabulous swag. Lots of product and small electronics—I got an MP4 player and a 9-megapixel digital camera. All this is great fun, and I'll continue on.*

But I've decided it's time to find a husband. Or a lover. Whichever comes first.

"What?" Becca said, reading that. "Ignore the person in-sinuating you killed someone?"

"There's nothing to implicate me, everything is circum-stantial, and no evidence of anything except we had a fight and Marianne left for the day and then didn't come home. Anything else is pure speculation. Nina hates me a lot, to have done that."

"Or she loved Marianne too much."

That gave her pause. "Loved her, like—*loved* her?"

"Like—*yes*," Becca said, imitating her tone. "She swings both ways, so Marianne's uninhibited sex life was a way for her to bond. There were lots of times Marianne wasn't play-ing with the guys."

Frankie tried to remember. "There *were* times she watched. She told me she was the ringmaster, that she liked to play head games."

"Yep. That was Marianne."

"Well, it's time for me to play head games, too. I'm having dinner tonight with a gentleman I met at the opera."

"Do tell. You're such an opera buff."

"I'm going high end, just as you advised. Notoriety is not a bad thing. I actually want to keep it going. I have the money, and I'm going to spend it. Limo, photographer, and big-bucks date. And I really hope Nina is watching."

Everyone seemed to be watching, to the point where her date became extremely uncomfortable.

His name was Joseph Martin and he was the CFO of a small manufacturing company in Westchester. Divorced, in his sixties, distinguished looking though not tall, and he had a sense of humor, though it wasn't quite enough to withstand the pressure of the press that had followed her limo from the house to Tavern on the Green, where they were to meet for dinner.

There they had some privacy, although her photographer managed a discreet shot of them via cell camera, with which she hoped to preempt any photo Blog-a-rella might post.

"All this public scrutiny is too hot for my taste," Joe Martin told her. "The *VF* article brought the rats out of the sinking ship, didn't it? Aren't you a little scared what else the reporter might have up her sleeve?"

"What more could there be? Everything in that article was conjecture. There was an inquest, and the coroner ruled it suicide. I have nothing to be afraid of."

When they left the restaurant, questions upon questions were shouted out in the bright glare of TV lights:

"Did you read the article?"

"Do you know what else the reporter knows?"

"Do you have any comment?"

"Who's the date?"

"Are you dating?"

"What did you have for dinner?"

And on and on until the limo managed to get out of the parking lot.

"That's enough for me," Joe said. "I'd love to see you again, but—"

The new story of her life.

And then, Blog-a-rella posted it first, the morning after, with a picture of them at the restaurant, and as they were leaving:

Sex-a-rella's Exploits

The man-eating money pit bought herself a date last night. What else can she do while she waits for the other shoe to drop? Momma can exclusively report there's still more to the story. And that we know Sex-a-rella went to bed all alone last night, her so-called fabulous life too much pressure for any sane man.

"That bitch! I won't be bullied." Frankie typed into her blog:

Had the most fun date last night with a very nice guy I met at the opera. Super dinner, great conversation. And let me tell you that every date doesn't have to wind up in bed. Sometimes you can *have a connection and let it simmer for a while.*

Anticipation is everything. A woman who jumps into bed with just anyone just because is obviously a low-rent slut.

"Oh God," Becca groaned.

"Yeah, it's come down to insubstantial allegations and teenage trash talk."

"And your strategy is?"

"I'm going to sleep around, baby. Because guess who called today, full of contrition?"

"Mr. Joseph Martin?"

"Oh yeah. Apparently hanging out with Sex-a-rella has given him new cachet. Pictures everywhere. Nobody reads the damned blog. They all read the *Post*. So tonight, my dear Becca, won't be just another date night."

"Is this where the simmering part comes in?"

"Boiling, actually. The guy was hot. And cool. A kind of irresistible combination. So let the blogs fall where they may."

The gossip columns:

The new game around town is guessing who Frankie Luttrell is sleeping with. Here, with Judson Clarke of Metric Manufacturing at the opera.

In the *Times* Evening Out page that Sunday:

The Museum of the City of New York Gala. Pictured: Frankie Luttrell, Theodore Daignan.

The following night:

Frankie Luttrell, the Cinderella Heiress, at the record release party of DJ Bodie Baker, in Brooklyn.

That Saturday:

Frankie Luttrell, the Cinderella Heiress, banking on an evening with East Side Trust Company's CEO Neville Captor, at Iridium.

And Sunday:

Joseph Martin, CFO of Titanium Sport, with Frankie Luttrell at Pastis.

Blog-a-rella on a tear:

Contrary to Sex-a-rella's high moral stance, she's been spreading herself around like cheap margarine. That highly touted anticipation gets stale after the first five minutes, obviously. Sooo Sex-a-rella. But then, that's her blue plate specialty . . .

"But I'm having sex," Frankie pointed out to Becca as she read that last Blog-a-rella rant.

"You've had a week and a half of teenage nooky . . ."

"*Not,*" Frankie interrupted. "Joe was good. Theodore, not so much. I like Joe."

Becca slanted a look at her. "But he's not Dax."

"Dax is a first-class bastard, and I don't even want to hear his name mentioned in my presence."

"Right, while you go on a girl-on-the-edge sex binge. What does that prove? It certainly won't mitigate whatever is coming in part two of Nina's article."

"No." That was enough to make her sober. "But it's enough to distract everyone."

"Not you."

"No," Frankie whispered, "not me." Because crawling into bed with a man with whom you had a tenuous acquaintance was a lot more fraught than raw, anonymous sex with no expectations.

It solved nothing, and it made her yearn for things she couldn't have.

Frankie Luttrell and Bodie Baker dancing up a storm at Club D2.

The Cinderella Heiress and her new man, the Swedish shipping magnate, at the International Ball inaugurating the Annual Run for the Sun.

Frank-lie, I don't give a damn, says the Cinderella Heiress, commenting on her seemingly endless serial dating. I'm having too much sex—I mean too much fun . . .

Has the Cinderella Heiress Found Her Prince Charming? Frankie Luttrell and Joseph Martin perusing the offerings at Harry Winston.

And chillingly, in the *Star,* a week later:

The shocking allegations you haven't heard—Preview, part two of the VF *Cinderella Heiress story.*

Leaked, a week before publication. On everyone's radar in the thirty seconds after the paper hit the stands, and the details were even more damaging than the circumstantial case that Nina had concocted in part one.

This is what we know, according to part one of the story: Marianne Nyland and Cinderella had a fight that morning: Marianne left the apartment sometime after and was not back by eight that night. Cinderella was the last person to see her alive that day. Late that evening, when Marianne had still not returned, Cinderella contacted all her friends who then initiated a search of her usual haunts and hangout spots. Cinderella had no witnesses to her whereabouts all of that day.

This is what you didn't know, to be published in part two of the VF *article next week: the terms of Marianne Nyland's will were leaked to the press before she was even buried. Three people in the family law firm were aware of its contents; one of them slept with Cinderella. The article claims there is irrefutable proof, and charges that there was collusion between Cinderella and the lawyer to bilk Nyland out of her money. In addition, a timeline was created, to further prove it was possible for Cinderella, whom no one saw that day, to have either gone with Nyland to Maine that morning by private jet, or followed her to Bar Harbor, committed the murder, and returned, and still have notified everyone she'd gone missing by eight that evening.*

Further—Cinderella vehemently tried to convince Marianne's friends that Nyland could not have gone to Maine because she wasn't intending to go to Maine this year, and then suggested that her mother be the one to check out the house anyway.

How did Marianne Nyland die? The coroner brought in a verdict of suicide. Did Marianne jump or was she pushed off that chair? Was the temptation of her fortune too much—for a poor girl from the country who got lucky and a scheming lawyer who was just too greedy? You decide.

Oh God. Nina was pointing the finger straight at Dax. This would kill his career, his life, his . . .
What kind of irrefutable proof?
She didn't know what to do.
Even the lawyers' statement, that Marianne had made the bequest of her own free will, and that Mr. Marcus Illingworth, Esquire, the head of the firm and the Nyland family's

longtime legal advisor, witnessed it, was not enough to beat down the news cycles that endlessly flogged the details in the article and called for exhumation of the body and another autopsy.

Blog-a-rella had a field day:

Poor Sex-a-rella. Paying for her sins, for her lies, for her prostitution—shall we say?—of the truth, and for her theft of what rightfully belonged to Marianne Nyland. Well, now we know how far she'll go, and how little she cared about the woman she claimed was her friend. All she wanted was the money, and in that moment one summer, where Marianne was so grateful for her life being saved by the then nonentity-a-rella, Sex-a-rella saw how she could worm her way into a life she never could have had, and find a way to get all that money as icing on the cake.

Who knew she was devious enough to plan thievery on such a grand scale—and take down one of the most eligible men in the city? But this is where Sex-a-rella truly shines.

Day after day.

So yesterday we had the tale of grand-theft millions. Today let me remind you of Sex-a-rella's perversions. The men. The sex. The clubs. The drinking. The sex tape. Remember the sex tape? The fourplex?

After day . . .

Sex-a-rella and Carl Moore. Did you think his fifteen minutes of fame was over? Oh no, I have resurrected him to take his rightful place in the pantheon of Sex-a-rella's conquests . . .

Now she understood Dax's concern about there being no buffer between her and the street. There was no escape. And the press was way too close, breaching the lines of civility to climb onto the windowsills to try to take pictures and shouting questions, and standing on the banister, trying to look over the transom.

She was a prisoner in her own house for the first couple of days after the preview and part two appeared, and on the phone with Illingworth twice a day, saying the same thing twice a day: "I don't care about anything, I'll do anything, I'll say anything, as long as they don't implicate Dax."

"Not smart," Illingworth would say twice a day every day. "Dax can take care of himself. I'm your unimpeachable witness, and it doesn't matter what they say."

"Sure it does," Frankie said bitterly. "Next they'll say I was in bed with you."

"That would be quite a compliment at my age, Frankie. Let them try it. I'll have my doctors in court in thirty seconds to testify I haven't gotten it up in twenty years."

That drew a small laugh. "I don't believe that."

"I'm seventy-five, Frankie. I'm not dead from the waist down yet, but I'm not stupid, either. Marianne wasn't all that stable, and there is evidence of that. So you just stay cool, stay put, and don't talk to anyone."

"I can't refute these charges at all?"

"It's all smoke and mirrors right now. Allegations by inference are not indictments. Nina Tyler is just a reporter with an ax to grind, and I could make a stunning case that this is pure jealous payback from a disgruntled lover who thought she would inherit those millions and didn't."

"*Oh.*" She had never thought that Nina might well have expected some reward for all that devotion.

"And if you want another little piece of advice, you'd be better off back at the apartment right now, where you have a doorman and an elevator between you and the fiction mongers out there."

Thank heaven she hadn't put the place up for sale yet. She could slip out in the wee hours, when the tattlers were a little less awake and aware. She could have Rollie park the limo where it wouldn't be that obvious. She could cloak herself in black and merge into the night.

For the first time in days, she felt as if this might not be an unmitigated disaster after all. Illingworth knew the truth about the will, and *he* felt that Marianne had been on the edge, and that Nina's motives were not altogether altruistic. So there was another case to be made—one that wouldn't defame her or destroy Dax.

She made all the preparations—put her lamps on timers, made certain the shutters were closed and that the curtains on the back windows and French doors were drawn. She didn't even pack a suitcase. She dressed in jeans, sneakers, a shirt, and sweater.

She grabbed a dark coat, found a black scarf for her hair, and alerted Rollie to be ready to roll.

An insane amount of subterfuge to leave her own home.

The basement entrance was her best shot. Three a.m. maybe. She could sneak out under the stoop and hope no one lingered there at that hour.

One a.m. It was so quiet.

Cross your fingers.

Two a.m. Dead silence. Just the occasional car going by.

She climbed up to the top floor, and looked out the front window. Street empty. Lights eerie. Little traffic. A couple of cars parked suspiciously close to the house. No loiterers, no one on the stoop.

Two thirty. Rollie had better be parked on the avenue.

Three . . .

She slipped out into the little courtyard.

Maybe someone in the cars, hopefully sleeping. A chance she'd have to take.

She opened the courtyard gate. Tiptoe, don't make a sound. Merge with the shadows, cross the street where the light isn't directly shining. Quick, quiet, down the street. The limo there? Oh thank God—and gone.

Chapter Thirteen

The apartment felt huge, like there was no safe corner to hide.

The air still carried the scent of fresh paint. The floors had been waxed. The kitchen thoroughly cleaned. Nothing in the fridge. Closets all empty. The rented furniture all crowded neatly under a tarp in a corner of her bedroom.

She brought the radio into the living room for company.

She huddled against the wall, listening to the excoriating voices of insomniacs who vented their feelings on late-night radio talk shows, everything from sports to politics and love-gone-wrong confessions.

She knew about that, big time.

But she'd chosen the bad-girl side of the road with her eyes wide open; she'd chosen to experiment with careless, heedless, anonymous sexual partners. Had chosen the kind of sex that led to betrayal and regrets.

And so here she was, on the cusp of Nina's sensational investigation into Marianne's death, just barely holding on, utterly demoralized by the attack and the accusations.

Too incriminating, every point. And worse, she remembered distinctly asking Dax if he had known about the will, and that he hadn't wanted to answer because he knew, on the surface, how it would look.

But what was Nina's so-called *irrefutable proof?*

Six a.m.—not too early to call for breakfast or to warn the doorman that the press might be hard on her heels and that she was expecting deliveries today.

She paced edgily through the apartment as she waited. Opened the closets in Marianne's room; all empty. Nothing in hers. Or in the linen closet, the bathrooms. What did she think she'd find?

And then that deep entrance closet where she and Rob had— *Don't let in the memories.* Piled in the far corner on the top shelf, way out of reach, was a jumble of wires—probably for the hidden TV and recording equipment.

There was no way to examine them either. Nothing in this damned apartment except the smell of off-white paint and her stupid memories.

Food arrived shortly after that, at which point she called her office supply store and bought a laptop computer and a TV set. Called the grocery store and ordered necessities. Called Illingworth and let him know she'd relocated to the apartment.

And now what? Sit and figure out how and why Nina had come to her conclusions?

She needed a table and chair. Wait—there was basement storage; maybe Marianne had put some things there. When she spoke to the building manager, she found that Marianne did indeed have storage space and that he had a key.

The storage locker was about six by ten feet, and, thank you, Lord, there was a chair, some lamps, and some end tables, which she arranged for the manager to bring up to the apartment.

When she returned, the groceries had arrived, and two hours later, the computer and TV were delivered. The TV went on one of the small tables, the computer on the other, and she booted up her email.

Hey, there, heiress—you might be nobody now, but somebody still wants you . . . in bed. Contact me . . .

God, like she was that desperate. His fifteen minutes were *over;* he couldn't seriously think she'd let herself be fodder for another man memoir.

Sex-a-rella's Exploits

Bye-bye, Sex-a-rella. The party's over, they found you out, and they're booting you out. Back to the double-wide, double-dealing trailer trash that you are. Back to where you came from. Back to being a low-rent slut. You'll leave behind a legacy of that smutty sex tape, the mouthy man toy, and the genius plot to steal millions that almost worked. We'll enjoy thinking about your primal encounters with the boys in the back room at home. They'll appreciate your naked body just that much more for all your carnal encounters in the big bad city.

Double God.

A smear blog was addictive. You kept doing it over and over again because you couldn't help wanting to see what new metaphors the bitch came up with.

On to the gossip columns.

Worse. The headlines, every one of them about her: Cinderella, could she, did she, would she?

Who was this interloper who'd come out of nowhere?

No one interviewed said a word about that fateful summer, about how Marianne had waved her wand and brought her into the fold. About the job that brought her to Manhattan, and Marianne's generous offer to let her stay at her apartment.

All of it was slanted to look as if she had instigated everything, she had wormed her way into Marianne's life and confidence.

She had to put *her* story out somehow. Except there was such an inundation of "facts" about her relationship with Marianne, she didn't see how she could breach the negative tide of public opinion right now.

Perception was everything. And it depended on which side of the road you were when you were looking.

The buzzer. "Miss Frankie, it's the board president."

Just what she needed: a scolding from the co-op board, whose perception was definitely on the side of the devil.

"Send him up."

He walked in, looking around warily as if he expected to find an orgy in progress. "Just a word of caution, Ms. Luttrell. The reporters and all that are very distressing to the board. The questions surrounding Ms. Nyland's death must be dealt with in a discreet way that doesn't reflect on the residents here. Too much intrusion, too much notoriety is being attached to this address. And now the doorman tells me you're back here again, when we thought the apartment was going up for sale."

"Perhaps I'm rethinking that," she snapped.

His brows went up. "Perhaps you ought not, Ms. Luttrell. The press is gathering yet again right in front of the building. It might be better if you were to stay at a hotel until all this furor dies down. Or someplace else in any event."

She didn't say another word, just opened the door so he had to take his leave. The only thing else he could say was to plainly ask her to go, and he'd already done that, in effect.

Stay off the internet.

Make lunch. Watch the noon news.

Never again watch the noon news.

The Cinderella Heiress is holed up in her luxury apartment on Central Park after the publication of the sensational second half of an investigative article in Vanity Fair *about the death of millionairess Marianne Nyland. Nyland insider Nina Tyler outlined motive, means, and opportunity for a possible alternative explanation of how Nyland, who was mysteriously found hanged in her fifteen-room Bar Harbor summer cottage, could have died. The death, nearly six months ago, was ruled a suicide.*

Motive, means, and . . . Nina meant to bring her down. She was doing a good job of it, too.

The cell rang, echoing over the drone of the afternoon anchors delivering the same story for the fifth time that day.

"Who?" she demanded tersely, without checking the ID.

"Hey, it's me." Rob. "Can I come up?"

"Sure."

She felt a wash of relief. Rob. Someone to lean on, someone comfortable, a known commodity.

He got past the snapping press dogs faster than she would have expected and wrapped her in a big bear hug.

"How did you get here so fast?"

"I was on the elevator when I called. There's a garbage exit on the side street."

She hadn't known about that. "Can't offer you much. Coffee maybe, some iced tea. A sandwich."

"I have something to offer you," he said, with a teasing note in his voice.

"Can you be serious? Nina just dumped a boatload of manure on my head."

"And I have a solution. I think Nina's insinuations are hogwash. And her sex life and her motivations wouldn't bear close scrutiny, either. She was obsessed with Marianne. Maybe even she loved her. So . . . look   marry me."

"*What!*" How did he get from Nina in love with Marianne to that?

"Marry me. It's the perfect solution. I'm a perfectly proper catch, my family name is gold in this city, and you'll be vetted in a way that no one can touch you."

"Omigod." She sank into the chair.

He went down on one knee immediately. "Frankie. We're good together. And where am I going to find a rich girl who's so down and dirty? Think, it'll be fun! *We're* fun. And it's kind of romantic, marrying your first."

"Kind of," she said faintly. Dear God. "Your family?"

"Not a problem."

Too glib. She didn't believe him. "I'm just . . . you just knocked my feet out from under me," she said finally.

"Well, of course. Look, Frankie, there's nothing we can't accomplish together. We're good in bed, we get along great, we like to party and have good times. People get hitched with way less going for them. And on top of that, we can kill the gossip and finally let poor Marianne rest in peace."

"Um. Very persuasive," she hedged.

"Is that a yes?"

"That's an—um—I'll think about it."

"What's to think?"

"It's too much to ask one person, one family, to put up with."

"My family's got strong shoulders, and you've got the money to make the good fight. So what's the problem?"

That was the problem. Her money, and his motives apart from good times, super sex, and sonic spending.

"I want to protect you," Rob went on when she didn't answer. "And that's how I can do it. To take care of you for the rest of your life, give you my name so no one can ever impugn yours again."

He was so sincere. He'd take on her troubles, and he'd banish them. She could be comfortable with him, have fun with him, be well sexed with him.

Maybe.

She started to tell him, again, that she'd think about it, but she was interrupted by a tumultuous pounding on the door. "Frankie!!!"

"Jesus—Dax?"

She flung open the door and he stalked in, all righteous rage, his eyes like cold stones. "I knew the son of a bitch would try to get at you."

"Dax, you can't *be* here. If they sniff out the fact that you are "

"I'll leave when he does."

"I don't have to leave," Rob said. "I proposed, and she's just going to accept me." He looked at Frankie. "Aren't you?"

"He proposed what?" Dax spat. "Marriage? Did he tell you he meant the marriage of money—yours to what's left of his? Yours to his daddy's firm to manage? Oh, you can bet old money will overlook anything for a fresh infusion of cash."

And there was the thing she felt so uneasy about. The money. Always the money, from Rob to Nina and everyone in between. They were all in a rage that she had inherited the money.

She couldn't even protest that she hadn't wanted it, since she'd dived into the good life with both hands.

This was worse than a mess. Rob had no right pressuring

her into a marriage she wasn't certain she wanted. And if the motive was just her money, for either of them, what was the point?

She felt sick. If Dax were caught up here with her, it was just to fuel the fire even hotter and give credence to all of Nina's conjectures about collusion.

And Rob couldn't really want to be photographed consorting with an untouchable, no matter how rich she was.

Maybe it was time to get away from them. From everyone—her alleged friends and her outright foes.

Out of Manhattan, where the stink from the article wouldn't continually waft in her face. Where she wouldn't have to keep telling herself that innuendo was not indictment, and no one was remotely interested in reopening the case.

Except, if the press, if Nina, through interviews and further articles, kept it alive and kicking.

Or just the prurient factor, once some other enterprising reporter delved into Marianne's secret sex life and dredged up all those excesses.

And hers.

If that happened—the pressure might just about kill her.

"This is not about money," Rob said stiffly. "This is about taking care of Frankie."

"*And* her money," Dax added caustically.

Rob shook his head. "Like your bank account couldn't stand a hefty beefing up. Can you match her dollar for dollar? Who can? You son of a bitch, intruding in my business, and look at Frankie—she's scared to death what you said is true."

"She should be," Dax snapped. "It is."

"And we haven't even gotten to the good stuff yet," Frankie said, sounding really weary.

They both turned to look at her. "What stuff?"

"Before you both leave, and you *are* both going in about two minutes, I need to know if Dax has any idea what *irrefutable* evidence Nina has that we slept together."

"Damn, I wish you hadn't brought that up," Rob muttered. "I refuse to believe you did that, Frankie."

Dax shook his head. "I could guess, but I don't want to upset Rob."

"You *slept* with her, *really*?" Rob asked.

"Yeah, that's where the collusion part comes in."

"God, that boggles the imagination."

"Back at you, bro'."

"All *right*." Frankie stamped her foot. "That's enough. Here's the deal. No to your proposal. No to either of you staying here. No to anything Dax suggests. No to everything. Yes, to your getting out. Both of you. *Now*."

"Aw, Frankie, you can't stay here like this. Come with me. We'll go to a hotel, load up on room service, massages, and sex, get away from the crazy crowd that wants to crucify you . . ."

"Nice thought, thank you. No." She looked at Dax.

He raised an eyebrow and opened the door. "Just keep saying no to everything, Frankie. My best legal advice."

She waited for Rob.

"I still think—"

"Don't think."

"Even better advice," Dax said as she closed the door behind them.

And then silence, so welcome but still reverberating with the impact of that proposal and Dax's daunting presence.

She felt like she needed a shower, but of course, there was no soap, shampoo, towels, or a change of clothes. Maybe a hotel was a good idea. A hotel far away from New York. Someplace where the air was fresh and clean and there was no traffic, human or otherwise . . .

The buzzer sounded. "It's Becca," her voice said.

Becca, now? It almost seemed that they'd planned how they would approach her.

"Come up."

Becca sailed in a few minutes later. "Love what you've done with the place. But look at you—what are you going to do with yourself?"

She knew what Becca saw—the worry-tossed hair, the strained look on her makeup-free face, the wrinkled sweater and jeans she'd slept in. But she wasn't actually certain of Becca's true concern.

She felt like she was walking a tightrope again. She needed a moment to get distance, to focus. "I have some coffee on. Want some?"

"Sure." Becca followed her into the kitchen. "So everything is painted, scrubbed, waxed, and ready to show, huh?"

"Pretty much. The board president is most anxious for the circus to leave the front of his building. Here you go."

"So what are you going to do?"

She gave Becca a sidelong glance. "You always have the answers. What do you think I should do?"

Becca shrugged. "What I always think. Deny everything and ride it out. Notoriety more often than not gives you cachet. I mean, please—look who you've been dating. And I assume your lawyers are actively monitoring things, so all you need to do is go about your business."

"I don't have any business, which I'm beginning to think is a big problem. Marianne did nothing except party; I can't do that forever. I have to do something."

"Okay, you could be someone's wife. Buy your way on to a committee. Do some good works."

"Rob's wife?" she asked slyly.

"You think *he'd* ever marry? Ha."

"He asked me."

Becca dropped her cup on the counter, and coffee splattered all over.

"He . . . what?"

"Asked me to marry him. What do you think? The womanizer and the outcast." She handed Becca a roll of paper towels.

"I think"—Becca chose her words very carefully—"he was trying to be chivalrous."

"I thought so, too. And of course, the money doesn't hurt." She threw that in almost as an afterthought.

Becca's expression tightened as she blotted up the coffee.

Oh? So the question of the money mattered to her, too?

"And you said what to that?" Becca asked after a moment.

"No. Of course."

"Of course. So when did that happen?"

"About a half hour ago. He and Dax—"

"God, *Dax*? How insane was that, him coming here?"

"It's insane."

"Well—" Becca said, then stopped. "Are you staying here? How can you stay here?"

"I'm thinking of going to a hotel for a week or so, go underground until this plays out a little more."

"The media won't let up. It's too juicy."

"No, and I don't think Nina intends to, either."

"You should tell your story."

"That story's been turned upside down and rolled over so many times, I don't even know what *my* story is. And who'd believe me now? I can't prove anything. And apparently Nina can. Do you know—?"

Becca stopped her before she asked the question. "No."

But she had the odd thought that Becca did. Becca was acting too tentatively for Becca.

"Maybe keeping out of the public eye for a bit is a good thing. Being elusive never hurt anyone, you know? And by that time, maybe they'll have run out of ways to play the story and it'll make them more eager to hear what you have to say."

"That's a strategy," Frankie said, knowing Becca liked the word *strategy*.

"I have a feeling you have something up your sleeve."

"No. I'm just tired and very unhappy. I've got Blog-a-rella still slandering me, Nina trying to hang me, Rob trying to tie me down, Dax trying to rip him up, and I don't know what you're trying to do, but whatever it is, I'm certain in some way it will be hurtful, and I just want it all to stop."

"Frankie, I *am* your friend. I'd never—"

Frankie interrupted her. "Why?"

Becca looked at her for a long time. "Because you're sane. Because you make people feel protective. Because I knew you were so innocent and in over your head when you came here, and I wanted to protect you. Because . . ."

Frankie waved off the rest of what she was going to say. "Okay—I got it."

"Do you?"

"Yes."

"So what are you really going to do now?"

"I'm really getting out of Dodge."

"Where?"

"Home." She hadn't even known she wanted that until she said it. *Home. Clean air, ocean breezes, Mom, apple pie, and a brand-new home . . .*

"I'll come with you," Becca offered.

"You don't have to." She was already dialing for Rollie and figuring out a way to avoid the press.

"You don't know what you might find there."

"What?"

"Look, you might be going home, but I think you *really* mean to go to the cottage. It *is* yours. Maybe you're still thinking it's Marianne's, but—"

"Yeah. No, I hadn't thought of it as mine. Maybe I do

need to . . . take stock. At least it's not in Manhattan, huh? Okay, you can come. I have a feeling you're more curious about it than I am. Rollie's going to meet us on Columbus Avenue. Do you know about this secret garbage exit? Good. I'll turn off the coffee, get my laptop, and we'll go."

Chapter Fourteen

"Wi-Fi's a bitch. It's too tempting, especially when you're on the road." Frankie closed the laptop down after reading her email. "Truck guy isn't giving up. I didn't even sneak a peek at Blog-a-rella, though I wanted to."

"Good, you're developing a backbone, and you need it right now."

They were just coming to the Connecticut Turnpike, and Frankie already felt antsy. Sneaking out of her own apartment building via the trash exit made her feel dirty. It was a narrow alley, out through the basement, and you had to squeeze past the Dumpsters, the smell, and a brick wall.

Pretty awful, very effective. They were out and walking west in minutes and no one the wiser. Rollie had been circling the block, and caught up with them before they reached Columbus Avenue. Now they were nearly an hour out of the city, yet it felt like they were barely on their way.

"Hell, it takes an hour just to negotiate the city streets onto the West Side Highway," Becca said.

"And it takes well over eight hours to get to Bar Harbor by car. Which means that Nina's timeline is wholly dependent on the theory that Marianne and I drove to Westchester County Airport and caught a flight to either Bangor or the local airport, or that Marianne went first and I followed, and both of us rented either a cab or a car to get to the cottage."

"But you needed to get back to the airport within a certain time frame."

"According to Nina's article, she found the record of Marianne's taking a car service from Bangor, but nothing to confirm that I had either flown in or rented a car that day."

"So all her suppositions don't wash," Becca said, "which kills her case."

"But she hypothesizes that I could have flown up to Bangor with Marianne in a private jet, committed the murder, and returned to the airport using that same car service, so my name wouldn't appear on any records. She also suggests I might have had access to Marianne's credit card, and used it to get to the cottage and back. And on top of everything else, there's that whiff of collusion. Dax knew about the provisions of the will, and Nina comes close to accusing him of leaking the details."

Becca raised a brow. "But there's no proof of any of this."

"No. There's just enough truth in her speculations to make our tabloid-worthy lives miserable."

"Dax hasn't asked you to marry him, has he?"

"Good God, no. He's into mercy mating. Turned a beautiful moment into major humiliation."

Becca looked askance.

"After the fund-raiser at the Boathouse, they asked me to

leave. You probably heard. It was one thing on top of another . . . and then him on top of me. I'm *so* stupid."

Becca said nothing to that.

They were passing Stamford now. It would be a long trip and they were taking the exact route of the Dirty Girls Road Trip. Too many memories along this route.

Her sins would drown her. She'd been too cavalier about sex, and too careless, too casual and too cocky. Becca had warned her all those months ago, and now she was reaping the consequences of all that purposeless promiscuity.

"Are we there yet?"

"What, you need games to occupy you?"

"The last trip, I had lots of fun and games. A PlayStation sounds about right."

"Depends on what you're playing," Becca said suggestively.

"Oh God, is everything about sex?"

"And money. And power. You might think about who has the power, Frankie. You think it's that truck guy, or Nina. But whoever has the power doesn't have to give a shit."

"Unfortunately, I do."

"Just act like you don't. That's the whole secret to playing this game."

Frankie mulled that over for a hundred miles while Becca slept. She thought she might have napped as well, but in her waking moments, she thought about what Becca had said and felt clarity coming with every mile closer to home.

*   *   *

Bar Harbor was a quintessential Maine vacation town, hard by Acadia National Park and full of quaint shops, sea captains' mansions, outdoor activities, whale-watching excursions, and a working waterfront. There were hotels, inns, restaurants, a village green, incomparable water vistas, and a public beach.

They drove into town late that night via Route 3 and over toward Hulls Cove, where Frankie's mother had bought a house overlooking Frenchman Bay.

It was impossible to see anything at night. You felt like you were the only one in the world as the limo slowly drove up the rural side roads with no lights anywhere.

"Your mom's expecting us?"

"She said she'd leave the lights on."

They went over the rise, the narrow road curving downward toward the bay, and there suddenly was a farmhouse with lights ablaze.

How weird. She hadn't seen her mother in nearly a year, hadn't even spoken with her very often; had bought the house for her on a quick whim, but had never come to see it.

And now, here it was—every would-be coastal resident's dream—the pure antique farmhouse, with the side porch to the driveway and barn, and the front porch overlooking the water.

There was a note on the door.

Make yourself to home. Two bedrooms to choose from: the one at the head of the stairs, and the one off of the living room. Your chauffeur can bunk in

*the guest room in the barn. Coffee on the timer, see
you in the morning.*

"I'm so wondering what your mother's like," Becca murmured.

"Just like me, only with gray hair and way more careworn."

She was glad to see the next morning that her mom looked younger and more carefree, now that she was retired and relieved of her money worries. Her hair might have been enhanced a bit, Frankie thought, but obviously she was happy. And obviously so pleased that Frankie was home.

But Pat Luttrell was not so pleased about what was going on with her daughter.

"I can't do anything about that," Frankie told her mother as she watched her fuss around the kitchen making biscuits. She would have loved to have her coffee on the porch, but it was nippy cold this morning, with Thanksgiving not two weeks away. She would be here for Thanksgiving, she thought. With her mom, her family.

"The rich kids always get picked on," she added.

"Speaking of rich kids, what are you going to do about that house?" her mother asked, setting out a fresh pot of coffee. "Lots of people have been asking about it. Real estate people call me every now and again. It doesn't seem like a suicide deters anyone."

"Not if there's a million-dollar view. I don't know. Becca just reminded me I own the damned thing. I haven't had two thoughts about it since Marianne passed away."

"So what do you plan to do?"

"Never go back to Manhattan."

"Nonsense," her mother and Becca said together.

"Umm . . . enjoy five minutes without media meddling?"

"You're not going to find that here, Frannie," her mother said, using her given name automatically. "They're still talking about Marianne Nyland's death every time the subject of the house comes up. Which is about every hour during the summer, and every two hours now in the off-season."

Frankie looked at Becca. "Do I have to deal with that here, too?"

Becca said, "I think you're going to deal with all of it the minute you step foot into that house. You should make sure the heat is on, by the way."

Her mother said, "I have the caretaker's number. Kept it just in case."

Oh Lord—she'd also put out of her mind that her mother had been on the scene that day. She hadn't found the body, thank God, but she'd been there when the police went in, and she was one of the first to hear that Marianne was dead.

After which, on Frankie's instructions, the house was locked up, sealed, and a cadre of guards and dogs hired. So the place had been empty and cold for these six months while she flirted, fucked around, and took fame and fortune as her due.

Five hundred miles from her home, light-years away from every value with which she'd been raised. Her mother should despise her for her defection; instead, she welcomed her home, wrapping her arms around her shoulders and saying, reassuringly, "Ah, Frannie. On the face of it, it was a good opportunity. And it got us here, so how bad is it, really?"

"Well," Frankie said, grasping her mother's hands, "if they don't arrest me on the basis of circumstantial evidence, not so bad at all."

"Good," her mother said. "I have to admit, the first month after it all happened, it was unsettling. Reporters poking everywhere, asking questions, taking photos. It was unnerving to see that trailer pictured in the tabloids, and me hiding behind the curtains." She shuddered. "But things have died down. The primary interest is in the real estate. Speculators coming in, talking about tearing the house down and building three waterfront mansions on a lot meant for that one, reaping big profits. Not what you want."

"No, all I want—I think—is to see where it happened. I think there's enough distance now."

"Don't look for answers," her mother cautioned. "There probably aren't any. The police went through the house very thoroughly."

Of course. Had she been thinking there'd be some kind of clue anyway? "I won't. We'll go there tomorrow. Today I want to show Becca the town, and then we'll go out to dinner."

There were four main thoroughfares downtown, with quaint alleys, side streets, and unexpected strips of shops in between. Fishing boats steaming into the harbor, yachts moored within hailing distance, fishmongers setting up to sell the afternoon catch.

And the sky was that rich, deep New England blue, not a cloud scuttling by, the sun a pinpoint of heat on the skin, and the cold as sharp as a knife.

"You okay, warm enough?"

"Warm enough," Becca said as they ambled down toward the harbor.

"Getting antsy yet? Feeling like you've been gone from New York too long?"

"Nope, I'm just fine," Becca said gamely.

"We should buy some walking shoes."

"That sounds practical and really good right now."

They turned onto Cottage Street where there were stores catering to outdoor sports enthusiasts.

A half hour later: "Way better." Becca groaned as she stretched out her legs to appraise the not-so-flattering hiking boots she'd bought. "I didn't think I could walk another inch in those high heels."

She'd bought walking sneakers as well and a down vest which was now under her jacket as they continued down Main Street.

"Ha, and you weren't cold."

"Well—how long do you feel we'll be staying here?"

"A couple of weeks, maybe." Frankie squinted at the sun. "I don't know. How long can I hide the limousine in the driveway? How long do you think it'll take before Rollie goes stir crazy with nothing to do?"

"Or you," Becca retorted.

"I was doing nothing anyway."

And now she had something to do: make a decision about that house. Make a decision about putting away the bad girl and becoming the good girl she used to be.

The kind of woman men like Dax married.

Damn. She thought she'd banished him from her mind. From her heart. He was a monster. He used her abominably. Just like the rest, he got what he could at a moment when she was vulnerable, when she needed *him*.

She didn't need him, or any man. She could lop off the past right now, and start over again.

But if there was one thing she had learned in these past months, it was that the past always caught up with you.

And so she wasn't all that surprised, when they all returned from having dinner that night, to find a strange car in the driveway and Dax sitting on the front porch.

Dax was the most charming man on the planet when he wanted to be. Her mother was utterly enchanted by his elegance, his manners, and those eyes.

"And you're here—why?" Frankie at her most abrasive. He had no business being here, no business even deducing where she'd gone.

"Just passing through. I wanted to revisit old haunts."

"You're such a liar."

"Where else would you go, Frankie? And you still have to lay Marianne to rest here."

"No, I don't. This is *my* domain. She was the visitor. She was the outsider here."

"Ignore that," Becca said to Dax. "She's going to the house. Tomorrow."

"Then I got here just in time."

"In time for what?" Frankie asked snippily.

"He'll share the guest room with Rollie," her mother decided.

"And Rollie can go back to New York since you've got a car," Becca added. "And then maybe we can all go back in a couple of days." She looked at Frankie and amended, "Weeks. Maybe years, at this rate. She won't admit it, but she's absolutely nerve-wracked at the thought of going to the house."

"Which is why *we're* here," Dax said easily. "It's time, and you have to make a decision about it anyway."

"I'll call the caretaker," her mother said, "make sure about that heat."

"Oh, there's some heat," Dax said, eyeing Frankie. "They never let the pipes freeze in the winter."

She was cold, cold as ice all night, and wide awake. Dax was in the house. Technically in the barn, but still. Close enough to make her mouth water, and far enough away he might as well have been in New York.

And she was scared. She didn't know why, but the thought of seeing the scene of the crime spooked her. And that was all it would be. Nothing else. The police had gone through everything, examined every possible clue, every possible, reasonable explanation for this self-destructive act.

And they'd come up with nothing. So what did she expect she would find?

Surely not Rob, pounding on the door at seven-thirty a.m.

"Jesus!" He nearly fell into the kitchen where Frankie's mother was baking again, and stoking the wood stove in the corner. "It's freakin' cold out there. Hi, Frankie. Hi, Mom. I'm Rob." He shook her hand enthusiastically. "Becca. I drove the whole damned night, once I realized that bastard had snuck away behind my back. Where is he, anyway? *Dax!* Get your butt down here . . ."

"Hold on, tiger," Becca said, "he's in the guest suite in the barn. And you'll be in deep manure if you don't stop shouting."

"Fine." He looked around the kitchen, focusing on the stove and rubbing his hands over the heat. "Got any coffee?"

Frankie set out a mug for him and he collapsed into a chair. "God, I'm dead. That is one hellacious drive."

"One could fly." And there was Dax at the door. "That's been suggested as a more efficient way to get here quick."

"Are we having fun yet?" Becca murmured, settling down at the table with her mug.

"Okay," Frankie said loudly. "Enough. Listen up. I—*we*, if you all want to come—am going to the big house today. It's time."

"You sure?" Rob asked, with some worry in his tone.

Frankie nodded.

"Two hours, people," Dax said, taking command. "Fed, washed, dressed, and out the door."

Rob took his coffee and a muffin. "Don't talk about me when I'm gone."

"He's a charmer, too," Frankie's mother said.

"Just one of the crowd," Frankie said dismissively.

"Who *volunteered* to marry her," Dax put in. "Noble, don't you think?"

"Right out of a fairy tale," her mother said. "Frankie, do you want me to come, too?"

"Maybe not today, Mom. Maybe when the cleaning out has to start?"

"That's fine with me."

They were ready to go at ten.

They had to park and walk a bit to the enclave of cottages on the Shore Path.

There was an air of disuse around the house. Even though the yellow tape was gone and there was nothing to suggest it wasn't occupied, it still looked empty and forlorn.

It hadn't been painted in years, so now the outside was somewhat shabby. The porch pillars and window frames were peeling in places. The stained-glass windows were encrusted with wind-blown silt.

The water view still was spectacular.

Inside, it was stuffy and airless. It hadn't been redecorated in about seventy-five years. All the furniture looked as if it dated from the thirties, and the oriental rugs were worm-eaten. The light fixtures had those custard glass shades so the interior seemed darker than it was.

It felt like a time capsule, stopped around 1935. Even the kitchen hadn't been modernized.

"I feel like Nancy Drew," Becca commented.

"They did live large," Frankie said. "We townies always thought these houses were up-to-the-minute elegant, but look at how it really was—"

"They're up-to-the-minute in some respects," Rob pointed out. "Big-screen TV, all the playback equipment."

The dining room featured an ornate carved table that could have seated twelve or more. The chairs looked as if they came out of a medieval dining hall, and the room was so big, it didn't feel crowded.

"Good lord," Frankie whispered.

"It's all yours, my darling," Becca kindly reminded her.

Dax hadn't said a word. Rob asked, "Ready for upstairs?"

Frankie nodded, and they tromped up the ornate winding staircase to the second floor, where they found five bedrooms, three facing the front of the house, and two at the back with an old-fashioned bathroom between.

"Which one do you suppose was Marianne's?" Becca asked.

"I guess we'll find out," Frankie said breathlessly, going for the door to the right, which was a corner bedroom with views on two sides. But it was not Marianne's room, nor were the other front-facing bedrooms.

Her room was at the back, on the left, strewn with clothes, underwear, makeup, jewelry, magazines, a computer, CDs and DVDs, and all the necessary electronic equipment.

In the corner, the unobtrusive open door to the fatal closet.

Frankie sank onto the bed, suddenly breathless. She could

see the closet from the bed. How many nights had Marianne looked into that closet stuffed with clothes and thought about doing what she did?

Dax touched her shoulder. "If you want answers . . ."

"But the police picked through everything already. And talked to all the summer residents who knew her," Frankie said.

"Except," Becca pointed out, "we were her real best friends. No one knew her like we did."

"Nobody knew her, period," Dax said. "Maybe there's something someone overlooked."

"Like what? A good-bye letter? A confessional tape?"

Becca was already on the floor, sifting through the clothes and rooting around under the bed. Dax took the closet, Rob the dresser drawers, and Frankie grabbed the CDs and movies since they were all piled on the bed.

"Okay," Rob said, starting the inventory, "big on filmy lingerie, B and D costumes, and sex toys. Wow. Who knew?"

"Lots of designer stuff," Dax said from the closet. "Lots of shoes, sportswear, evening clothes . . ."

"This is like when we searched her room the day she disappeared," Frankie fretted. "We found nothing. There was nothing *to* her. She was like . . . like cotton candy—all whipped up and no substance. She was partial to scream queen horror movies. She listened to eighties rock and single discs of titles I never heard of—'Bad Girl's Lament,' 'Which Side Are You On'—What? 'Frankie and Johnny.' "

She froze, looked at Becca, who had popped up from the floor.

"It's an old folk song," Dax said, his voice dry.

"Why would *she* have folk music?" Frankie countered, her voice just a bit wavery. "It's not her taste, by anything I see here."

"But listen to the titles," Becca said. "'Bad Girl's Lament'? 'Which Side Are You On'? And 'Frankie and Johnny'?"

"Maybe we've come across the hitherto unknown depths of Marianne."

"Or maybe it's something the police overlooked, because it meant nothing to them."

"Maybe it's a message," Rob said. "Maybe she recorded something and burned a CD. Let's try it." He took the discs from Frankie. "Hell. Look at this: she's got a tape and DVD deck; a digital camera hooked into the TV; a TV-to-DVD setup. And a five-changer CD and radio. Man."

He pressed switches. "Ready?" First CD into the changer. Music. Second CD, "Which Side Are You On." Music. "Hmmm." Third CD, "Frankie and Johnny."

Silence.

They looked at each other.

"Okay," Rob said, his voice tight. "Trying the DVD player."

Instantly a white haze came up on the TV screen. And then, Marianne, dressed in white, obviously staged in this very bedroom.

Rob stopped the player. "Jesus God. Are you guys ready for this?"

Frankie felt like she couldn't breathe. "No. But we have to, don't we?"

"We don't have to," Dax said.

"Do it," Becca commanded.

Rob pressed the play button and there was Marianne, almost as large as life.

"Hello. I knew you would get the symbolism of the titles when the police wouldn't, so Frankie, I know you're here. Hopefully not for long. And I hope you're alone. And I hope you've lost everything, and they're on the cusp of hauling you off to jail for my murder. Because you took everything away from me, and now I've taken everything away from you.

"You thought you were so smart, right from the beginning. That day, I wanted Dax to rescue me, and you interfered. You had to be a heroine, grabbing my dress, my hair, bringing me to life, instead of Dax.

"God, I hated you right then. And in the hospital—it was so obvious something had happened between you and Dax. Every time I saw you, it was perfectly plain to see, yet you kept denying it and denying it. What else could I do but make you my best friend, so I could keep an eye on you?

"I thought I was rid of you after that summer, but four years later—there you were again, coming to New York. How did you *ever* think you'd fit in with any crowd in New York? Of course, I had to offer you hospitality. Otherwise, you'd have gone behind my back and sought out Dax. I couldn't have that, Frankie. Couldn't have you within a hundred miles of him, if I could help it.

"Nobody cared about my feelings about him. You two just struck sparks all over the place. So, I got you into sex.

Every dumbass who comes here gets seduced by freewheeling sex, especially the town tramp from the boonies. I wanted to make Dax wholly disgusted with you. Guys like him don't marry trailer trash, Frankie. I made you into trash, and I loved every minute of it.

"He didn't come around so much then, did he?

"But then you took Becca away from me. Suddenly you were buddy-buddy pals, having lunch behind my back and everything. Fine.

"So I hired you. I couldn't have you free after your work-study stint was done. I got you in debt to me so I'd have a hold on you for*ever*. But on that road trip—you got all the guys. All the good ones. You took the ones I wanted, each time. I couldn't believe it. Not an iota of gratitude for everything I'd done for you.

"You showed your true face by your theft of my best friend and the man I always wanted. You wouldn't even take Rob, would you? You wouldn't do *anything* I wanted you to do. So when we went to France, I arranged for that tape to be made. That was going to be my *coup de grâce*. If you hadn't left Dax alone by then, he would leave you *all* alone after that became public. Nina released it, in case you haven't figured it out.

"And to ensure you cemented your reputation as a whore, I invented a reason for that road trip and made certain he heard about it.

"And the strip club? I wanted him so fed up with you that he'd never go near you again. I never expected he'd fuck you that night, or set up meetings in some sleazy motel.

"So, I arranged it that you'd inherit everything. And then, when I'm found dead, here in Maine, something further to connect you to my death, you'd be the primary suspect and eventually be arrested for my murder, and you'd lose everything and everyone.

"Nina's investigative report will be the fallback position, in case they bring in a verdict of suicide.

"Do you think my decision is extreme? Well, Becca knows that I've practiced a compression form of autoeroticism for a long time. I love that exact moment when everything is constricted and I feel light as air, part of the universe, and in control of everything, even life, and the pleasure comes and comes and comes until I almost die that little death . . .

"Knowing that it could kill me—that's the purely orgasmic part, the danger, the risk. Cheating it every time, aware there could be one time you might not. But I would pass away in ecstasy knowing that you, Frankie, will experience the death of your ambitions, your dreams, and your holy love. Your losing everything makes my sacrifice so much the sweeter."

She stared at the screen with her flat, dead eyes, and as the light slowly faded, she added, "But do *not* think for a moment that this confession will exonerate you." Then she disappeared into the white.

Becca looked sick. Frankie was white, shaking, speechless. No one moved.

"No one was ever going to arrest you," Dax finally said into the shocked silence, his voice a little uneven.

"She was freakin' nuts!" Rob exploded.

"She just loved to push the boundaries," Becca whispered. "She just finally went beyond—reason. God . . ."

"Are you all right, Frankie?" Rob turned to her, still shocked himself.

"This will never go away. How can it? How can you guys go on, knowing all this about her?"

"We just will," Becca said consolingly. "You'll take that thing and either destroy it, or put it in a safe deposit box, and just . . . forget it."

"I can't forget," Frankie whispered. A vendetta like that, against her? Marianne killing herself in sick vengeance because Dax had never wanted her and she didn't want *her* to have him?

It was mind-blowing. It was life-changing.

"Let's get out of here." Dax was in charge again, taking Frankie into his arms as Rob popped out the disc and pressed it with suppressed violence into its jewel case.

"Leave it," Frankie said, her voice muffled against Dax's chest. She shouldn't be there. She shouldn't let him hold her, shouldn't still want him so much. This had all happened because she wanted too much, and it had cost some one her life.

"I'll take it," Dax said, holding out his hand. "I'll keep it. As someone famously once said, that's what lawyers are for."

Frankie did not return to New York with Rob, Becca, or Dax. She needed the time, the space, she needed the cold, fresh air, the bright sun; she needed her mother and she needed perspective.

And she began to get the Nyland house ready for sale.

"It's a nice old house," her mother said. "You know, people rent out their houses for the season. You could probably make a nice dollar doing that if you cleaned it up and modernized it."

"This is a notorious house, Mom. No one's going to want to stay here."

"Better that than a teardown. And people *will* want to stay there."

Frankie looked at her speculatively. Her mother was barely fifty-five, and in this past year, she'd regained some of the vigor and energy she'd once had. Maybe, just maybe, her mother was looking for something to do. Maybe . . .

"O-kay. So you think this property is more valuable as a rental than as a teardown."

"Yes, and it should be to you, and it certainly would be to the town."

"Then what if you took charge of the project? What if I funded the rehab, and you got it cleaned up and refurnished? What if you ran the operation?"

"It's not a bed and breakfast, Frannie. People who rent take care of themselves, and you hope they take care of the house for the few weeks they live there."

"That's even better—no extra work involved. Why don't you think about it?"

"I'll do that. And you, what have you been thinking about?"

"Changing my life," Frankie said. "I just don't know how."

She couldn't bear to go near the house, but her mother

had no such qualms, and after Thanksgiving, which they spent together, she began work in earnest.

Phone calls from Becca, Rob. Rob reiterating his offer to take care of her.

"You should marry Becca," she told him.

"You should *not* marry Dax," he retorted.

"Not likely. Unlike you, he never asked."

The next step: not opening email. Not even turning on the computer. Not knowing what was happening in New York, not knowing if anything was still being said or written, if Blog-a-rella was still banging the drum of her decadence.

She didn't care. It was the most liberating thing, not to care, just as Becca said. She could afford it, too. And she didn't have to pretend.

Her mother came home one day the first week in December with two boxes full of decorative items and jewelry, and one filled with videotapes.

With Frankie's name on them.

"Where did you find those?"

"Way back in her closet when I was cleaning out her clothes. What do you think they could be?"

Frankie shivered. "I don't know." She was scared that she did, though—Marianne, reaching out again from the grave. She waited for her mother to leave the room before she turned on the VCR and shoved in the first tape.

The perspective was from above, as if the camera was on a window or door frame. Dimmed lights. It looked like Marianne's living room. It looked like . . . her.

And—Rob.

"Mom . . ." she said warningly.

"I'm in the kitchen."

And the next. Rob again. Next: the guys from the tasting party.

Once again, she was speechless. Sick. She clicked off the VCR, popped out the tape, ripped it out with her bare hands, got a pair of scissors and cut it to pieces. She did the same with each of the others, stunned at how degenerate, how utterly hardened Marianne had been, that she'd resorted to *this* for entertainment.

All that time, recording her, recording Becca, recording all her friends.

Thank heavens, not Dax.

She froze as something occurred to her. She was in love with Dax. Marianne would have taken him any way she could get him. And that had to be Nina's *irrefutable proof*—a tape of Dax—and *her.*

It was just a small leap from that conclusion to envisioning Marianne watching that tape over and over and over . . . Frankie and Dax, in the living room. Their conversations. Their kisses. Their lovemaking.

There were probably cameras all over that apartment. It was sickening to imagine everything that was on those clandestine tapes.

All destroyed now, except that *irrefutable* one which Nina would probably never give up.

Christmas was coming. It was already freezing cold, snow-on-the-ground weather. Her mother and she went to a farm and chopped down a tree, they wrapped presents, they listened to music, baked cookies, went to town events, sang carols, and went to midnight mass.

She would never have done this in New York. She *needed* to do this in New York, to bring the home values back with her. Because Christmas blew away all the sins of the past, and made her eager to start over. To do it differently, do it right this time.

It was almost the new year. One year ago, she'd gone to New York and gotten sucked into Marianne's sex-saturated world.

Who had that girl been?

She didn't know her. Two months out of the spotlight made the events of last year seem so very far away.

She could live without all that—the cameras, the gossip, the notoriety, the internet catfights, the trash talk. She was ready to forge ahead. Her mother would manage the Nyland house as a guest house, which would keep her busy and content, and the architecturally valuable old house would be preserved.

The tapes were destroyed; Dax had possession of the DVD. Marianne was now well and truly buried, unless Nina ever made the irrefutable proof public. It was conceivable the lawyers could convince her not to.

By now the Boutique sex tape should be yesterday's news, and Carl Moore should have taken his couple hundred thousand dollars and bought himself a business and perhaps had found another sexually voracious partner.

She called Illingworth and asked him to arrange to have

the furniture in the town house moved back to the apartment, and to put the town house up for sale.

She called Becca and told her she was coming home.

"Guess what," Becca said. "Marianne's confession disc was destroyed. She put something in the jewel box that abraded it when Rob pressed down on it. So no one ever has to know that it was anything more than a suicide."

"Mom found a box of tapes in the house. Marianne had cameras all over the apartment and she taped everyone. She probably spent hours watching us."

"You and Dax, you mean." Becca guessed. "Pouring gasoline on the fire."

"Anyway, I'm going back to the apartment. But I have to sell it—too many memories."

"Selling might be good," Becca agreed a little cryptically. "Talk to you later."

It didn't take an hour after she returned for Rob to come by. "I'm taking you out," he told her preemptively. "Find something bright and sexy to wear. We're celebrating."

"Exactly what do we have to celebrate?"

"The end of one chapter, the beginning of another?"

"What other?"

"Go get ready, Frankie. This is the change-your-life moment."

"Please—not another proposal."

"Frankie . . ."

She threw on a slip dress of red matte jersey and matching shoes, brushed her hair around her shoulders, put on minimal makeup, grabbed an evening purse and coat. "Where are we going?"

"Rollie's waiting. Come on."

"Rob—where are we *going*?"

"Out, I told you." And he wouldn't say more.

The limo crept east through Midtown, turning onto Lexington Avenue a block above the Waldorf-Astoria, and swinging into line behind dozens of other limos.

"What's this?" Frankie demanded.

"This is the beginning of the rest of your life," Rob said, and he was dead serious. "There's a fund-raiser here tonight. Absolutely star studded, so there'll be lots of cameras. You're done with all the scandal and sex, so this is your coming out party. Just look gorgeous and deny everything. And *smile*."

She smiled. Rollie inched the limo up the line and finally stopped at the red carpet and a porter opened the limo door. She slid her leg out and immediately cameras started flashing. Suddenly someone blocked her sight line, and his hand reached out and touched her knee.

She knew that touch, that hand.

Dax. In a tux, so tall and elegant, his eyes soft for her, love-soft.

Her heart stopped. She looked at Rob.

He shrugged. "He won."

"Frankie. You look gorgeous."

"You too," she whispered as her breath caught in her throat.

He reached out his hand for her. "It's not too soon anymore."

"No?" Barely a breath of a word.

"No," as horns started honking and cameras kept flashing and he pulled her toward him and leaned in closer to her. "It's our time now. And the hell with everyone else out there—I need to kiss you."